ROBIN
THE PLEASURE CRUISE MYSTERY

Robin Forsythe was born Robert Forsythe in 1879. His place of birth was Sialkot, in modern day Pakistan. His mother died when a younger brother was born two years later, and 'Robin' was brought up by an ayah until he was six, when he returned to the United Kingdom, and went to school in Glasgow and Northern Ireland. In his teens he had short stories and poetry published and went to London wanting to be a writer.

He married in 1909 and had a son the following year, later working as a clerk at Somerset House in London when he was arrested for theft and fraud in 1928. Sentenced to fifteen months, he began to write his first detective novel in prison.

On his release in 1929 Robin Forsythe published his debut, *Missing or Murdered*. It introduced Anthony 'Algernon' Vereker, an eccentric artist with an extraordinary flair for detective work. It was followed by four more detective novels in the Vereker series, ending with *The Spirit Murder Mystery* in 1936. All the novels are characterized by the sharp plotting and witty dialogue which epitomize the more effervescent side of golden age crime fiction.

Robin Forsythe died in 1937.

Also by Robin Forsythe

Missing or Murdered

The Polo Ground Mystery

The Ginger Cat Mystery
(*aka* Murder at Marston Manor)

The Spirit Murder Mystery

ROBIN FORSYTHE

THE PLEASURE CRUISE MYSTERY

With an introduction
by Curtis Evans

DEAN STREET PRESS

To

BEATRICE

Robin Forsythe (1879-1937)
Crime in Fact and Fiction

Ingenious criminal schemes were the stock in trade of those
ever-so-bright men and women who devised the baffling puzzles
found in between-the-wars detective fiction. Yet although scores
of Golden Age mystery writers strove mightily to commit brilliant
crimes on paper, presumably few of them ever attempted to
commit them in fact. One author of classic crime fiction who
actually carried out a crafty real-life crime was Robin Forsythe.
Before commencing in 1929 his successful series of Algernon
Vereker detective novels, now reprinted in attractive new editions
by the enterprising Dean Street Press, Forsythe served in the
1920s as the mastermind behind England's Somerset House
stamp trafficking scandal.

Robin Forsythe was born Robert Forsythe—he later found it
prudent to slightly alter his Christian name—in Sialkot, Punjab
(then part of British India, today part of Pakistan) on 10 May
1879, the eldest son of distinguished British cavalryman John
"Jock" Forsythe and his wife Caroline. Born in 1838 to modestly
circumstanced parents in the Scottish village of Carmunnock,
outside Glasgow, John Forsythe in 1858 enlisted as a private in
the Ninth Queen's Royal Lancers and was sent to India, then in
the final throes of a bloody rebellion. Like the fictional Dr. John
H. Watson of Sherlock Holmes fame, Forsythe saw major martial
action in Afghanistan two decades later during the Second Anglo-
Afghan War (1878-1880), in his case at the December 1879 siege
of the Sherpur Cantonment, just outside Kabul, and the Battle of
Kandahar on 1 September 1880, for which service he received the
War Medal with two Clasps and the Bronze England and Ireland
until his retirement from the British army in 1893, four years after
having been made an Honorary Captain. The old solider was later
warmly commended, in a 1904 history of the Ninth Lancers, for
his "unbroken record of faithful, unfailing and devoted service."

His son Robin's departure from government service a quarter-century later would be rather less harmonious.

A year after John Forsythe's return to India from Afghanistan in 1880, his wife Caroline died in Ambala after having given birth to Robin's younger brother, Gilbert ("Gill"), and the two little boys were raised by an Indian ayah, or nanny. The family returned to England in 1885, when Robin was six years old, crossing over to Ireland five years later, when the Ninth Lancers were stationed at the Curragh Army Camp. On Captain Forsythe's retirement from the Lancers in 1893, he and his two sons settled in Scotland at his old home village, Carmunnock. Originally intended for the legal profession, Robin instead entered the civil service, although like E.R. Punshon, another clerk turned classic mystery writer recently reprinted by Dean Street Press, he dreamt of earning his bread through his pen by another, more imaginative, means: creative writing. As a young man Robin published poetry and short stories in newspapers and periodicals, yet not until after his release from prison in 1929 at the age of fifty would he finally realize his youthful hope of making his living as a fiction writer.

For the next several years Robin worked in Glasgow as an Inland Revenue Assistant of Excise. In 1909 he married Kate Margaret Havord, daughter of a guide roller in a Glasgow iron and steel mill, and by 1911 the couple resided, along with their one-year-old son John, in Godstone, Surrey, twenty miles from London, where Robin was employed as a Third Class Clerk in the Principal Probate Registry at Somerset House. Young John remained the Robin and Kate's only child when the couple separated a decade later. What problems led to the irretrievable breakdown of the marriage is not known, but Kate's daughter-in-law later characterized Kate as "very greedy" and speculated that her exactions upon her husband might have made "life difficult for Robin and given him a reason for his illegal acts."

Six years after his separation from Kate, Robin conceived and carried out, with the help of three additional Somerset

House clerks, a fraudulent enterprise resembling something out of the imaginative crime fiction of Arthur Conan Doyle, Golden Age thriller writer Edgar Wallace and post Golden Age lawyer-turned-author Michael Gilbert. Over a year-and-a-half period, the Somerset House conspirators removed high value judicature stamps from documents deposited with the Board of Inland Revenue, using acids to obliterate cancellation marks, and sold the stamps at half-cost to three solicitor's clerks, the latter of whom pocketed the difference in prices. Robin and his co-conspirators at Somerset House divided among themselves the proceeds from the illicit sales of the stamps, which totaled over 50,000 pounds (or roughly $75,000 US dollars) in modern value. Unhappily for the seven schemers, however, a government auditor became suspicious of nefarious activity at Somerset House, resulting in a 1927 undercover Scotland Yard investigation that, coupled with an intensive police laboratory examination of hundreds of suspect documents, fully exposed both the crime and its culprits.

Robin Forsythe and his co-conspirators were promptly arrested and at London's Old Bailey on 7 February 1928, the Common Serjeant--elderly Sir Henry Dickens, K.C., last surviving child of the great Victorian author Charles Dickens--passed sentence on the seven men, all of whom had plead guilty and thrown themselves on the mercy of the court. Sir Henry sentenced Robin to a term of fifteen months imprisonment, castigating him as a calculating rogue, according to the Glasgow Herald, the newspaper in which Robin had published his poetry as a young man, back when the world had seemed full of promise:

> It is an astounding position to find in an office like that of Somerset House that the Canker of dishonesty had bitten deep....You are the prime mover of this, and obviously you started it. For a year and a half you have continued it, and you have undoubtedly raised an atmosphere and influenced other people in that office.

Likely one of the "astounding" aspects of this case in the eyes of eminent pillars of society like Dickens was that Robin Forsythe and his criminal cohort to a man had appeared to be, before the fraud was exposed, quite upright individuals. With one exception Robin's co-conspirators were a generation younger than their ringleader and had done their duty, as the saying goes, in the Great War. One man had been a decorated lance corporal in the late affray, while another had served as a gunner in the Royal Field Artillery and a third had piloted biplanes as a 2nd lieutenant in the Royal Flying Corps. The affair disturbingly demonstrated to all and sundry that, just like in Golden Age crime fiction, people who seemed above suspicion could fall surprisingly hard for the glittering lure of ill-gotten gain.

Crime fiction offered the imaginative Robin Forsythe not only a means of livelihood after he was released in from prison in 1929, unemployed and seemingly unemployable, but also, one might surmise, a source of emotional solace and escape. Dorothy L. Sayers once explained that from the character of her privileged aristocratic amateur detective, Lord Peter Wimsey, she had devised and derived, at difficult times in her life, considerable vicarious satisfaction:

> When I was dissatisfied with my single unfurnished room, I tool a luxurious flat for him in Piccadilly. When my cheap rug got a hole in it, I ordered an Aubusson carpet. When I had no money to pay my bus fare, I presented him with a Daimler double-six, upholstered in a style of sober magnificence, and when I felt dull I let him drive it.

Between 1929 and 1937 Robin published eight successful crime novels, five of which were part of the Algernon Vereker mystery series for which the author was best known: *Missing or Murdered* (1929), *The Polo Ground Mystery* (1932), *The Pleasure Cruise Mystery* (1933), *The Ginger Cat Mystery* (1935) and *The Spirit Murder Mystery* (1936). The three remaining novels—*The Hounds of Justice* (1930), *The Poison Duel* (1934, under the pseudonym Peter Dingwall) and *Murder on Paradise Island* (1937)—were non-series works.

Like the other Robin Forsythe detective novels detailing the criminal investigations of Algernon Vereker, gentleman artist and amateur sleuth, *Missing or Murdered* was issued in England by The Bodley Head, publisher in the Twenties of mysteries by Agatha Christie and Annie Haynes, the latter another able writer revived by Dean Street Press. Christie had left The Bodley Head in 1926 and Annie Haynes had passed away early in 1929, leaving the publisher in need of promising new authors. Additionally, the American company Appleton-Century published two of the Algernon Vereker novels, *The Pleasure Cruise Mystery* and *The Ginger Cat Mystery*, in the United States (the latter book under the title *Murder at Marston Manor*) as part of its short-lived but memorably titled Tired Business Man's Library of adventure, detective and mystery novels, which were designed "to afford relaxation and entertainment" to industrious American escape fiction addicts during their off hours. Forsythe's fiction also enjoyed some success in France, where his first three detective novels were published, under the titles *La Disparition de Lord Bygrave* (The Disappearance of Lord Bygrave), *La Passion de Sadie Maberley* (The Passion of Sadie Maberley) and *Coups de feu a l'aube* (Gunshots at Dawn).

The Robin Forsythe mystery fiction drew favorable comment for their vivacity and ingenuity from such luminaries as Dorothy L. Sayers, Charles Williams and J.B. Priestley, the latter acutely observing that "Mr. Forsythe belongs to the new school of detective story writers which might be called the brilliant flippant school." Sayers pronounced of Forsythe's *The Ginger Cat Mystery* that "[t]he story is lively and the plot interesting," while Charles Williams, author and editor of Oxford University Press, heaped praise upon *The Polo Ground Mystery* as "a good story of one bullet, two wounds, two shots, and one dead man and three pistols before the end....It is really a maze, and the characters are not merely automata."

This second act in the career of Robin Forsythe proved sadly short-lived, however, for in 1937 the author passed away from kidney disease, still estranged from his wife and son, at the age of 57. In his later years he resided--along with his Irish Setter Terry, the "dear pal" to whom he dedicated *The Ginger Cat Mystery*--at a cottage in the village of Hartest, near Bury St. Edmunds, Suffolk. In addition to writing, Robin enjoyed gardening and dabbling in art, having become an able chalk sketch artist and water colorist. He also toured on ocean liners (under the name "Robin Forsythe"), thereby gaining experience that would serve him well in his novel *The Pleasure Cruise Mystery*. This book Robin dedicated to "Beatrice," while *Missing or Murdered* was dedicated to "Elizabeth" and *The Spirit Murder Mystery* to "Jean." Did Robin find solace as well in human companionship during his later years? Currently we can only speculate, but classic British crime fans who peruse the mysteries of Robin Forsythe should derive pleasure from spending time in the clever company of Algernon Vereker as he hunts down fictional malefactors—thus proving that, while crime may not pay, it most definitely can entertain.

Curtis Evans

Chapter One

Anthony Vereker, known to his friends as Algernon unabbreviated, sat, the picture of dejection, in an easy chair in the studio of his flat in Fenton Street, W. His long legs were thrust out straight in front of him; his thin nervous hands fiddled uneasily with the keys and money in his trousers pockets; his chin was sunk on his breast and his eyes were fixed gloomily on the toe-cap of one of his brown shoes. At a table in the centre of the room sat his friend Manuel Ricardo, glancing eagerly at a highly coloured and illustrated folder setting forth in the magniloquence of the publicity expert the delights of pleasure cruises on the Green Star Company's luxury liner "Mars." Every now and then his features expanded in a grin of amusement as some particular phrase tickled his malicious sense of humour.

"Algernon, my old wimple, listen to this blurb; it's inimitable; a second-rate publisher couldn't do better: 'Each state room on the "Mars," the *dernier mot* in sumptuous luxury, is fitted with every modern convenience that can appeal to the man or woman of culture and refinement, from electric fans and radiators'—er, well, you wouldn't need the last."

"Need what last?" asked Vereker drearily.

"Electric curling irons," replied Ricardo, glancing at his friend's thin fair hair and laughing boisterously.

"Ricky, I really can't descend to your depths of humour at the moment. You're becoming more infantile every day."

"I'm sorry you're not *en rapport.* As I've warned you before, you'll have to give up this itch for painting. Painting's a degrading vice. Once you become an addict you're no longer fit for human company. You neglect your fellow men to hobnob with landscapes, you make bosom pals with still life and other inanimate objects, you have unblushing intimacy, only visual to be precise, with repulsive nudes! There's only one thing more debasing than Art, and that's Art criticism."

"Even Art criticism couldn't be worse than your last serial, Ricky. *The Cost of Loving* I think you called it."

"It went a long way to meet the cost of living, Algernon. It served its purpose. Painting—I mean your painting—serves no purpose at all. It's merely an exasperating excrescence on your mental life. Since the critics slated your last atrocity you've been unfit to live with. If I could afford it I'd leave your hospitable flat at some distant future date and seek sanctuary in a common lodging-house. You'll end in acute melancholia."

"And you suggest a pleasure cruise, Ricky. The very epithet 'pleasure' makes me recoil!"

"What better antidote to the poison of paint, Algernon?" asked Ricardo and, opening out the folder, continued: "Listen to this. 'A holiday cruise in luxurious comfort. You visit lands of sunshine, mystery and romance. Dances, carnivals, fancy-dress balls, bathing pool, gymnasium, deck sports...' You see, Algernon, there's everything for geniuses like you and me who seek relaxation from the rigour of the Ideal!"

"Um!" grunted Vereker.

"Wait; the best is still to come. 'A carefully selected supply of wines, spirits, tobacco and cigars at moderate prices. Bar open from 7 a.m. till 12 p.m.' Try to realise that. It meets the best of thirsts with a British sense of fair play. A barber's shop too! 'Scalp massage one and sixpence. Chiropody from three shillings and sixpence.' Inexpensive peace for tortured tootsies! 'Cheques cannot be accepted.' That's the only snag so far, and sounds like a pub on shore. 'Deck chairs free; rugs five bob. Further details from the purser or...'"

"I don't want any further details, Ricky."

"I'm glad you've decided to come."

"I don't know, I don't know," said Vereker reflectively and after a pause; "it might be an escape from life, though carnivals, dances, fancy-dress balls, deck sports sound rather painful."

"Listen once more, Algernon," said Ricardo, turning to the illustrated folder. "This I think's the sublime, the irresistible appeal: 'You meet people of culture and refinement, people with good taste and savoir vivre. You make new friends, you enter at once into a charming social life...'"

"Good Lord deliver us!" exclaimed Vereker.

"Don't fall back on the Lord in your present state of mind, Algernon; it's cowardly. For a man like yourself, disgustingly bourgeois, what you need is a few delightful weeks with the right kind of people, people with savoir vivre and all that. No use sticking your nose into a palette of colours and thinking you're kissing the skirts of the shy goddess of Beauty. It's high time you learned that she's always just out of mortal reach. Now on board the 'Mars' you'll be having a high old time in a new low way. Not a moment to think—thinking's a disease, anyway. As you walk briskly round the promenade deck imagining yourself a sea rover—Vereker the Viking—you'll regain physical health. You'll be a healthy animal in a week. Didn't my old friend Epicurus say that animals were the mirrors of Nature. Algernon, you'll go about looking like a cheval glass. Then there are beds instead of bunks, enchanting diddler machines, the ship's Lido or bathing pool, with alluring women unabashedly undressed, bridge parties, violent flirtations with a fortunate time limit to avoid the distress of love, dancing and dining and wining and a two bob deposit on a book to prevent you reading rubbish..."

"Ricky, you almost persuade me to be a Christian."

"Thanks for the interruption; I was out of breath. Now I've got my second wind I'll be serious. Your concentration and bad luck in the Armadale murder took it out of you. Inspector Heather won in a common canter while you were nibbling grass somewhere near the starting post. Your one-man-show of pictures that followed demoralised you. You must get back to mere living. It's terribly difficult but not impossible. I'm suggesting to you the easiest and quickest way back—a cruise on the 'Mars' with me as your inseparable companion. You'll be immersed in the joyous inanities of a charming social life, while around you, just to remind you of reality, will be the terrible beauty of the sea, vast, restless, indifferent, but profoundly disturbing at times. Every now and then you'll experience an inexpressible thrill when her cruel grandeur pokes a mischievous finger into the cosy mental tent of your self-satisfaction. Momentarily she will take you by the collar of your dress shirt and haul you roughly into the presence of the Unintelligible Infinite—nearly as disrupting as being hauled before your C.O. for appearing dirty on parade. I've done my rhetorical damnedest—are you coming on this bally cruise or not?"

"You're going, of course?"

"Indubitably. I'm writing up a little brochure for the Green Star Company to cover the cost of my fare. You can lend me the rest. It's a bit of a literary descent from the *Cost of Loving*, but I must stoop to conquer the present adverse state of my financial world. Like my namesake I'm an economist!"

"I've half a mind to accompany you, Ricky."

"You never had more than half a mind in any case, so the matter's settled, Algernon. Now what about a *soupçon* of lunch? Your sherry's a great appetiser. You'll have to order some more shortly."

"Your presence in my flat's a constant reminder, Ricky. Shall we go round to our old friend Jacques?"

"Anywhere for lunch, my dear Apelles, except a modern drapery store. Being persons of refinement and culture about to enter the charming social life of the 'Mars' on a footing of equality, we must adhere strictly to our social code. No civilised being could sip a choice wine with *brassières* at four eleven three in the offing. It simply isn't done."

"When does this pleasure cruise start, Ricky?"

"The 'Mars' leaves the Thames on Monday, March the 26th, a week hence. Lean on me. I know young Wheble up at the Green Star's offices. His guv'nor is one of the directors. He'll wangle us the nicest berths and get us a seat at the captain's table. I've met the latter—I mean the captain, not his table—before. Bluff old mariner who keeps up the proud traditions of the British Mercantile Marine and all that sort of bravura, so we'll have our knobs well in as they used to say in the Army when I was a corporal in the H.A.C. without 'a marshal's baton in my kit-bag!"

"But, Ricky, what's this going to cost us?"

"Cost us? Cost you, you mean. We can compute that better on our return, Algernon. When you, I mean we, were busy unravelling the Bygrave case, you promised to take me afterwards to Provence. Fond of romaunts, I was eager to join you as a troubadour, but you dashed off in the scented wake of that provoking jade, Ida Wister, and left me in the lurch, alone in London. I always thought you were a man of principle..."

"The man who acts on principle instead of being guided by intelligence is a fool, Ricky."

"Then I was right, Algernon. On principle you're going to redeem your debt to me. After lunch I'll run up to the Green Star's offices and put the matter on an irrevocable footing. Before lunch what about another spot of your old golden Sherry?"

"Not for me, thanks, Ricky."

"Being guided by intelligence, I'll wait till we reach Jacques'; your bottle's empty. Shake yourself and we'll beat it, Algernon. I'm famished. There's no time to lose. Some time this afternoon I must root out Aubrey Winter. He'll be able to lend me deck shoes, a tropical kit and a decent dinner jacket—in fact he'll think it almost an honour."

"Aubrey's a charming fool," replied Vereker quietly.

Chapter Two

The luxury liner "Mars" lay with her bow up-river and her stern to the incoming tide. Punctually at twelve o'clock the ship's siren blew a warning blast for departure; friends of those about to start on the well-advertised cruise hurried down the gangway and waved spasmodic farewells from the quay to the ranks of happy, excited travellers lined along the taffrails of the upper decks of the ship. Two fussy tugs tackled the monster, pulling her stern towards mid-river and swinging her nose round to the wharf. In a few minutes, with almost off-hand efficiency, the "Mars" was under way, breasting a light wind and the lazily rolling river. Gradually she drew into the widening estuary of the Thames, and the receding banks became flat bluish-grey stretches dotted with clumps of elms and touched here and there with the lighter coloured splashes of farms and dwellings. Anthony Vereker and Manuel Ricardo stood leaning over the rails of the upper promenade deck, gazing at a determined tug plugging up-river with oil barges in her wake, her black and scarlet prow nosing into a bouquet of snowy spume.

"It's the first time I've realised the truth and beauty of Walcot's Thames etchings, Ricky," said Vereker.

"Hang Walcot's etchings, Algernon! Have you noticed the high standard of good looks aboard? Hollywood afloat but not on its own conceit. There's one dark-looking Argentine maid with eyes, large, Latin, lustrous. I'd like her for keeps. I scent romance, Algernon."

"Ricky, my boy, when will you learn that a woman is seldom romantic. She hasn't time for imagination; she's always too busy trying to make a man practical. You'll be horribly disappointed. By the way, did you see her mother?"

"Oh, yes, the old wisp with onyx eyes and saffron skin. Looks like a compendium of all the vices bound in crepe rubber. I shall have to snooker her. What do you think of our cabins?"

"I'm glad you got them on this top deck. We're not quite in the thick of the refinement and culture. If we run into rough weather I dare say we'll get too much motion."

"They're O.K. even in rough weather. I never mind being rocked in a Ritz of the deep, but I bar cradles. Have you seen your next-door neighbour?"

"Just a glimpse. She was going to emerge from her cabin as I was entering mine, but on seeing me changed her mind and quickly closed her door. Her action rather puzzled me."

"Easily explained, Algernon; her complexion was temporarily dismantled. If you're searching for mysteries you needn't look further than a woman's nose. Was she pretty?"

"I saw her for an instant only."

"Beauty is always instantaneous: character requires a time exposure."

"You mean a bad character," corrected Vereker with a slight twitch at the corners of his mouth.

"*Bien touché*, Algernon; almost up to my standard of brilliant flippancy."

"I suppose flippancy's the name you give to other people's wit, Ricky?"

"Only when I'm reviewing a smart book. Wholesome deflation so to speak. But to return to the lady, was she dark or fair?"

"Fair and English I should say."

"But her name's Mesado."

"How on earth did you discover that?"

"Natural inquisitiveness; my birthright as a journalist. I read the label on a monstrous cabin trunk that was left for a few moments in the corridor outside her state room."

"'Pon my soul, Ricky, what will you poke your nose into next?"

"Anything but a bad smell, Algernon. What makes you think she's English?"

"She wears brogues, a signet ring on her left hand, smokes Players and says 'damn' deliciously."

"Did she damn you when she was about to come out of her cabin?"

"I flattered myself that she was impersonal; she was cursing circumstance."

"She probably thought you weren't worth a damn or looked suspiciously like circumstance. You seem to have gathered a lot of information in a 'palpebral flicker' as we used to say when we were young enough to think it funny."

"Observation's one of my confirmed habits, as you know. I caught a glimpse of a beautiful left hand holding a fifty box of Players fags, a neat left foot, the line of hip and thigh encased in check tweed, but her face disappeared behind the door before I saw more than a flash of nicely waved fair hair. As I said before, her action puzzled me; it was so unnecessary. I wasn't unduly inquisitive."

"A grave fault in your attitude to a pretty woman, Algernon. She's out to rouse your curiosity, of course."

"Then why did she mutter a faint damn? It was a clear indication of annoyance."

"Simulated hostility is the oldest gambit in the game of intrigue. Immediately a woman begins to make you think you're a nuisance she has definitely removed your apathy. You've acquired momentum. You will either run away from her or bally well run after her. If she's beautiful the deduction's obvious. Even if you run away she prefers that to your being static. You've proved to her that she's significant. There's nothing the feminine gender hates more than to be thought neuter."

"You'd be the last person to give her the opportunity, Ricky. The petticoat's an obsession with you."

"Most emphatically. I give it its correct status in a world of misplaced values. The only people who think that there's anything more important than woman are either scientists or lunatics, and it's damned hard to differentiate between them. Do you think that this lady who has already roused your interest is married?"

"Yes, I saw her left hand."

"A wedding ring's not unimpeachable evidence; nowadays it frequently extends rather than circumscribes freedom."

"She may be a widow. She's travelling alone. I saw her talking to the married couple in the next cabin. The Colvins are friends or relatives. Mrs. Colvin's her sister, I should say; they're very much alike."

"So Colvin's their name. More natural curiosity on your part, Ricky?"

"Yes. I looked at the label on an exactly similar trunk to Mrs. Mesado's that was finally dumped in their cabin."

"You're devilishly interested in your fellow passengers."

"I see no other way of entering into the charming social life of the 'Mars.' We must all get matey. Lands of sunshine, mystery and romance are only verbal flummery in connection with a pleasure cruise."

"You've seen Mrs. Mesado at close quarters?"

"I saw her back view when she was chatting with the Colvins in their cabin. She and Mrs. Colvin have the same proud carriage of the head and there's a marked similarity in their fuselage. Of course they're not to be compared with my Argentine maid."

"You always preferred the Latin type."

"Always; the Nordic's a calculating barbarian."

"What's the male Colvin like?"

"Short stature, ginger hair, rufous eyed, rubicund. Looks as if he had been suckled on beer but will now drink anything from Schnapps to Tarragona. I passed the time of day with him, and he has a forced heartiness that's almost ecclesiastical. He's a lanigerous gent—the kind that wears Harris tweeds, a woolly jumper and superabundant stockings, May be a good fellow, but his chin's in the wrong quarter and his mouth's a bit medusal. I like his wife better."

"She's fair like her sister?"

"I don't know about her sister, but Mrs. Colvin's almost platinum. Soft-eyed and sweet-mouthed, self-sacrifice will be a pleasure rather than a virtue with her. I should say Colvin trades on her complacency. Ah, there's the bugle for lunch! Come on, Algernon, I yearn for a little nutriment."

Algernon Vereker took a last glance at the beautiful wide sweep of the grey estuary, every detail softened by an exquisite silvery haze, and accompanied Ricardo down the companion to the dining saloon.

After lunch, which Ricardo asserted was the best he had eaten since he was paid for his last serial six months previously, the two men wandered up to the lounge where coffee was served. After coffee Vereker became absorbed in Miss Sackville-West's *Edwardians*, which he had borrowed from the library.

"This was worth the two bob deposit, Ricky," he remarked at length to his companion, who had sunk into the depths of an armchair beside him. A faint snore was Ricardo's only reply, and noticing that he was fast asleep Vereker rose and wandered out on to the main promenade deck. On the north side of the river the "Mars" was passing a gigantic oil station with its gleaming silver tanks, and some time afterwards a bluish-grey mist swallowed up the coastline and all around seemed limitless ocean. Accustomed to a considerable amount of exercise, Vereker joined in the usual steady pacing round the promenade deck. He noticed the dark, beautiful Argentine of Ricardo's fancy and her mother, a shrivelled, desiccated edition of the daughter. They were lounging in deck chairs, wrapped in rugs and in earnest conversation with a swarthy fellow countryman who gave Vereker an impression of being all eyes, a mobile moustache and a large diamond ring. Later he passed on his round a man and woman whom he at once recognised from Ricardo's description as Mr. and Mrs. Colvin. They were walking arm in arm, and Colvin's red face seemed unduly serious and preoccupied. They were conversing in undertones, and from the expression on Mrs. Colvin's soft features the subject was evidently distasteful to her. From the passengers Vereker's thoughts reverted to his own personal affairs. He was engrossed in them when his attention was attracted by a spasmodic hooting on the starboard. It was the warning siren of the Girdler

Light. He ceased walking and leaned over the rails, gazing at the ship with idle curiosity, when he was joined by Ricardo.

"Damned thing woke me up," said Manuel. "Sounds like a cow with milk fever. I was dreaming I was back at Chalk Farm, where my landlady used to keen periodically for her sons lost in the Irish rebellion. What's the book?"

"*The Edwardians.* Have you read it?"

"Yes. Jolly good, but I'm now wandering wearily through the Crystal Palace of fiction built by John Galsworthy. To change the subject, it's time for tea in the garden lounge and I'm going to get busy with my future playmates."

"I'm going to dump this book in my cabin, Ricky, and will join you in the lounge for tea," said Vereker and, leaving his friend, lightly ascended the companion to the upper promenade deck. As he passed along the alleyway to his cabin, No. 88, a woman swiftly emerged from No. 90 and hurried into No. 89. She was still dressed in her shepherd's tartan tweed suit, and one glance at her figure informed Vereker that she was Mrs. Mesado. She seemed eager to avoid meeting a fellow passenger and disappeared without giving him an opportunity for close observation. On returning to the garden lounge he found Ricardo sitting at the same table as the Argentine lady and her mother, talking volubly over tea to the daughter, who, evidently amused by his light chatter, took every opportunity of displaying a dazzlingly beautiful mouthful of teeth. Vereker chose a seat in a secluded corner of the lounge and was joined at his table by a Scotsman called Ferguson, whose conversation was a questionnaire as to his views on the modern conception of God. Tiring at length of this examination, Vereker lit a cigarette, excused himself and sauntered out on to the deck once more. He felt idle and a trifle bored and began to wonder why he had allowed Ricardo to persuade him into entering on this adventure. Of course the lands of "mystery, sunshine and romance" were ahead, but at the moment they appeared insufferably remote. He glanced at his watch. It was half-past five. Suddenly a commotion among the travellers attracted his attention. He joined the eagerly chattering throng to discover that Gris Nez had suddenly thrust its impressive mass through the haze. Later in the evening a blast from the "Mars's" siren called attention to the approach of a pilot boat from Boulogne. The white, red and green stars of her lights were reflected in twisted beauty on the sombre ripple of the sea. The simplicity of the dark outline of the boat and the brilliance of the colours awakened his artistic appreciation.

"Nice little subject for a decorative poster," he thought.

The pilot boat sheered off and the lights of Boulogne swam into view, a diadem of ruby, gold and emerald on the swiftly darkening sky. Away on the port side the lighthouse on Gris Nez exploded intermittently with dazzling radiance. At length Vereker went below to dress, and as he passed Mrs. Mesado's cabin door, which was partly open, he caught a glimpse of her putting the final touches to her toilet assisted by her maid. She was wearing a pale blue georgette evening gown, and beneath her neatly trimmed hair there glittered on the white nape of her neck the emerald butterfly clasp of a fine necklace of diamonds. She had evidently dressed for dinner. While he was tying a black evening tie Ricardo, who had already changed, sauntered into his cabin smoking a cigarette with lazy self-satisfaction.

"How do I look in borrowed plumes, Algernon? Aubrey's guzzle garments fit me to a nicety. He was out when I called at his flat in Clarges Street. I persuaded his valet that I had Aubrey's authority to take them. Wrote him a letter of condolence immediately I got on board. They're really too good to return, and in any case Aubrey can afford another suit. Also tried on his deck shoes, but they were miles too big. Aubrey would be a tall man if he hadn't so much turned up to make feet. He's a bit lacking upstairs; balance of Nature I suppose. I had to hump round to Buhl's in the Arcade and make a costly investment which depleted me considerably."

"I see you've already made the acquaintance of the dark lady?"

"Bit of luck, wasn't it? Got off the mark as if I were being chased by a man with a writ. She's a Miss Penteado. Saw her and her mother having tea together and pounced on the psychological moment, whatever that may mean. Some fool with a preposterous diamond ring tried to intermeddle, but I outflanked him and put him in a conversational barbed wire enclosure with the mother. He finally wriggled free looking a beaten man, and afterwards I met him at the bar standing our neighbour Colvin innumerable cocktails. Managed to bullock in discreetly and get treated. Thinking it was safe I generously offered a return. It was an error of judgment. I hadn't reckoned on Colvin. Dias, the chappie crouching behind the diamond, refused. Colvin said he never drank more than one cocktail but graciously expressed a desire for a large whisky and soda. He remarked that he was feeling cold. I succumbed gallantly but wished him in a very warm place. From their conversation when I came over the horizon I should say they weren't strangers to one another. I don't like the look of Dias; he's an untidy bit of sculpture."

"I saw the Colvins on deck this afternoon. His wife's a good-looker, but I wasn't too favourably impressed by him," remarked Vereker.

"In my opinion, he's not a bad sort on the whole, Algernon. Suffers from a common form of throat trouble; the only remedy is alcohol. I'd be a martyr to it myself, but my pocket keeps it fairly well in check. See anything of Mrs. Mesado?"

"She had just finished dressing for dinner when I passed her cabin. She has her maid with her."

"I know. I met the maid in the fairway just now. She's a pirate's prize. Has wet lips and swings her hips imperially. Her eyes are a misfit; they're distrustful and tell you that man alone is vile. I stepped aside like a courtier to let her pass and smiled appreciatively. I was declined without thanks and crept into your shelter feeling thoroughly unbuttoned. Still, I'm not defeated. I must live romantically, and it's either Mrs. Mesado's maid or the dark lady from Buenos Aires. I shall have to toss up and decide some time tonight. The dark lady is an heiress to untold wealth, and I'm afraid it gives her a cynical bias against disinterested flirtation. She thinks every admirer is making a knight's move on her fortune, while the maid fears you are making a frontal attack on her virtue."

"Come along, Ricky, I'm ready."

"About time too. I'm feeling in the mood for a Trimalchian feast."

The orchestra were playing the first few bars of Lincke's waltz, "Venus on Earth"; the dining saloon was swiftly filling up with a vivacious and well-dressed throng of passengers; the air was humming with the noise of their movement and talk, the clatter of crockery, the clink of silver; every now and then the joyous pop of a wine cork came to the surface of this murmurous tide of sound; waiters hurried to and fro or bent attentively to take their orders; the wine steward, wearing his chain and key of office, moved with the dignity of a mayor; the *maitre d'hôtel* sauntered about, keeping deftly clear of his staff, a prandial commander-in-chief, his dark eye taking in every detail of his well planned campaign. Ricardo was critically studying the menu. Vereker was gazing interestedly at the little groups of people that moved together to their tables and then suddenly sank out of his sight into their seats.

"Yes, *consommé printanier royale* sounds a good foundation, and then *suprême de barbue à l'anglaise* to follow," said Manuel with gusto to himself. Turning to Vereker he exclaimed, "By Jove, Algernon, eating's a great game played in moderation. I wish you'd attend to business instead of gazing yearningly at the beautiful feminine back at the next table. Your chit for a bottle of wine wouldn't be out of order."

"Being lazy and ignorant, I'll leave you to conduct the meal, Ricky. I'll follow your lead. What on earth are *paupiettes* of Dover Sole?"

"God alone knows, but don't ask Him. They'll be Dover sole anyhow, and that's good enough to take a running jump at. Ah, there's Miss Penteado just come in. That claret-coloured gown shows off her dark beauty to perfection. What art—only one large ruby ring!"

Vereker glanced towards the entrance to the dining saloon and saw Miss Penteado, accompanied by her mother and the gentleman with the conspicuous diamond ring, moving leisurely to her table. A moment later a figure in pale blue georgette followed.

"There's Mrs. Mesado, Algernon!" exclaimed Ricardo in an eager whisper. "Beautiful but marmoreal. Still, with a breath of romance she might come to life. I prescribe Heidsieck when you've got past the prologue and first chapters with her. She's positively lit up with diamonds; her necklace would keep me in luxury for the rest of my life. She has joined the Colvins. Damn this table; we're a million light years away from them. If she's not a widow she ought to be for the duration of the cruise. It's not fair for such a lovely creature to entrench herself behind her marriage lines."

"What are you choosing to follow the fish?" asked Vereker, not deeply interested in the doings of Mrs. Mesado and her companions.

"*Chapon de France rôti*, my lad, and then *crêpes au citron*, devilled sardines on toast, coffee and an orange curaçao with a nip of old brandy. I reckon that's fairly sound architecture."

"Order the same for me, Ricky. And what on earth are you going to do with yourself after dinner? I'm bored with this cruise already; there's absolutely nothing to do!"

"Nothing to do? Why, there's conversation in the lounge; there's a card room; you can pirouette on the light fantastic in the ballroom; you can lose money at the diddler machines, if you enjoy losing money. If you're merely out for a restful time, I can give you a packet of chewing gum and you can sit in your cabin and read Professor Dorsey's *Why We Behave Like Human Beings*. It's science with a pizzicato touch and goes down well with chewing gum. I'll lend it to you if you'll promise to be good and not cry any more."

"I suppose you'll be found in the ballroom if wanted?"

"Certainly, if Miss Penteado dances. I'd like to hold the floor with her and dance a Tango Ranchera. It's the nearest thing in human life to a dance of the butterflies. Most significant, Algernon, most significant! You'd enjoy the symbolism. You needn't want me unless you're prepared to stand iced fizz. Friendships are tested by time, and as you know time's money!"

"Very good. After dinner you can lend me your Dorsey, and I'll try and digest him over a cigar."

"Algernon, you're ossifying. You're losing your capacity for enjoyment. You're beginning to live in a straight line instead of rhythmically. A book and a cigar! You prefer them to the enchantment of music, the swing of a waltz and the perfume of a woman. I must dig you out of this spiritual tomb, strip you of the cerements of asceticism and lead you back naked and unashamed into the noisy market place of life. It was one of the reasons why I persuaded you to come on this bally cruise."

"I'm beginning to regret…"

"Don't interrupt me. You can go and incubate in your cabin tonight, but after tonight I'm going to pull you by the nose into the charming social life of the 'Mars.' Tomorrow you'll emerge an imago—Algernon the mayfly! I should take a couple of liver pills on retiring; they're an excellent beginning for a spiritual catharsis!"

After dinner both Vereker and Ricardo chatted for some time over their coffee and liqueurs in the lounge, and then the latter wandered off to the ballroom, having first lent his friend the book he had promised. Vereker lit a cigar and withdrew to his cabin, where he could read with complete absorption. He was immersed in the opening chapters of Dorsey's book when he heard voices in Mrs. Mesado's cabin. There were two voices; a man's and a woman's. First there would be a passage spoken in a deep undertone, and then would follow the higher and more penetrating feminine notes. For some time he continued to read, keeping his mind free from their interrupting influence, but all the while they beat an insistent tattoo on the outer doors of his consciousness. Gradually his concentration on his book weakened and transferred its awareness to the conversation proceeding beyond the dividing wooden wall of his cabin. He dropped the extinct butt of his cigar into an ash tray, lit another, closed his book and threw it on to his bed. As he lounged in his easy chair, his hands clasped behind his head, his eye lazily following the wreaths of smoke from his cigar, his extremely acute hearing began to pick up the more loudly spoken words of the speakers beyond.

"You'll have to do the job as soon as possible, Dick. I can't stand this any longer," came a clearly spoken sentence from the woman.

"All damned fine talking! How the hell... be reasonable, Beryl... risks... consider the awful risks..."

"You've got to take them... your suggestion..."

"Don't talk so loud..."

The agitated voices sank until they were inaudible once more. Vereker, who had listened to the conversation with only casual interest, was now roused to inquisitive alertness. Dick and Beryl! Dick was undoubtedly the Mr. R. Colvin of the passenger list which had been handed out that evening to all the diners at their tables. Vereker drew the list from the pocket of his dinner jacket and glanced through the names again. Mrs. G. Mesado and maid. Was Beryl Mrs. Mesado or Mrs. R. Colvin? he wondered, and then came to the conclusion that the matter was irrelevant. At least it didn't concern him. Strange how intriguing an overheard conversation could be! It set one thinking; the mind seized on a few broken sentences and began to weave them busily into a glowing pattern—an idle if amusing pastime.

"You'll have to do the job as soon as possible. I can't stand this any longer."

Here was the foundation for some grim imaginative edifice. Interested in crime and the detection of crime, Vereker seized on the very word "job" as significant; it was the generic term that criminals applied to any of their sinister acts from common larceny to a gigantic fraud, from blackmail to murder. The male reply had been defensive; it had thrown up obstacles to an immediate accomplishment of the mysterious job; it had asked the speaker to consider the "risks." Risks! Did the word "risks" prove conclusively that the job was one which might bring in its wake the consequences which follow detection of an infringement of the law? It was a reasonable inference. No danger, no risks. The injunction, "Don't talk so loud," was an admission that their conversation if overheard might prove disastrous. It all looked very suspicious when viewed from a certain angle. Here were a gathering of people, bent on a pleasure cruise which was only possible to those blessed with a certain amount of leisure and means. These wealthy holiday-makers carried money and valuables. They were of the type that were notoriously careless, and many of them from their very circumstances of birth and affluence, circumstances which had shielded them from contact with their predatory fellows, unbelievably credulous and trustful. There would be human sharks among this company, ready to prey on the unwary; for them it was not a pleasure cruise to lands of sunshine, mystery and romance; it was a business undertaking which might yield a profit on their investment and the risks incurred. And yet this overheard conversation might have an altogether innocent interpretation. The conclusions one arrived at were entirely coloured by one's mood. For some minutes Vereker's thoughts wandered into the obscure and complex subject of human emotion. It was emotion which magically formed one's settled convictions rather than reason. It entirely depended on one's emotional mood whether a statement was a terminological inexactitude or a damned lie. Words were the mysterious criteria framed by feeling which made things culpable or venial, right or wrong.

"I detest this man Dias... he's a crook..." came again the woman's voice in raised tones.

"Old Miguel's all right... prejudice..."

"You simply sponge on him for drinks!"

"Shut up, Beryl..."

Again the voices subsided and a smile crossed Vereker's face. The lady evidently disliked Mr. Miguel Dias. It bore out Ricardo's first impression of that gentleman. Ricky had called him "an untidy bit of sculpture," and Manuel was gifted with a very shrewd insight into human nature, an insight which was almost as instantaneously intuitive as that of a child or a dog.

A period of silence followed, and then the woman's voice was raised in a distinct note of alarm.

"Dick, Dick, Maureen's necklace has gone!"

"Necklace? What necklace?"

"The one Guillermo gave her—the one that caused all the trouble."

"But you don't mean to tell me she had it on?"

"Of course she had. I wouldn't touch the accursed thing. I felt it was obscene!"

"Impossible! You must be dreaming, Beryl!"

"I know... I know..."

"All rot... distracted... no one has access..."

"For heaven's sake speak quietly! You'll be overheard."

The voices died out, and at this juncture a knock sounded on Vereker's cabin door and next moment Ricardo walked in.

"Hello, Ricky; enjoyed yourself?"

"Famously. I've already made a wide circle of admirers."

"Dance with Miss Penteado?"

"Several times. She's an incarnation of Terpsichore. I also sat out in the deck garden with her, and she became quite confidential. I'm joining her tomorrow at the bathing pool or ship's Lido. We shall admire one another's figures shamelessly."

"Was Mrs. Mesado dancing too?"

"No. She and Colvin disappeared together after dinner, and I haven't seen them since. Mrs. Colvin, her sister, was there. I had the pleasure of one dance with her. It was unimpassioned perambulation to be truthful. Her name is Constance and bears out my first impression of her. A name's a terrible thing; the subconscious mind moulds one's whole character to fit it. Arnold Bennett was doubtless scared to death of Enoch, and Oscar Wilde must have trembled at the O'Flaherty."

"So her name is Constance, and her sister's is Beryl!"

"Algernon, you've been at your old game of sleuthing. By what cunning ruse did you discover it? I knew Mrs. Mesado would put a lighted match to you."

"I happened to hear Colvin call her Beryl."

"Amazingly clever! I wish I had your powers of deduction."

"Was the man Dias in the ballroom?"

"Oh, yes, old Koh-i-noor was tripping it with Latin energy. I managed to ditch him beautifully, as the Americans say, whenever he wanted to dance with Rosaura—that's Miss Penteado. She told me frankly that Miguel Dias had a crush on her but that she had no intention of crumpling up under the pressure."

"You seem to have entered rapidly into the charming social life of the 'Mars,' Ricky."

"Taken a header, my boy. I never stand on the brink of flirtation and shiver at the possibilities of marriage. In and out again and a rub down with the rough towel of indigence is my philosophy—*pace Veneris*."

"Dias seems to be an old friend of the family?"

"Merely an acquaintance of Mrs. Mesado's husband, Guillermo Mesado. The latter's an Argentine millionaire according to Rosaura. Mrs. Mesado and Mrs. Colvin are English."

"How did Mesado make his pile?"

"Argentine meat trade. I didn't ask too many questions. Must leave some topics of conversation for the remainder of the trip. Even I can't make love at the Herculean pitch."

"What does your Rosaura think of Colvin?"

"Didn't say much about him, which may mean she thinks a lot or nothing at all. Possibly doesn't know him very well. I should say he was a feckless idiot, and the gods always bless feckless idiots with millionaire brothers-in-law. From what I can gather he's Mesado's mentor when he's living in England. Mesado has bought a beautiful country place called Firle House at Jevington in Sussex, and likes to do everything in our fashion. *Plus anglais que les anglais.* Colvin advises him on the outdoor side of how to be a Britisher. He has taught him to sing 'Rule Britannia,' which shows he has a sense of humour."

"You say the Penteados are wealthy too?"

"Filthily. Meat packing business. Rosaura's the only daughter and will come into the doubloons when the packers cease from packing and the weary are at rest."

"I suppose your flirtation will have an ulterior motive, Ricky?"

"God forbid, Algernon! I belong to the noble army of artists in prose fiction. With us money's a secondary consideration. The primary condition is how to get it and spend it recklessly. But I'm tired and feel like a reviver. You haven't a bottle of Scotch hidden anywhere?"

"I'm afraid not."

"Poltroon! Have a Haig and Haig ready tomorrow night. I'm accustomed to a nightcap. I saw Colvin at the bar and think I'll join him and gather some more gossip. I feel I've interested you in some of your fellow passengers of culture and refinement. Good night!"

On Ricardo's departure Vereker once more picked up his book and continued to read, but soon felt an overwhelming desire to sleep. Drawing the curtains of the windows, for there were square glass lights instead of portholes on D deck, he undressed and got into bed. The wind had freshened and the "Mars" had acquired a slow heel and toe motion that Vereker found decidedly pleasant. For some time he lay awake and then fell off into a light doze. He was awakened by the sound of footsteps on the promenade deck without and wondered what time it might be. He was about to switch on the electric light and look at his watch when he heard the ship's bell. It was two bells of the middle watch. He remembered that that was one o'clock in the morning and became inquisitive as to the identity of the late promenaders. As the footsteps became audible again he glanced through a chink in the curtain and saw a man and woman pass. They were well wrapped and muffed, so that it was impossible to see their faces clearly, but as their receding figures became silhouettes against one of the deck lights he distinguished them as belonging to Mrs. Mesado and Colvin. He lay back once more in his bed and tried to sleep. At regular intervals he heard the passing footsteps of the two patrollers as they made their circuit of the promenade. Remembering their conversation which he had overheard in the adjacent cabin some time previously, he wondered what might be the object of this strange nocturnal meeting. He had a curious persuasion that it was not altogether innocent, and at the back of his mind there lurked the suspicion that it had some connection with the "job" which Dick had been enjoined to do as soon as possible. He recalled the various items of information he had gathered from Ricardo's gossip, and gave himself up to lazy conjecture about these strangers who had thus merged into the area of his observation. Before the end of the voyage they might be his enemies or friends or merely those polite acquaintances who are mere puppets on the stage of life, that are seen awhile and pass away, leaving nothing but an impersonal memory. Lost in idle dreaming, he heard once more their steady pacing as they passed outside his cabin and then in the ensuing silence he heard three bells. It was half-past one; the half hour had seemed hours.

Gradually his thoughts became more diffuse and detached from reality and he fell into a sound slumber.

Chapter Three

The wind of the previous night had dropped and a thick, sleepy haze hung over a calm sea. The day passed with the usual lively routine of life aboard a liner. Physical health enthusiasts in bathing costume were up early and exercising vigorously with the medicine ball, the rowing machine or stationary bicycles in the gymnasium; others trudged determinedly round the promenade decks to awaken an appetite for breakfast. The majority of the passengers, however, emerged from their cabins at the breakfast hour. During the interval between breakfast and lunch the pari mutuel, under the direction of the deck steward, did a lively business in shilling tickets on the ship's run for the twenty-four hours ending at noon. On the games deck deck-tennis, deck-quoits, shovelboard, bat-tennis, a species of glorified ping-pong, were in full swing. After lunch an air of lethargy settled on the company, who read or gossiped in the lounge smoke room, or from deck chairs in sheltered corners. The elderly retired to their cabins for their habitual afternoon nap. Tea followed at four o'clock with a musical programme by the ship's orchestra, Cocktail time preceded dinner, and after dinner there was a cinema performance in the dining saloon, which had been quickly transformed into a theatre for the purpose. Light-hearted dancers thronged the ballroom, while bridge enthusiasts sat in grave concentration over their cards in the card room.

Through this day Vereker went with moody resignation. He experienced at moments an exasperating sense of precious, unrecoverable time slipping away relentlessly in utterly futile idleness, and then argued himself into quiescence by reminding himself that he needed a rest. As far as his art was concerned, he knew that he was feeling jaded: he was convinced that he must leave paint and brushes alone until zest and courage and sensitive enthusiasm revived to act as merciless goads to fresh work. He spent a considerable part of the intervals between meals in strolling idly round the deck; in casual chatter; in noting the extraordinary variety of colour assumed by the sea under the ever changing light; in quietly observing his fellow passengers from some coign of vantage and furtively caricaturing them in a few forceful and illuminating pencil strokes.

Captain Partridge, Captain of the "Mars," had been present at dinner. Ricardo, who had met the sailor before, had laughingly introduced Vereker as the well-known amateur detective and third-rate professional painter. Captain Partridge, a clean-shaven, ascetic-looking man with a penetrating eye, a square jaw and a firm mouth, showed a lively interest in Vereker's criminal investigation and clearly remembered the "Polo Ground Mystery," as the Press had called the sensational factors surrounding the murder of Sutton Armadale, "the millionaire sportsman." Vereker at once liked Captain Partridge, and the dinner hour was his first complete escape from the boredom which he had suffered since the start of the cruise. The ship's doctor, Macpherson, a taciturn Scot, had also been present at the meal, but had taken little part in the conversation though he had listened to it with grave concentration.

During the day Vereker had seen little of Ricardo. With his usual zest, Manuel had entered into every scheme devised by the passengers for killing time joyously. At one moment he was one of a mixed four playing deck-tennis with rope rings, or partnering an enthusiast in a game of quoits; at another he was romping with a party of children, a species of entertainment at which he was singularly adept, thereby becoming a great favourite with his playmates' parents. After dinner he joined the dancers; an hour later he was in the card room making a four at bridge; the rubber finished, he was one of a syndicate trying to scoop the pool at a diddler machine. At ten o'clock at night he sought out Vereker and joined him in a whisky and soda in his cabin.

"Our syndicate scooped the pool tonight, Algernon," he said.

"I'm glad to hear you've made a little pocket money, Ricky. What did you win?"

"Scooping the pool is high falutin for spending seventeen shillings and winning back nineteen and threepence. The winnings were then pooled for drinks, so we are square with Chance and not too elated with our luck."

"See any more of our new acquaintances?"

"Dias the diamantiferous delivered his riposte tonight. Carried off Rosaura from under my nose to join a party who were drinking champagne as if it were as cheap as municipal water. I was left out in the cold, but on parting she gave me a squeeze of the hand which assured me that I was nearly as dear as the fizz. I retreated to the card room and bought solace exorbitantly. Then I made a forced march on the bar. There I found Colvin had dug himself in. We exchanged drinks, but I soon discovered from the squish he talked that his back teeth were awash. I left him and came here to be comforted. Comfort me with apples."

"Help yourself, Ricky."

"Thanks. I'm glad you're accelerating on the uptake. On coming to your cabin I passed Mrs. Mesado in the alleyway."

"Did you get a good look at her?"

"No; to tell the truth I was too much interested in her diamond necklace. It must be worth some thousands of pounds. Only ugly women should wear resplendent jewels. Jewels distract your attention from their wearers' faces. Besides, it's unfair to thieves; it must be difficult to rob a beauty if you're at all susceptible to feminine charms."

For some moments Vereker was lost in reflection, and then he turned to Ricardo and asked inconsequently: "By the way, Ricky, in your conversation with Rosaura Penteado was the name Maureen mentioned?"

"No."

"Are you quite sure?"

"Absolument, mon brave. I would have noted it. Surely you haven't forgotten Maureen?"

"I can't say I remember the lady."

"The only girl I ever became engaged to."

"You never told me about the engagement."

"Perhaps it was too painful. We were engaged for a week. Her parents objected to her marrying a penniless scribbler and persuaded her that it was madness to take a chance on my future royalties. Today I admire their commercial vision."

"It wasn't your past history, Ricky?"

"No, that would have been an exciting excavation among ruined romances. It was the economic argument, the financial purview. *Mort aux industrialistes*! Excesses of the heart are venial; an overdraft with your banker a mortal sin. Algernon, the world's growing ugly. We've built altars to mass production and smashed up the shrines to Venus. When I remember Maureen I always think of Siegfried Sassoon's lines:

"Can my night-long thoughts regain
Time-locked loveliness and laughter?
Can your presence in my brain
Be rebuilt such aeons after?
Can it be so far away—
Yesterday, yesterday?"

"Shut up, Ricky; remember you're on a pleasure cruise."

"I was trying to make you forget it, Algernon. But what's this about Maureen?"

"Oh, nothing, nothing at all, Ricky."

"Very well, if you're going to be so confoundedly mysterious I'm going to turn in."

Manuel Ricardo finished his whisky and rose slowly to his feet. At that moment the ship's siren gave a prolonged blast and the two men, listening intently, heard her engines gradually slow down almost to the point of stopping.

"Looks as if we'd run into a belt of fog, Algernon. It was getting blankety when I came down. That tootling will probably continue and keep us awake all night. If it does I'll get up and have a gambade round the deck for exercise. It's now eleven o'clock. So long."

On Ricardo's departure Vereker picked up the bottle of whisky from the table in his cabin and, opening a small cupboard in which were neatly fitted a vacuum-flask jug of drinking water and glasses, locked the spirit up. He glanced at the electric clock on the mantelpiece above the radiator, a clock which was altered daily to agree with the chronometer on the captain's bridge, and compared it with his own. He then stood for some moments as if wondering what to do. He was debating whether he should resume his reading of Dorsey or go to bed. He was not feeling sleepy and decided to read, but before settling down in his chair he pressed a bell for the cabin steward. The wine he had drunk at dinner had made him thirsty, and he was now assailed by a sudden longing for a cup of tea. Fuller the steward appeared, took his order and a few minutes later returned with a tray.

"When would you like your tea in the morning, sir?" he asked as he was about to depart.

"About six o'clock, Fuller. No tea. A little fruit, please."

"Very good, sir, and your bath about half an hour later?"

"That'll do nicely."

"Good night, sir." Fuller closed the cabin door quietly and Vereker, having poured himself out a cup of tea and lit a cigarette, picked up his book once more. He had been reading for about an hour or more when he again became conscious of voices in Mrs. Mesado's cabin, but their speech was no longer audible as it had been the night before. The occupants of No. 89 had doubtless heard Ricardo's penetrating, high-pitched voice and, aware of the possibility of being overheard, had taken the precaution to converse in more subdued tones. Again Vereker's attention strayed from his reading, and his thoughts reverted to the information Ricardo had gathered from Miss Penteado. Mrs. Mesado's husband was Guillermo Mesado, and judging from Ricardo's appraisement of the lady's diamond necklace the husband was evidently a very wealthy Argentine. Now that Vereker was certain that she was the Beryl to whom he had overheard Colvin speaking his interest in her redoubled. But who was Maureen, and what was the interpretation of Mrs. Mesado's dramatic exclamation that Maureen's necklace had disappeared? It was the necklace that Guillermo had given her and had very unpleasant associations for Beryl Mesado. What was the secret trouble it had caused? Vereker found himself becoming more intrigued in this fair traveller than he would have deemed possible. Strange that so far he had been unable to get a good look at her! Ricardo had said she was beautiful, but Ricardo's criterion of beauty was extremely elastic; it ranged from La Gioconda to any comely ballet girl, from society beauties to half the barmaids of London. As an artist, Vereker was more than discriminating; he was exacting. As he pondered on the subject he became almost annoyed with himself for his preoccupation with Mrs. Mesado; it amounted almost to an impertinence. Let Ricardo enter into the passing friendships that pleasure cruises afforded! He would keep aloof, his detached critical self, an amused spectator of this "magic shadow show." As he mused thus he heard footsteps pass his cabin door and enter No. 89; a third person had joined Colvin and Mrs. Mesado. He came to the conclusion that the newcomer was probably Mrs. Colvin, whose voice he had not yet heard. Curiosity to confirm the correctness of his conjecture made him doubly alert. He sat patiently listening for the newcomer to cabin No. 89 to reveal her identity by speech. In this he was for the time being disappointed, for if the occupants of No. 89 were now conversing they were doing so in whispers. He could hear nothing but the dull sounds of occasional movements. Losing interest in this occupation, Vereker picked up his borrowed copy of *The Edwardians* and was about to resume reading when he heard a voice exclaim:

"Gone? But it can't be gone. If some one has stolen it all our plans must be known!"

"For God's sake be quiet, Constance, or you'll be overheard. There's probably some mistake, came the admonition in Colvin's deep voice."

The words confirmed Vereker in his surmise that Mrs. Colvin had joined her husband and her sister. There followed once more the hum of lowered voices, and after a further period some one quietly left the cabin. Vereker listened, and judging by the sound of the receding footsteps and the opening and closing of another door one of the party had left cabin No. 89 and entered No. 90.

Vereker now glanced at his watch and, finding that it was nearly one o'clock, undressed, got into bed and switched off the light. He composed himself for sleep, but the regular hooting of the ship's siren now became irritatingly obtrusive. Again and again he was on the borderland of unconsciousness when its melancholy boom hauled him back to wakefulness. He was on the point of deciding to switch on his light once more and bury himself in his book when a knock sounded on his door and Ricardo entered. He had put on a thick, warm overcoat over his dress clothes, and wore a tweed cap and a muffler.

"Well, Ricky, what's your trouble?" asked Vereker after he had pressed the electric light switch above his head.

"I simply couldn't turn in with that infernal hooting going on. No sober man could unless he were dead beat. It's as bad as being on a lightship. Did you manage to doze off?"

"In spasms, but for some time I've been lying awake thinking."

"Thinking? It sounds incredible, but in any case a reasonable being can't lie awake thinking all night; he'd disintegrate. I don't know why they want to keep up this bally row when there's not another ship within a stone's throw."

"To avoid collisions, but evidently you believe in a miss being as good as a mile."

"Certainly, and that a pretty Mrs. is dangerous at any distance, Algernon."

"I'm sorry I can't ask the skipper to stop the noise on your account, so what are you going to do about it?"

"I'm going to scamper round the ship until I feel comatose and then I'll ask the nicest stewardess to put me to bye-bye. So long. I wish you brighter thinking."

With these words Manuel Ricardo left Vereker's cabin and, passing along the alleyway and up the short companion, let himself out on D deck, which was the upper promenade deck of the ship. For some moments he glanced round at the surrounding white globe of mist lit up by the lights of the "Mars," and then began to pace determinedly round the deck to induce physical weariness. At this hour there was not another soul on the deck, so he paced alone, but Ricardo's temperament was almost aggressively cheerful and he whistled the soldier's chorus softly to himself as he covered lap after lap of the monotonous course. Once as he passed the officers' quarters, which were situated at the bow end of his rectangular journey, an officer descended from the bridge and was about to disappear when he caught sight of Ricardo.

"Sorry we've got to keep you awake," he remarked cheerily, "but it's pretty thick to-night."

"How long do you expect to be wrapped up in this cotton wool?" asked Ricardo.

"No saying. Probably clear before morning. Good night."

On Ricardo's departure Vereker once more decided to try and sleep and gradually dropped into an uneasy slumber, troubled by fantastic dreams. He was being chased across an endless desert by some hideous monster which kept bellowing like a ship's siren in his wake. His feet sank deeper and deeper into the desert sand, causing him to drag his weary legs along at a ridiculously slow pace. The monster was gaining on him relentlessly and escape seemed altogether hopeless. Its bellowing grew louder and louder. Now it seemed immediately behind him, and he awoke with a start.

"Damn this fog!" he exclaimed when he realised what had awakened him. He switched on his light and sat up in bed. He was reaching to take his book from the book rack beside his bed when he was startled by a loud scream from Mrs. Mesado's cabin. That scream was followed by the sound of stifled sobbing and the agonised exclamation:

"Dick, it's all up!"

"You're not going to leave this cabin, Beryl!" came the stern rejoinder.

"Remember it's murder. Damn you, get out of my way!"

A brief silence ensued, and was broken by the sounds of a sharp struggle. For some moments the noise of scuffling continued. The cabin door slammed and all was silence. Vereker, now awake and somewhat alarmed, sprang from his bed. He was momentarily at a loss what to do. Should he go and inquire what was wrong and if he could be of any assistance? A moment's reflection made it clear that any interference on his part in the private quarrels of strangers might be reckoned by them as an unwarrantable impertinence. After all, it was not his affair, and the wisdom of minding his own business became more cogent as he stood in his pyjamas wondering what course to adopt in such an exigency. At that moment he heard the sharp rattle of something striking his cabin floor, and wondered what it might be. To his half wakened senses it sounded as if something had fallen from his dressing table—his keys, pocket knife or fountain pen—and he immediately turned round and made his way to that article of furniture. On examination he found that all his belongings, the usual articles that a man carries in his pockets and habitually turns out on a dressing table when retiring, were still where he had left them. He glanced at the floor beneath the table, but found it clear. He at once ceased to trouble about the

matter; there was no accounting for the innumerable sounds to
be heard in a ship's cabin at sea. A chilly mist was slowly filtering
in at his window, which he had left half open, for he was almost
fanatical on the subject of fresh air during sleep. He shivered
slightly, pushed the window up with a quick thrust and drew
the curtain across it. The action riveted his attention on the fact
that he had ostensibly forgotten to draw that curtain earlier in
the evening. Strange! He was almost positive he had done so
immediately on entering his cabin. The slight breeze caused by
the slow motion of the ship must have blown it back while he was
dozing. Feeling cold he switched on the electric radiator, thrust
his feet into bedroom slippers and pulled on his Jaeger dressing-
gown. In a state of nervous agitation he fumbled in his pockets
for his cigarette case and then, opening his wardrobe, extracted it
from his dinner jacket. Having lit a cigarette he sat down on his
bed and smoked as his mind flitted restlessly over the incidents
of the night. That there was something unusual afoot between
Mrs. Mesado and the Colvins was apparent, but again it was
none of his business. The old inquisitive itch, the hunger of the
detective to probe into a mystery, was now insistent, and out of
the general lethargy in which he had lately been steeped sprang
a sudden liveliness, a bright vivifying enthusiasm. He would find
out all about it, burst through the tegument of mystery which
shrouded the actions of these next-door neighbours of his on
board the luxury liner "Mars." To dismiss the subject from his
mind and stand aloof disinterestedly was alien to his explorative
mind, and as he pondered on the matter the boredom which he
had already associated with the term "pleasure cruise" vanished,
and he rose from his bed and began to pace his cabin floor with
quick nervous steps, his hands thrust into the pockets of his
dressing-gown, an eager light burning in his eyes. At last he had
found something congenial to do. Rapidly he began to work out
a plan of action. He would keep his ears alert and his eyes open.
He would not rouse suspicion by any eagerness to ingratiate

himself with these strangers, but gradually he would gather his information, piece it together patiently as a player assembles the components of a puzzle, and in the end he would have in his possession a solution of the problem. The end might not justify the labour and concentration he would have to bestow, but to Vereker the intricacies, the disappointments, the excitements of investigation were a sufficient incentive; they were the elements of the enthralling game of detection which he loved. And Manuel Ricardo was fortunately on board. He had made use of his friend on innumerable occasions in the past. Ricardo was invaluable in his way; he had a genius for friendship, for those cheerful and transient acquaintanceships in which so many people pass their time, and which Manuel called "the gentle art of living like sheep." He was, moreover, a great favourite with the opposite sex and possessed an extraordinary power of eliciting confidences which, useless to himself, were frequently vital to Vereker's theories. He greatly admired his friend Vereker, and took a whole-hearted delight in assisting a man who he was convinced was one of the greatest amateur detectives in England.

"Yes," thought Vereker, "Ricky will be indispensable; he always was a first-rate mixer, and on this occasion the circumstances will be peculiarly suited to his penchant for living like a millionaire. A costly stalking horse at times, but the game's worth it and one must always pay for one's hobbies..."

His reverie was at this point suddenly shattered by a sharp rapping on his cabin window, and kneeling with one knee on his bed Vereker swiftly drew aside the gaily coloured cretonne curtain which screened his cabin interior from the publicity of the deck and peered out. Looking from this brightly lit chamber into the outer gloom, he could only discern the vague silhouette of a head and shoulders. He switched off the light and looked again. Now he could see clearly that the head and shoulders belonged to Ricardo, and that Ricardo was beckoning him frantically to come out and join him. Vereker was seized with a swift spasm of annoyance. Was Ricky indulging in one of the idiotic pranks to which his mercurial temperament was addicted? He was not going to encourage him in any of his freakish practical jokes.

"Some tomfool game or other, I'll bet," he exclaimed petulantly. "I'm not joining in at this godless hour!"

At that moment he heard the ship's bell strike four. It was four bells of the middle watch and two o'clock in the morning. He switched on his light once more and was about to draw the curtain of his cabin window when he noticed that Ricardo's short thick nose was flattened against the pane. His eyes were wide and startled, and his lips kept framing the words "Come out here, Algernon. Quick! Quick!"

Without further hesitation Vereker pulled on trousers, socks and shoes and, enveloping himself in an overcoat, quietly let himself out of his cabin. A few minutes later he was out on the starboard sweep of D deck and, glancing towards the stern, noticed in the half light that Ricardo was still standing outside the window of his cabin. He was bending down over some dark mass lying prone at his feet. On hearing his friend, Manuel stood erect and gesticulated wildly, urging haste and pointing to the object over which he was standing guard. In a flash Vereker saw that Ricardo was in no joking mood and at once hurried along the deck to his assistance.

"What's the matter, Ricky?" he asked breathlessly, and at the same moment realised that the mass lying at Ricardo's feet was the body of a woman. "Good Lord, who is it? Has she fainted?"

"It's Mrs. Mesado, Algernon," replied Ricardo in a strained whisper, "and if I'm not mistaken she's dead. I can't rouse her."

"Impossible!" exclaimed Vereker and, stooping down, caught hold of the recumbent figure's hand. To his surprise it was encased in a chamois leather glove. Quickly pushing down the soft gauntlet of the glove, he laid his finger on her wrist. Delicate as was his sense of touch he could feel no throbbing of her pulse, and the flesh of the forearm was unpleasantly cold.

"By Jove, I'm afraid you're right, Ricky!" he said. "Run and get the ship's doctor while I stay here and keep an eye on things."

"Where on earth does he hang out?" asked Ricardo.

"I don't know, but hunt up one of the night stewards and he'll dig him out. There's no time to lose!"

Ricardo promptly disappeared, and Vereker, pulling out a small pocket torch which he always carried on him, made a swift examination of the body. Mrs. Mesado was dressed in the pale blue georgette dress which she had worn at dinner the previous evening, and the fact reminded him that he had not seen her at dinner that night. Strange that he should have missed her, for he had been particularly anxious to get a good look at her. He at once observed that she was not wearing her valuable diamond necklace. Flashing his torch from one point to another, his sharp eye took in every detail of the figure as it lay in an ungainly sprawl on the deck. Again he experienced a sharp sense of surprise on noticing that Mrs. Mesado was wearing a pair of ordinary chamois leather gloves with her evening gown. This fact struck him as so unusual that, in spite of his ingrained scruples to leave the body untouched, he quickly removed the glove of the left hand in order to examine it, and in doing so found that the material of the glove stuck to the fingers. Flashing his torch on the bare hand he discovered that the flesh of all the knuckles was cut and bruised, and that the adhesion of the fingers to the leather of the glove had been caused by the blood that had flowed from the wounds and dried. A swift inspection of the right hand showed that it too was cut and bruised in a manner similar to the left. Before replacing the gloves on Mrs. Mesado's hands he noticed that the letters C. C. had been written in purple indelible pencil on the inside of the gauntlets.

"An interesting point," he murmured, and as he replaced the right-hand glove Vereker began to whistle to himself a mournful little air from a forgotten Viennese opera, a sure indication that he was beginning to get excited. Then as he was about to slip on the left-hand glove he suddenly dropped it and switched the light of the torch on to that badly injured hand.

"More and more interesting!" he exclaimed as he saw on the index finger an emerald and ruby marquise ring, two of the stones of which were missing. Without further delay he pulled the glove on to the apparently lifeless hand and made another examination of the body. The extreme pallor of the face struck him as remarkable, and then his quick, restless glance settled for a moment on the high-heeled blue satin shoes that Mrs. Mesado was wearing. At once his hands caught hold of her feet and felt them all over with great care. The action imparted some recondite information which elicited a slight grunt of satisfaction, and, hearing footsteps approaching, Vereker straightened himself, extinguished his torch and thrust it into the pocket of his overcoat. Next moment three figures appeared from the door leading into the cabins situated on the starboard side of the upper promenade deck and hurried up to where Vereker stood beside Mrs. Mesado's body. As they came within the radius of light flung from the window of Vereker's cabin he saw that the men were Ricardo; the ship's doctor, Macpherson; and Fuller, one of the night stewards for the range of cabins on D deck. The doctor, without speaking a word, pressed the button of an electric lamp which he was carrying in his hand and flung a wide circle of light over the body lying on the deck. Thence he swung the lamp upwards and enveloped Vereker in its rays.

"Oh, it's you, Mr. Vereker," he said, and added quietly, "I'll be glad if one of you gentlemen would give Fuller a hand to carry the lady back to her cabin. Mr. Ricardo has told me she's a Mrs. Mesado and her cabin is No. 89 on this deck."

At once Vereker stooped and lifted the recumbent body by placing his hands under her arms. Fuller raised her lower limbs by embracing her round the knees, and the party made its way carefully along the deck.

"Not any more noise than you can help, gentlemen," warned the doctor as they proceeded along the alleyway; "the less the other passengers know about this matter the better."

A few minutes later they had entered Mrs. Mesado's cabin and deposited the body gently on the bed. The doctor then made a swift examination and grunted ominously.

"Is she dead, doctor?" asked Ricardo impatiently.

"I'm afraid so. Just passed away," he replied without looking to see who had addressed the question.

For a brief period the four men stood in silence, and Doctor Macpherson, who was quietly reviewing the matter from a wider angle than the particular death of a human being, silently produced a loose cigarette from one of his pockets and lit it. Turning slowly to Fuller he asked:

"Is Mrs. Mesado travelling alone, or has she her husband or friends on board?"

"She has her maid with her, sir—a Miss Gautier—and Mr. and Mrs. Colvin, in the next suite of cabins, are relatives if I'm not mistaken."

"Mrs. Colvin is Mrs. Mesado's sister, I believe," added Ricardo.

"Oh, that so!" commented the doctor, and after a pause, "You might tell Mr. and Mrs. Colvin to come here quietly, Fuller. Never mind the maid for the present. Tell the Colvins that Mrs. Mesado has taken suddenly ill and that I'd like to see them as soon as possible."

Fuller departed and Doctor Macpherson, puffing unconcernedly at his cigarette, turned to Vereker and Ricardo.

"Thank you very much, gentlemen, for your assistance and the trouble you've taken. I won't detain you any longer; I'm sure you must be tired. Captain Partridge may want to see you to-morrow. If so he'll send for you. In the meantime I must ask you as a great favour not to let this matter go beyond yourselves. I'm sure you'll see the necessity for keeping the other passengers in the dark. The matter doesn't concern them, and a sudden death isn't a particularly happy occurrence at the beginning of a pleasure cruise. May I rely on you?"

"Certainly, doctor," replied Vereker and Ricardo together.

"Thanks very much," replied the doctor, and, wishing him good night, Vereker and Ricardo left Mrs. Mesado's cabin and returned along the alleyway to Vereker's quarters.

Chapter Four

The pontifical manner leeches assume always gets my goat," remarked Ricardo with heat as soon as Vereker and he were alone in the latter's cabin. "I suppose Hippocrates started the stunt to cover his deficiencies, and his disciples have made it part of the ritual of medicine ever since."

"Sound psychology, my dear Ricky. The public demands omniscience from the hierarchs of healing. The only way you can prevent the public from discovering that a certain amount of knowledge is not omniscience is to be mysterious and authoritative. Assurance is the greater part of suggestion, and suggestion the greater part of most cures."

"So that's the simple explanation, is it? Well, I wish Macpherson wouldn't try to work the spoof off on me. Any fool could twig that he hadn't the haziest notion of what had happened to Mrs. Mesado, and he didn't take the slightest trouble to ask us anything about the business. Promptly took the attitude that the matter didn't concern us at all, and told us to run away and play. Ergo, Macpherson's an ass, and a Scots ass at that. He ought to have been brought up on carrots instead of oats."

"You're annoyed because you didn't get more of the spotlight, Ricky. After all, the matter doesn't really concern you. You were an accident."

"I never was an accident, Algernon. My parents considered even my birth an answer to prayer. I claim to be a protagonist in this drama. Didn't I find Mrs. Mesado's body?"

"Yes, and your vanity's hurt because Macpherson ignored that minor fact in his general concern about major things. A death's a pretty serious business on a pleasure cruise when you come to think of it."

"I suppose it is. When they find out, half the company, with smug hypocrisy, will go about with long faces as if they were deeply grieved. They'll discuss it eagerly and pretend it has cast the inevitable gloom—yes, gloom's the word—over the ship. They'll have a high old time with condolences, and after fairly wallowing in a burial at sea they'll forget all about it. In any case, that doesn't justify Macpherson's heavyweight manner with us. If I hadn't given him my word I'd chastise him by blowing the gaff to all the passengers tomorrow morning. That'd cook his goose—I mean his porridge—for him!"

"Forget your grouch against Macpherson for the moment, Ricky, and tell me just how you came to discover Mrs. Mesado's body lying on the deck," asked Vereker calmly.

Ricardo promptly opened Vereker's cupboard and produced a bottle of whisky and glasses. Having poured out a liberal dram for his friend and himself, he flung off his cap, muffler and overcoat and sat down.

"Phew! I feel as if I were disrupting. This business has shaken me badly," he exclaimed and drained his glass. Replacing the glass on the small cabin table, he once more sat down, thrust his hands into his pockets and stretched his legs out in front of him.

"Let's begin at the beginning," he said. "Do you remember the exact time I left your cabin for a stroll round the deck, Algernon?"

"Well, not the exact time, Ricky, but it must have been about quarter to one; perhaps a few minutes before."

"Very good. I immediately got out on deck and began to pace round the usual course. There's a brass plate fixed up somewhere which tells you that so many times round the deck is one mile, but I never compute distance by such an abstract thing as measurement. Mathematical abstractions are the bane of modern thinking because they're so illusorily concrete. I measure distance by feeling and know that I've walked far enough when I'm tired. My intention was to get thoroughly tired and then go to bed and fall asleep in spite of the ship's siren. Well, I began to pace round the course, and around me was a globous world of mist, eerie and wonderful but damned cold. I don't know how long I'd been tramping when I ran into one of the ship's officers. I think it must have been the chief officer from the number of gold stripes on his sleeve. He looked a perfect zebra. He had evidently come down from the bridge, and after a cheery word disappeared into the officers' quarters, which are, as you know, situated on this deck some distance nearer 'the neb of the ship' as Macpherson would probably say. There were no further interruptions to my pensive circumambulation until about one-thirty or perhaps a little later. As I came along the starboard deck, which is the right side looking forrard, in case you're not sea-minded, I was surprised to see a man and woman locked in one another's arms standing against the outer wall of our cabins not six paces from the door leading on to the deck. I couldn't see them very clearly in the gloom, and with my customary delicacy I naturally didn't go up and ask them what they thought of the political situation in Europe as a conversational gambit. I soon recovered from my surprise because it's quite irrational to be surprised at anything lovers may do under divine impulse..."

"I wish you'd cut out the embroidery, Ricky; I want to get at the facts," interrupted Vereker impatiently.

"Sorry you object to my narrative style, Algernon, but you must remember it's my profession to make dull facts interesting. A gripping serial isn't a bald statement of facts; it wouldn't pay at two guineas a thousand. Half the fun of eating a nut is cracking the shell."

"Well, get along and don't make the shell too thick. What did you do after finding the couple—interlocked, so to speak?"

"I proceeded on my way. I remember thinking that I might dig out Rosaura and ask her to come up and admire the fog. Concluded it was out of the question, so I wandered round to the port deck. Not wishing to embarrass the lovers on the starboard deck, I began a kind of sentry-go instead of completing the usual lap. I got tired of sentry-go, had enough of it during the war, so I glanced at my watch and found it was nearly two o'clock. I know half an hour's a very short time to tell a girl you love her and persuade her you're a superman, but I wasn't going to let the couple make a golden age of it. Thought I'd reappear as a memory tickler. Remind them that life's brief and one side of the promenade not long enough for exercise. When I turned on to the starboard deck I was surprised to see that the lovers had gone, and promptly quickened my pace. Then came a painful shock. I caught my foot in something soft but inert and found myself full length on the deck. Picked myself up quickly, almost apologised and investigated. Struck a match and discovered that I'd tripped over the body of Mrs. Mesado. Even then I didn't realise the seriousness of the affair. I thought at once that she had fainted and that her companion had vanished in search of a restorative. I automatically stooped and felt her heart. It was not beating, or rather I couldn't feel it beating. I listened for her breathing: there was not the faintest sound. I experienced a quick start of fear. Death in any circumstances has a tendency to put the wind up you, but when you stumble over it on a pleasure cruiser's deck you get panicky. Comparable to meeting the devil in Paradise. My first thought was to spring up to the bridge and bring down the skipper or shout for help. Then I noticed I was standing exactly opposite your lighted cabin window. I could just see your mug through a chink in the curtain. I hammered on the pane, and it seemed ages before you deigned to take the slightest notice."

"To tell the truth, I thought you were up to one of your usual silly pranks and wasn't going to be caught. Then I concluded you weren't good enough an actor to put on such a scared look, and I jumped to it. But tell me, Ricky, was it Mrs. Mesado you saw in a lover's embrace on the first occasion?"

"How the devil should I know? I only looked at the pair through the tail of my eye, but now you mention it the lady of my first encounter was certainly wearing a light-coloured dress. That's as much as I can say for certain; it wasn't a moment for kit inspection."

"That of course means nothing. Seventy-five per cent of the evening gowns worn at dinner tonight were pale tinted affairs. You couldn't see who the man was?"

"No, but he was much taller than the woman was as far as my recollection goes, His head was certainly bending down over her. I took it to be the conventional osculatory pose."

"It wasn't Colvin, was it?" asked Vereker as if his thoughts were following some definite line of conjecture.

"I don't see how it could have been Colvin," replied Ricardo. "In the first place he's a very short, thick-set fellow, and certainly not much taller than Mrs. Mesado, though she's a pocket Venus. Secondly, it's not likely he'd be making love to his sister-in-law in such dangerous proximity to his wife. There are remoter nooks to make the world safe for infidelity. Still that's an obvious point of view. Colvin may be of a different temper, like a street bookie I knew who used to work right in front of a police station."

"Was there anything unusual about Mrs. Mesado that caught your attention, Ricky?"

"Well, I didn't expect to find her lying full length on the deck to say the least of it."

"Yes, I know, I know, but was there anything about her clothes, shoes, face and general appearance that you found in any way remarkable?"

"Let me see. I'm being put through a test for observation. In the first place, her dress, blue georgette, was the same as she wore at dinner last night. Her shoes were blue satin; I hadn't spotted them previously. Her face had, of course, changed terribly; it seemed thinner, the cheeks were more sunken and it wore that indefinable expression which seizes a human face in death. As for her general appearance, her clothes looked as if they had been pulled about... she looked badly mauled."

"As if she had been struggling?" interrupted Vereker.

"Exactly! But do you think there had been a struggle, Algernon?" asked Ricardo eagerly.

"I was wondering. I noticed that her hair was all over the place."

"Yes, now that you mention it, I remember the fact distinctly. But, my hat, I nearly forgot a major point! She was wearing a pair of chamois leather gauntlets!"

"Yes," drawled Vereker in his pensive way, "I had a good look at them."

"But, Algernon, surely a woman doesn't wear chamois leather gauntlets with an evening gown?"

"I'm not a fashion expert, but I should say not. In Mrs. Mesado's case, however, she had slipped them on for a definite purpose. While you were searching for Doctor Macpherson and I was alone with the body I yanked off those gloves, which by the way were much too large for her, and found the knuckles and fingers of both her hands cut and smashed very badly."

"Good Lord, that's strange! How could she have come by her injuries?"

"I'd like to know. The point, however, is when did she come by them. Did she wear those gloves at dinner?"

"I didn't see her at dinner tonight. I only met the lady once at close quarters, and that was in the alleyway. I was much too interested in her necklace to notice her hands."

"She wasn't wearing that necklace when you found her lying on the deck, in any case, Ricky!"

"No, by Jove, she wasn't. I say, Algernon, do you think...?"

"Tell me, Ricky, could you identify that necklace if you saw it again?"

"Without fail. There was an emerald pendant attached, and the clasp on the back of her neck was a large emerald butterfly. I took particular notice of it."

"That's satisfactory," remarked Vereker, and rising from his chair began to pace slowly up and down the cabin. "It's a great pity," he added almost in soliloquy.

"What's a great pity?" asked Ricardo eagerly. He knew that his friend's preoccupation was a sure indication that a significant problem had presented itself to him, and that he had encountered some difficulty.

"It's a great pity I never got the chance of seeing Mrs. Mesado close at hand. She always seemed anxious to avoid being seen too closely by her fellow passengers. Do you remember when I almost ran into her as she was about to leave her cabin?"

"Very clearly. She damned you incontinently and swiftly disappeared. Didn't you see her face on that occasion?"

"No, merely the parting in her hair, the curve of a permanent wave, the line of a fine figure and a beautiful left hand holding a box of Players cigarettes."

"The hand was not in a glove?"

"No. I saw it very distinctly even to a signet ring she wore on her little finger."

"Are you quite sure that it was Mrs. Mesado?"

"I had no reason to think otherwise. Why?"

"Because it may have been Mrs. Colvin. The latter's not unlike her sister and wears a signet ring on the small finger of her left hand. I noticed that point when I was dancing with her."

"But does Mrs. Colvin wear a shepherd's tartan tweed suit?"

"Oh, yes, she was wearing one on the promenade deck this morning. A brown and white check; very smart I thought it."

"That complicates matters," murmured Vereker as he slowly lit another cigarette, "but I'm almost certain that Mrs. Mesado's was a black and white check, though it'd be dangerous to be positive considering the brief glance I got of her."

For some minutes the two men sat in ruminative silence. Then Ricardo, after helping himself to another whisky and soda, exclaimed: "Look here, Algernon, I know this mood of yours. You smell a rat. Personally I've never wanted to smell a rat, but I can see you think there's some hugger-mugger behind the sudden death of Mrs. Mesado."

"I've gone beyond mere thinking, Ricky. I'm certain of it. I'm convinced there's been murder!"

"Good heavens, Algernon, you don't mean to say it's as serious as all that! What makes you suspect murder?"

"Several incidents that have occurred since we started on this cruise. To avoid being mysterious about the business I've overheard remarks passed in Mrs. Mesado's cabin by her and by Colvin, words spoken in distress or in anger, which at once roused my curiosity. To tell the truth, the bally cruise was boring me till I ran into the fringes of this mystery."

"Tell me exactly what you overheard, Algernon. I may be useful..."

"Be patient, Ricky. You're going to be useful all right. I shall ask you to help me as I've done on former occasions. There's a mystery on board this ship, and I'm not going to rest till I get at the bottom of it."

"Relentless sleuth! But for goodness' sake tell me what you overheard."

"The first thing that caught my attention was the fact that Mrs. Mesado wished to avoid her fellow passengers. There was nothing very extraordinary about that. Some people are painfully shy at all times, but such people don't indulge in pleasure cruises. She has practically kept to her cabin, except for a brief appearance at dinner last night, ever since the 'Mars' left London. You might explain her conduct by illness, but to all appearances she was not ill. Then last night, when I was sitting alone reading your book by Professor Dorsey, I happened to overhear voices in No, 89. I am now certain that the two people who were talking were Colvin and

Mrs. Mesado. I very clearly heard Mrs. Mesado tell Colvin, 'You'll have to do the job as soon as possible, Dick.' Dick remonstrated and asked her to consider the risks, and was told that he'd have to take them. Now you know the word 'job' is a very common one among criminals, though I'm not prepared to say right away that either Colvin or Mrs. Mesado is of that class. The expression, however, made me prick my ears, especially when coupled with the idea of risks. Then Colvin warned the lady not to talk so loudly, which showed he was conscious of the danger of being overheard. The tentative conclusion to draw from this was that the job, whatever it was, was not an innocent one."

"Too many was's about it, but it sounds reasonable on the face of it," said Ricardo, rubbing his hands excitedly, for his interest was now thoroughly roused.

"From that moment I began to sit up. To use your own expression, I smelled a rat, and though I went on reading I was all ears for any further morsel of information. It was not long before Mrs. Mesado told Colvin that she detested the man Dias, expressed her opinion that he was a crook and accused Dick of sponging on him for drinks."

"He's a sponger all right, but not at all selective. A mass sponger you might say. And then?"

"The conversation became inaudible once more."

"Damn it, Algernon, you're a born serialist. Get on with the yarn. I'm pining for the next instalment."

"Well, for some minutes I could hear nothing clearly, and then Mrs. Mesado in a very excited voice exclaimed, 'Dick, Dick, Maureen's necklace has gone!' Dick asked her which necklace, and was told that it was the necklace that Guillermo had given her. 'The one that caused all the trouble,' were her words, to be exact."

"Of course you know that Guillermo is Mrs. Mesado's husband," exclaimed Ricardo.

"Yes. I have to thank you for that bit of information. You've already been a great help. But who is Maureen?"

"Ah, now I know the reason of your eagerness to know who Maureen is. I can't tell you at the moment, but leave that line of inquiry to me. What a pity your old friend Detective-Inspector Heather isn't here! He'd solve the problem without your assistance and save you all the trouble."

A wry smile stole over Vereker's thoughtful face as his memory travelled back over the famous cases in which he and Heather had been good-natured rivals.

"It's not a case which would suit Heather's peculiar genius. He always blames me for exercising a too lively imagination. He prefers something concrete to work on, and so far I'm working entirely on conjecture. But to return to the subject, there was evidently a violent quarrel and a scuffle between Colvin and Mrs. Mesado in No. 89 tonight, and the very word 'murder' was mentioned."

"At what time was this, Algernon?"

"That's a pertinent question. I can't be exact, but a little before two o'clock. As I was working purely on conjecture and didn't expect anything so serious as Mrs. Mesado's death, I was rather lax in noting the exact time. One point, however, I can be definite about: just after you discovered her body on D deck it was four bells of the middle watch."

"And pray what time was that?"

"If you were sea-minded you'd know it was two o'clock in the morning."

"And you mean to say she was alive between one-thirty and two o'clock?"

"Of that I'm positive. We can take it for granted that it was sudden death, rather too sudden to be innocent, unless of course it was heart failure."

"Looks pretty fishy when you come to think of it, especially after a row and a struggle," remarked Ricardo, and for some minutes both men sat in silence, lost in their own thoughts.

"I wish Macpherson hadn't been so eager to get rid of us after he had summoned the Colvins," said Vereker at length. "I'd have given something to see Colvin's immediate reaction to the news of Mrs. Mesado's death. It might have been informative. I suppose the doctor was being tactful."

"Yes, I know—the old hush-hush trick. Do you think there'll be any sort of private inquiry tomorrow?"

"It all depends on Macpherson and Captain Partridge. They may be satisfied by such explanation as the Colvins can give, and we may hear little or nothing further about the matter. If the skipper is inclined to discuss the subject of Mrs. Mesado's death with me I may be able to get him thinking. But we must tread very warily, Ricky. This affair will certainly make Partridge use nautical language even if he only soliloquises. You see, he has the success of this cruise to think about. His responsibility is a heavy one. He's answerable to his company in the first place, and naturally a pleasure cruise isn't a joy ride for them; it's a commercial undertaking, with profits as the main issue. Partridge's job is navigation, and that's a big enough job without the addition of a murder mystery on board his ship. If there's anything fishy about Mrs. Mesado's death he'll be obliged to take notice of it. He's literally between the devil and the deep sea."

"I see your argument, Algernon, but Macpherson annoyed me tonight. I'd take a delight in shaking his self-assurance. He simply asks to be baited."

"Now, Ricky, for Heaven's sake go canny with Macpherson. You'd better leave him to me. I'll manage him better than you. He's inclined to be friendly with me in his dour Scots way, and I'll profit by it. We've got to keep in mind that this affair of Mrs. Mesado is really no concern of ours. To me of course it presents a problem to be solved. The question of culpability or punishment isn't strictly my affair, though I may have to take steps eventually in the cause of common justice. But I'm determined to solve the problem whatever may happen."

"Well, I'm determined to go to bed and sleep in spite of everything. I'd clean forgotten the ship's siren in my preoccupation with this business. Lord! What a row! He must have been a humorist who called that infernal instrument a siren, after a sea nymph with a melodious voice. A minor key is always a major irritant to me."

"What time are you going to get up, Ricky?" asked Vereker as he commenced to undress again.

"Depends on when I fall asleep. I asked the steward to bring tea at six-thirty. It's now three o'clock. You'll see me at breakfast in any case; I'm feeling hungry already."

"I'd like to see you fairly early. I shall have several odd jobs for you tomorrow and you'll need all your wits about you, so try and get a couple of hours' sound sleep."

"It'll be sleep in spite of the sound, Algernon. Good night!"

"Good night!"

Chapter Five

I

To put it very mildly, this is a damned nuisance, Mac," said Captain Partridge to the doctor.

They were closeted together in the master's cabin not long after the doctor had interviewed Mr. and Mrs. Colvin and told them briefly that Mrs. Mesado was dead. They had thrown off all official restraint and were chatting very confidentially with one another.

"I agree," replied Doctor Macpherson curtly as he lit a cigar.

"Any nasty complications from our point of view?" asked the captain quietly as he flung off his cap and ran his fingers through his thick grey hair.

"On the face of it, no. The Colvins—Mrs. Colvin, by the way, is the dead woman's sister—say that she was suffering from heart disease and knew herself that she might have a fatal seizure at any moment."

"What d'you think yourself?"

"Considering the circumstances it might be advisable for me to think they're right."

"I see your point," remarked the captain slowly. "Do you think there's anything not quite straight in the business? Suicide for instance?"

"Might be suicide, but that would be clear only after a post-mortem examination."

"Suicides are a bit of a nuisance. I've had four of them in my time. Three on the 'Nereid', my last ship. In every case they occurred the day before we put into port. The poor devil who's sick of the world dreads the very sight of land. The choice of time in each case was rather convenient, because I put the body ashore next day and sent my coded message to the company, as well as my report to the Home Office, before I forgot all the particulars."

"Speaking professionally, there's something not quite straight in this case. I don't altogether like the look of it," said the doctor reflectively.

"Between you and me and the binnacle, what d'you think's wrong, Mac? You needn't mince matters. We're alone."

"It's terribly difficult to say just off-hand. I'm not so sure about that heart disease."

"But the Colvins say it was heart disease, and they ought to know."

"That's true."

"Well, then that's good enough for us. Simple case of death at sea. Who found the body on D deck?"

"Your young friend Ricardo, and he summoned his pal Vereker. Ricardo collected the night steward, Fuller, who dug me out, explained matters, and I went straight to where Mrs. Mesado's body lay on the starboard side of D deck. Fuller and Vereker carried the body to the lady's cabin, No. 89 on the same deck. By this time life was extinct. Cautioning Vereker and Ricardo to keep their own counsel owing to the nature of the trip, I dismissed them tactfully and told Fuller to bring in the Colvins."

"They were terribly upset of course..."

"Yes, but they gave me to understand that they knew that such a seizure might occur at any moment. They say the patient took a digitalis preparation for her ailment, but after a search I could find none of the medicine among her things."

"Is digitalis poisonous?" asked the captain gruffly.

"Very much so, and the worst of it is that the effects vary with different people."

"I suppose you've just mugged that up in your library," commented the captain, smiling.

"Well, yes, a man can't remember everything, though my memory's a first-rate one as far as memories go."

"Most Scots have good memories. They haven't forgotten the Battle of Culloden yet. Could she have taken an over-dose?"

"Possibly, but in that case she'd probably have been deadly sick prior to death. Again, if Mrs. Mesado was in the habit of taking a digitalis preparation she might have died from the cumulative effects. In such a case a patient may go into a fainting fit and die without any warning. What's more, there'd be no appreciable post-mortem sign. These vegetable poisons are tricky things. You never know exactly where you are with them."

"That's good enough, then, from the Green Star's point of view, Mac. As far as we can judge it's an unfortunate occurrence, perfectly straightforward, and it's no damn good your getting mysterious about it. Has the lady a husband alive?"

"Yes; she's English by birth, but married to a very wealthy Argentine."

"Where's her husband?"

"They don't know at the moment. There seems to have been a bit of a rumpus some weeks ago, and the husband went off in a huff. The lady was evidently used to his nasty habits and didn't trouble herself about his departure. She shut up her house in Sussex and decided to console herself with a cruise aboard this ship."

"Usual burial unless they want to take the body home or bury it in Lisbon. We've no facilities for keeping a corpse in any of the refrigerators."

"The sister says she'll take all responsibility on behalf of her sister's husband, and wishes a speedy burial at sea. They can't communicate with Mesado by wireless because they don't know where he is, although they think he may have gone to Buenos Aires."

"She's a sensible woman. You've explained, Mac, that it's not desirable to make a public function of the burial?"

"Yes, yes, I took care to put that aspect of the affair very clearly. They agreed with me wholeheartedly."

"Excellent. We'll bury her tomorrow night. Beyond her relatives it won't be necessary to have anybody else present, though I dare say some of the passengers will find out and put in an appearance where they're not wanted."

"They like burials at sea as a rule," commented the doctor dryly.

"Well, they're jolly well not going to get one this trip," replied the captain firmly. "We'll drop her overboard tomorrow night. Bit of a nuisance. Dancers and card players hang about the ship till all hours. Damn these cruises. We've been turned into variety entertainers. We're no longer seamen."

Doctor Macpherson was silent for some moments, smoking lugubriously.

"There was one rum thing about the body that I could not quite understand," he remarked at length.

"What the devil was that?" asked the captain, casting a troubled glance in the doctor's direction.

"She was wearing a pair of chamois leather gloves. I took these off and found that both hands were very badly cut and bruised. A valuable ring on one of her fingers had had some of its stones knocked out."

"How did you account for that?" asked the master sharply.

"I didn't account for it," replied the doctor.

"Well, what had the Colvins to say about it?" asked the captain impatiently.

"They said Mrs. Mesado had a motor smash on the way from London to Tilbury, and had thrust her hands through the windscreen of the car she was driving."

"Ah, well, that's a satisfactory explanation," sighed the captain, as if some unpleasant matter had been definitely settled.

"I wasn't quite satisfied with the explanation," remarked the doctor.

"Good Lord, Mac, you're always seeking trouble. The thing seems quite feasible to me."

"But her hands weren't bandaged, as they certainly would have been if such had been the case. The wounded flesh of both hands was sticking to the leather of the gloves."

"I see. It's a rum sort of point to raise, Mac, but we must leave well alone. It's not our job to try and fathom the idiosyncrasies of all our passengers. Did you probe the Colvins further on the subject?"

"No. I couldn't very well give them the lie, and I diplomatically let the subject drop."

"Good. We're famous for diplomacy on the Green Star Line. Now I think that's all we can do about this rather unfortunate occurrence at the moment. If anything unusual transpires let me know. We must be careful."

"Very good," agreed the doctor, and wishing his skipper good morning, for it was seven bells of the middle watch, he retired to his cabin and was soon sound asleep.

II

Not long after Ricardo had left Vereker in the early hours of the same morning, and before the latter had completely undressed and returned to his bed, a gentle knock sounded on his cabin door. Slipping on his dressing-gown, Vereker quietly opened his door to see who the untimely visitor might be and was confronted by Mr. Richard Colvin.

"May I come in and speak to you for a few minutes?" he asked uncertainly.

"By all means," replied Vereker and, closing the door, pushed an easy chair over to his guest. His eye roved quietly over Colvin, noting his general appearance. From his twitching mouth and shaking hands he learned that the man was in a highly nervous and distressed state.

"I hope you'll forgive my intrusion at this hour," he said, "but I felt I had to see you before I turned in. I would have come earlier, only Doctor Macpherson kept Constance, my wife, and me jawing over things, and we've just managed to get rid of him."

Colvin's shifty eye wandered furtively round the cabin and at length alighted on the bottle of whisky standing on Vereker's table. He looked at it yearningly for a few seconds and then asked:

"I wonder if I might help myself to your whisky? I'm terribly upset."

"Take a good stiffener," replied Vereker warmly, and added, "Wait a minute. I'll get you a clean glass."

Colvin poured himself out a plentiful potion with a shaking hand and drained the glass greedily.

"Don't be afraid to punish it," urged Vereker cordially. "I have another bottle in my cupboard. You've had a rough passage tonight and it won't do you any harm. Take another shot, and I'll join you."

To his satisfaction the invitation was promptly accepted. It was at once evident to Vereker that the quickest way to this man's confidences was through his throat, and he had decided to get Colvin to talk at all costs now that chance had flung him the occasion. The moment was particularly opportune, he thought, for a man is less guarded in highly emotional states.

"Your friend Ricardo found my poor sister-in-law's body on the deck tonight. I wanted to thank him. I went to his cabin next door, but found it in darkness. Thinking he was asleep I didn't like to disturb him. I noticed your light was still on, so I risked dropping in on you. I believe you were with him."

"Not at the moment of the discovery. Ricardo knocked me up. Rapped on my window, and I joined him."

"Ah, I see. Still it was very good of you both to take so much trouble. Constance and I are very grateful."

"Glad to be helpful. Most unfortunate occurrence. I sympathise with you and Mrs. Colvin. Mrs. Mesado has been ill for some time, I suppose?"

"More or less. She suffered from heart trouble, and we were always led to expect that she might die suddenly at any time."

"To expect misfortune tends to lessen the shock when it arrives," remarked Vereker, at a loss for more appropriate words, for his thoughts were not in his speech. He was trying to fathom the reason for Colvin's visit. A conventional expression of gratitude for the trouble he had taken seemed to him at the moment hardly a strong enough motive. It had the insincerity of exaggerated feeling; Colvin seemed to be over-acting his part. His disturbed mental state might account for his deviation from the acceptable norm, but it had roused Vereker's lively suspicion.

"She was apparently well when you saw her last?" he remarked, as if eager to avoid any uncomfortable hiatus in their conversation.

"Seemed quite well. We saw nothing unusual and she herself didn't complain."

"What time would that be?" asked Vereker in as casual a tone as he could assume.

"Let me see, let me see," replied Colvin with studied innocence; "it must have been ten o'clock when she left Constance and me and went to bed."

"As early as that," remarked Vereker and, instantaneously aware that he had made a dangerously false step, asked impressively, "And you never saw her alive again?"

"Never," replied Colvin with a theatrical pathos which he did not improve by helping himself to further whisky.

For some moments Vereker's thoughts were vigorously occupied in seeking a motive for such a deliberate lie, for he had heard Colvin's voice in Mrs. Mesado's cabin as late as quarter to two in the morning. Either the man was a fool or was boldly attempting to safeguard a dangerously weak spot in some defensive scheme. Vereker's face was as impassive and expressionless as that of a Chinaman. He gazed blankly in front of him and heard Colvin utter an instinctive, almost inaudible sigh of relief. At once the reason for this unexpected visit flashed on him. Colvin had surmised that Vereker was the only person on the ship who might know that he had been in Mrs. Mesado's cabin just prior to her sudden death. He would be aware of this through having overheard their conversation in the adjoining cabin. He had come to find out and, satisfied that Vereker did not know, was obviously relieved.

"I'm not keeping you out of bed, Mr. Vereker?" he asked in a more natural tone.

"No. I'm particularly wakeful after the incidents of tonight, and I seem to have done nothing but sleep since this cruise started. I don't suppose you feel too eager for bed either?"

"No. I couldn't possibly sleep if I turned in. Apart from our bereavement, I'm extremely worried."

"Can I help you in any way?" asked Vereker sympathetically.

"Well, one of the main objects of my looking you up was to ask your advice. You may be able to put me wise. Did you see Mrs. Mesado at dinner last night?"

"I thought I saw her enter the dining saloon. Our table is on the opposite side of the saloon from yours, and as I didn't know Mrs. Mesado very well by sight I can't be positive."

"Ah, then you would hardly notice that she was wearing a very fine diamond necklace."

"As a matter of fact I did even at that distance, and thought to myself that it must be worth a small fortune. I was right in my surmise that it was Mrs. Mesado?"

"That was she all right. Her necklace is a very valuable one. You couldn't see it clearly from where you sat, but I can assure you the stones are really magnificent. Her husband, however, is very wealthy and can afford these expensive trifles. It'll be a terrible blow to him when he hears of his wife's sudden death. I suppose you'll send him a marconigram?"

"Well, no," replied Colvin after some hesitation. "As a matter of fact, we don't know where he is at the moment. Beryl and he quarrelled and have been estranged from one another for some time. Doubtless it would only have been temporary, but now..." Shrugging his shoulders dramatically he continued, "To return, however, to my sister-in-law's diamond necklace. I'm afraid it's missing."

"Good heavens! You don't mean to say so!" exclaimed Vereker with surprise, and at once all his wits were on the alert. "It certainly wasn't round Mrs. Mesado's neck when we found the body," he added significantly.

"No, I know that," said Colvin immediately and, evidently feeling that his certainty might be informative, qualified the statement: "At least we were fairly certain that it couldn't have been. You see, Mrs. Mesado always took her necklace off after dinner and locked it in her jewel-case. It was a confirmed habit with her when she was staying in hotels or on board ship."

"These expensive gewgaws are more trouble than they're jolly well worth," remarked Vereker slowly as his mind rapidly reviewed every aspect of the situation.

"I agree. I don't know why women carry the damned things about with them; they're a constant source of worry, even of actual danger where desperate men are concerned," said Colvin with apparently unfeigned distress.

"You've thoroughly searched Mrs. Mesado's belongings?" asked Vereker, looking up at his visitor quickly.

"Well, not thoroughly. We were too much upset for that, but on finding that Beryl was not wearing her necklace we ran hastily through her jewel-case. It's certainly not there."

For some moments Vereker was silent, his face stonily impassive, but a certain brightness in his eyes and a thinning of his lips, undiscernible to those not intimately acquainted with him, declared that he had resolved on some audacious plan to serve his own purposes.

"You know that I was in Mrs. Mesado's cabin for some time tonight with Doctor Macpherson, Ricardo and Fuller, the night steward?" he asked.

Colvin nodded assent and glanced up expectantly.

"Well, I'm almost certain I saw Mrs. Mesado's necklace when I was casually looking round her cabin. I'm trying to remember where it was. Some unusual spot, I know. The fact struck me forcibly at the moment, though I was naturally too preoccupied with the gravity of the occasion to worry much about jewellery."

This information at once brought an eager light into Colvin's rather watery reddish-brown eyes.

"Look here, Vereker," he said impetuously, "would you, would you mind just popping into her cabin with me now and having another look round? It might help you to recollect where you saw it. I'd be very grateful."

This was the opportunity for which Vereker had been longing, and to secure which he had not been strictly truthful. He excused the ruse by telling himself that the means were justifiable when dealing with a liar, perhaps even a criminal.

"If you're particularly anxious..." he began.

"I am anxious," interrupted Colvin emphatically. "We'll have to account to Guillermo Mesado for the loss of his wife's necklace. Knowing the gentleman, I can assure you it won't be a pleasant job."

"I suppose not. Perhaps if I had another look round Mrs. Mesado's cabin I might remember where I saw the thing. You've got a key to her cabin?"

"Oh, yes. We've locked the cabin, and I have a duplicate in my pocket. The body is still in there and will be removed to the sick-bay later. Are you ready?"

Vereker rose to his feet as if to signify his readiness to proceed, and the two men quietly entered the adjoining cabin and switched on the light.

"Now let me see. I was standing here when I thought I saw it," said Vereker impressively, and his glance wandered swiftly round every nook and corner of the bedroom of Mrs. Mesado's suite. "I'm afraid I see no signs of it now," he added disappointedly after a few minutes of scrutiny. His eyes finally came to rest on the gruesome white sheet which discreetly covered the dead body lying on the bed. He turned towards Colvin, who stood patiently awaiting the result of his examination."

"Look here, Mr. Colvin," he said at length, "I have an idea it was somewhere on that bed, and I've a proposal to make. If you will just run quickly through Mrs. Mesado's personal belongings once more I'll make a thorough search of the bed and the cabin. I've done a lot of detective work at different times and am quite expert at rapid searching."

He turned and looked Colvin direct in the face to note the effect of his words. He was not astonished that the very mention of detective work seemed to exercise an immediate and disturbing effect on his companion. An uneasy look came into his eye and his brows knitted uncomfortably. He recovered from his discomposure with marked celerity and agreed to the proposal with forced heartiness.

"That's an excellent idea," he said. "If you'll just run your hand over the bed I'll go through Beryl's jewel-case and belongings. I hope you're not squeamish?"

"No, not at all," replied Vereker quietly, and crossing quickly over to Mrs. Mesado's bed he pulled down the sheet covering the body and began his search. It did not take him many minutes to satisfy himself that the diamond necklace was not there. He had, indeed, never expected to find it, and was really seizing another opportunity to have a very careful look at Mrs. Mesado's face and hair and hands. There was something about the dead woman's hair which apparently puzzled him. He stood for some minutes lost in conjecture and then, taking advantage of Colvin's preoccupation with Mrs. Mesado's valuables, discreetly produced from his pocket two picture post cards of the "Mars" several of which he had bought at the ship's shop. They were of the highly glazed variety common to this type of photograph. Removing the glove from the right hand of the dead woman, he pressed the fingers firmly against the mirror-like surface of the post card and slipped it into his pocket. Having gone through the same process with her left hand, he crossed over to the dressing table and, picking up an ordinary white celluloid comb which lay on it, dropped it into his pocket beside the post cards. He glanced quickly round at Colvin and was satisfied that his action had not been noticed by him. Pulling out the right-hand drawer of the dressing table, he found it contained gloves, handkerchiefs neatly arranged, a pair of discarded silk stockings rolled into a ball and tucked carelessly into a corner, an odd leather handbag and a small phial containing capsules. He glanced at the label on the phial and found that the capsules were nembutal. He was seized with a sudden impulse to pocket the phial, but on second thoughts replaced it and withdrew a pair of chamois leather gauntlets from the drawer. They were of exactly similar pattern and size to the pair on the dead woman's hands. Glancing inside the gauntlet he saw that the initials B.M. were marked on the leather with purple indelible pencil. The remaining drawers of the dressing table contained nothing but articles of wearing apparel and yielded little of importance to his investigation. He turned towards Colvin, who was rapidly going through the contents of a small dressing case and jewel box, taking out the articles and placing them one by one on an occasional table. Vereker carefully memorised these articles, especially the items of jewellery. There were no necklaces, but several bracelets and three magnificent rings. He noted the absence of wedding ring and signet ring, both of which Mrs. Mesado must have discarded for the evening when dressing. Among these articles, however, was a passport, and as Colvin busied himself with his search Vereker picked up the passport and examined it. He glanced rapidly down the descriptive particulars: Height, 5 ft. 2 in.; colour of eyes, grey; colour of hair, fair. The item "Special peculiarities" had been left blank. Taking a good look at the photograph, which like many passport photographs was a very poor likeness of the bearer, he tossed the book back on the table and made a rapid search of the cabin. During this procedure he carefully examined several pairs of the dead lady's shoes, noting they were size 5 and scrutinising the soles, especially those of the right foot. He opened the cabin wardrobe and glanced at the dresses hanging there. As he took careful stock of them a look of amazement was born on his face, but was instantly suppressed.

"I'm afraid I've drawn blank," he remarked to Colvin, who, heedless of Vereker, was now busy replacing Mrs. Mesado's belongings in her dressing case.

"The confounded thing's not here either," said the latter and, closing the dressing case, carefully relocked it and rose to his feet.

In one corner of the cabin stood a very capacious cabin trunk, which had caught Vereker's eye on his first entry.

"Have you gone through that Saratoga?" he asked.

"Yes, once, fairly carefully," replied Colvin and seemed about to give up the search as fruitless. Then, as if assailed by some swift doubt, he crossed to the trunk, unlocked it and flung up its lid. Vereker came and stood over him as he knelt down and ran swiftly through its contents. The latter consisted of one or two dresses, some silk stockings and underwear which only half filled the trunk. These articles of clothing too had apparently been thrust into the trunk in great haste, for their arrangement was singularly unlike a woman's tidy method of packing. Vereker was struck by this fact, and concluded that they had been disarranged by Colvin during his first search for the missing necklace.

"No, I'm afraid it's gone," said Colvin in a despairing tone. "I wonder what the devil she could have done with it?"

"It may have been stolen, though that appears an unlikely contingency. Barring yourselves, Doctor Macpherson, Fuller, Ricardo and me, no one so far as we know has entered the cabin."

"Suppose for a moment it has been stolen, what am I to do?" asked Colvin, turning to Vereker.

"Report the loss to the purser. The captain's omnipotent on board his ship, and I dare say he could order every cabin to be thoroughly searched if he felt that the necklace had been stolen."

"That'd be an unpleasant sort of thing at the commencement of a pleasure cruise," remarked Colvin ruefully.

"Yes, like a politician, the captain would doubtless explore every avenue before resorting to such a drastic expedient. In any case you can report to the purser later on. He'd probably suggest something helpful in the circumstances. Such losses must have occurred before in his experience. He'll certainly impress on you that the company isn't responsible."

With these words Vereker glanced at his watch and uttered a mild exclamation of surprise.

"Thanks very much for your help, Vereker. I don't see that we can do any more," said Colvin, taking the hint, and added, "I'll get back to Constance. She'll be wondering what has happened to me."

The two men left the cabin. Colvin switched off the light, locked the door and thrust the key in his pocket. In the alleyway he again thanked Vereker for his assistance and, bidding him good morning, turned and disappeared into No. 90.

Back in his own quarters, Vereker sat down once more in his easy chair and gave himself up to thought. He was not quite sure of this man Colvin. There was something insincere about him, something which certainly did not inspire confidence. He was genial, plausible, easy-mannered, but his face suggested shiftiness rather than weakness. He was apparently no fool, and his adroit adaptation of action to conceal his hidden purpose, his swift, suspicious awareness warned Vereker that he must not take his man too lightly in any battle of wits. From Colvin his thoughts turned to Mrs. Mesado, to the quarrel in her cabin, to the missing necklace, to various incongruous factors that obstinately refused to fit into any rational scheme of things, and he grew more and more amazed as he slowly began to piece all he had learned into a constructive theory. At last, weary of speculation, he rose from his chair. The light of dawn was already throwing up the brilliant hues of the cretonne curtain drawn across his window. In a few minutes the steward would bring his morning fruit. It was hardly worth while trying to sleep. He drew the curtain of his window and looked out. The fog was dispersing and the ship's engines were beginning to throb with a livelier pulsation. He picked up his safety razor and began to fit in a new blade. He was proceeding with this operation, his mind still intensely preoccupied with other matters, when he dropped a portion of the nickel-plated mechanism of the razor. He stooped to pick it up, but on striking the cabin floor it had bounded somewhere out of immediate view. He knelt down to search for it, and instantly his eye caught the glitter of something lying under the electric radiator. Thrusting his hand underneath the radiator, to his unbounded astonishment, he drew forth a rope of dazzlingly brilliant stones. One glance at the emerald pendant and the large emerald butterfly clasp forming part of the ornament informed him that it was Mrs. Mesado's lost necklace.

"Well I'm damned!" he exclaimed, and stood for some moments admiring the flashing blue and white radiance of the magnificent diamonds that hung in a shimmering loop from the fingers of his left hand.

"Now, how the devil did it get there?" he promptly asked himself, and at once his thoughts flew to Colvin and to Colvin's unexpected visit to his cabin an hour or so previously. No, there seemed no explicable connection between Colvin's visit and this amazing discovery of Mrs. Mesado's necklace. Colvin had been sincerely enough distressed at its loss; either that or he was a consummate actor. Then, as Vereker stood dumbfounded trying to fathom the import of this astonishing find, he remembered that arresting moment when he had heard the impact of some article striking his cabin floor, an incident which at the time he had been unable satisfactorily to explain. At once, too, his memory flashed back to the half-drawn curtain of his window, which he felt certain he had fully drawn on entering his cabin and switching on the light. Some one must have pushed back that curtain. A curious smile spread slowly across his features as he gathered the necklace of scintillating gems into a blazing heap in his left hand and then thrust them into his trousers' pocket.

"That sheds a little more light on the subject," he remarked to himself, and at that moment Fuller brought in a tray on which was a plate of fruit. Having eaten a few grapes, Vereker shaved, enjoyed the invigorating stimulus of a hot sea-water bath and quickly dressed. Leaving his cabin, he knocked on Ricardo's door and was greeted with a sleepy "Come in!"

"Not up yet, Ricky!" he exclaimed on seeing his friend still huddled up in bed, his dark head almost completely hidden beneath the clothes.

Ricardo moved lazily, rubbed his eyes and finally sat up.

"How now, Algernon? Anything important to discuss with your chief? I thought it was the steward. I see he has left my tea. I didn't hear him come in."

"Drink a cup and pull yourself together, Ricky. I want to ask you a few questions."

"A police interrogatory at this unearthly hour! Algernon, you're an outrage. I was dreaming I was a pirate and was boarding

'A stately Spanish galleon coming from the Isthmus
Dipping through the Tropics by the palm-green shores
With a cargo of diamonds

Emeralds and amethysts
Topazes and cinnamon and gold moidores!'

and you shatter the dream by saying you want to ask me a few questions. You've robbed me of an adventure of the soul. I was about to savour the delight of cutting throats, of rapine..."

"Shut up, Ricky, and listen to me."

"Perhaps you're a fair substitute for sudden death. I'm listening. Anything serious happened?"

"Yes. In the first place, do you remember on which side of her head Mrs. Mesado parted her hair?"

"This is momentous, Algernon; I'm glad you're not being frivolous before breakfast. A woman's hair is a subject to which I've always given considerable thought. I used to think a woman parted her hair on the side she thought most becoming to her face. This is, of course, an error into which a fashionable hairdresser might fall. If she's right-handed she always parts it on the right side; if she's left-handed, on the left. The ambidexterous, and most women are more or less so, part it on either side. The final test, however, is on which side does her hair part in a dead straight line?"

"Did Mrs. Mesado part her hair on the left of right side?" asked Vereker with a shade of curtness. He was in no mood for Ricardo's airy trifling.

"On the left side. Next question, please."

"You're certain?"

"I took particular notice. You remember her perm wave, don't you? It fell in shining breakers over her right ear."

"I do. Your answer's a confirmation."

"They're usually an education, but proceed."

"When you were pacing round the deck this morning, Ricky, did you notice how many cabin windows were alight on the starboard side?"

"Yours was the only one on the whole deck—a lone star in a world of Cimmerian gloom!"

"You're sure that Mrs. Mesado's cabin was in darkness all the time?"

"Positive. A lighted window has an overwhelming attraction for a vulgarly inquisitive man like me. I'd have remembered."

"Do you know what your statement implies, Ricky?"

"It implies that the story of Lady Godiva will always appeal to human beings, and that deaf, natural Peeping Tom will be held up for ever as a nasty example by nastier people."

"I'm not referring to your peculiar type of curiosity, Ricky. You remember my mentioning that I heard Colvin and Mrs. Mesado talking in her cabin between 1.30 and 1.45 this morning?"

"Yes."

"Well, doesn't it strike you that they were talking in the dark? Why had they put out the light?"

"An intriguing question, Algernon," replied Ricardo, smiling. "It reminds me inconsequently of where was Moses when the light went out? To be blunt, they were doing something in that cabin which they were anxious to hide from the outer world. I was the only outer world at the time you mention."

"Exactly, and I've a shrewd idea of the nefarious game they were up to."

"You're not letting your erotic imagination run riot, Algernon?"

"Even my imaginative efforts are rather practical, Ricky, and I'm beginning to think I've made an amazing discovery."

"Let's have the story; I'm all agog."

"Not yet. When I'm certain of my facts I'll tell you more. In the meantime you've got to give me a hand. I feel sure that a murder has been committed. How I don't know, but I'm going to find out. It will be a tricky business, for we're dealing with a clever man in our friend Colvin."

"You've met him?"

"He paid me a visit this morning. First he called on you, but you were asleep, and then he descended on me."

"What did he want?"

"He wanted to thank us for all the trouble we had taken in this business of his sister-in-law."

"His gratitude seems a bit devastating. I lost nothing by being asleep."

"He was fishing for information. I'm sure he wanted to find out if I'd overheard anything of the row between him and Mrs. Mesado in the latter's cabin."

"You left him guessing, if I know you, Algernon."

"Naturally. He also wanted to ask my advice. He says that Mrs. Mesado's necklace is missing and was eager to know what steps to take."

"Good Lord, he doesn't suspect me or you of having pinched it, does he?"

"No, I don't think so."

"She wasn't wearing it when I found her body on the deck. I'm positive of that because I wasn't tempted."

"Somehow or other he seemed certain on that score."

"I'm glad. Where the devil can she have put it? Did she hand it over to the purser?"

"No. I've got it here," replied Vereker, drawing the necklace from his pocket. "You said you could identify it if you saw it again."

"Great heavens, that's it all right," gasped Ricardo in sheer astonishment, "but how the dickens did it come into your hands?"

"It was flung into my cabin through the open window in the early hours of this morning, just before you came across her dead body on the deck."

"Do you think she threw it in?"

"I'm not certain. You see, my window is next to her own, and whoever threw it in must have thought he or she was returning it to Mrs. Mesado's cabin."

"I follow you, Algernon, but if there was murder committed for the sake of that necklace, why return it to Mrs. Mesado's cabin?"

"She may have thrown it in for safety, but it's more than I can explain at the moment. Later we shall find an answer to the question."

"What are you going to do with it? It must be worth a couple of thousand pounds."

"Hang on to it for the present and say nothing. I may have to have a confidential talk with your friend Partridge to avoid dangerous complications. Now I'm going to tell you how you can lend me a hand."

"Fire away, Algernon; I'm simply too excited for anything." With these words Ricardo sprang from his bed, slipped on a dressing-gown, lit a cigarette and sat down in a wicker chair. He looked up expectantly at Vereker, who stood rubbing his chin thoughtfully.

"You've a knack of making friends, Ricky, and I want you to cultivate Miguel Dias. Learn all you can about him. He'll probably mislead you, but Miss Penteado may prove less discreet, and she knows him fairly well I should say. Another task—perhaps more congenial to your temperament, is to pay delicate attentions to Mrs. Mesado's maid. She may be informative under tactful pressure."

"You mean Renée Gautier? I've already got on nodding terms with her and wouldn't mind exerting tactful pressure; she has an inviting waist. Leave her to me. She's of French parents and, though English in outward respects, I'm sure she has the racial characteristics highly developed. *Elle meurt d'amour!*"

"Sounds promising, but be most discreet. There's more than one in this affair, I feel sure, and we mustn't rouse the faintest suspicion. I'll see you at breakfast."

III

On leaving Ricardo, Vereker was about to enter his cabin when he ran into Colvin in the alleyway. He was the very man he wanted to meet.

"Can I have a word with you?" he asked.

"Certainly," replied Colvin, and on Vereker's gesture preceded him into No. 88.

"I've been thinking over this affair of Mrs. Mesado's missing necklace since we met this morning," began Vereker, "and would like to make a suggestion. As I told you, I've done a considerable amount of detective work in very similar cases, and I might be able to recover the property for you without creating a scandal on board. I'd naturally work in secrecy. I would, of course, lay the whole matter confidentially before the captain, who is a friend of mine. Beyond him, yourself and perhaps Fuller, the steward, no one need know anything about the matter. I'm sure Captain Partridge will fall in with my plan. As you know, his aim is to make this cruise a thundering success. This is the Green Star's first venture in this direction, and they've taken the 'Mars' off the ordinary passenger route to Canada for the purpose. The competition in pleasure cruises is now getting terribly keen, and any unpleasant occurrence on board would go dead against that desired success. That's how the matter stands. If you don't quite like the idea, turn it down and we'll say no more about it. I can assure you, however, that I'm confident I can get Mrs. Mesado's necklace back without setting the whole ship by the ears."

For some moments Colvin stood hesitant. He was ostensibly reviewing the matter and envisaging other possibilities than were apparent to Vereker.

"I don't want to get anyone into trouble," he said at length. "It's the last thing I want to do. If the property were mine I'd rather stick the loss than kick up a dust about it. But the necklace is worth some thousands of pounds; they are all specimen stones and we shall have to account to Mesado for it being missing. I suppose the captain must know?"

"I suggested telling him in order to safeguard myself. Without him my task might be impossible. A captain is 'It' on board his ship. He can do anything except marry a couple. He can order a cabin or cabins to be searched if necessary. He can clap a man in irons. I think the best thing I can do is to have a quiet chat with him and lay all our cards on the table. But it's for you to decide... What d'you think?"

"Then I should say go ahead. If there's any likelihood of trouble arising, unexpected trouble I mean, of course you'd let me know. I don't want to make myself a nuisance or the cynosure of all eyes for the remainder of the trip."

"You intend to complete the cruise?" asked Vereker, rather surprised.

"Constance and I have talked it over and think it's the best thing to do. There'll be a burial at sea. She will take all responsibility on that score, for she's Mrs. Mesado's sister. We see no purpose in taking the body ashore to be buried in a foreign land or getting it embalmed and taking it back to England. The latter is costly and is hedged in by all sorts of irritating formalities."

"I see your point of view," remarked Vereker with grave sympathy, "Perhaps you're doing the best thing in the circumstances."

"I'm sure of it, and my wife agrees with me. She feels the loss of her sister terribly; they were very fond of one another. The cruise will switch her mind off her troubles and give her other and happier interests. As for her sister's necklace, I hope you can get it back. Naturally I can't ask you to do the work for nothing..."

Vereker raised a deprecatory hand. "We won't discuss that side of the question. I ask nothing for my work. If I can recover the necklace I'll be delighted. I'm not a 'pro.' at the detective game. Must try and keep up my amateur status so to speak."

"Very well, we'll leave it at that," said Colvin and hesitatingly extended a hand.

Vereker shook it with more graciousness than warmth. He was particularly anxious not to be too friendly with Colvin at this juncture of his investigation, and yet he felt he must rouse no inkling of his purpose to probe deeper into the mystery surrounding Mrs. Mesado's death. In his own mind he was still uncertain in what relation Colvin stood to his sister-in-law's sudden death. That he was concealing something was to Vereker a fairly safe assumption, but such concealment, he felt, might in the light of further discoveries have either an indirect or no connection at all with such a serious thing as murder. In his statements Colvin had lied, but falsehoods are often uttered by men who, by ordinary criteria, would never be classed as criminals. He felt that he must keep an open mind. On reflection he decided that he must not be prejudiced against Colvin. Whatever weaknesses of character the man might display could not wholly efface a certain natural likableness, a kindly, easy-going disposition. Feeling that there was no reason for prolonging the interview he moved towards his cabin door and opened it.

"Now for breakfast," he said, and then by one of those flashes of inspiration for which there is no accounting he suddenly turned to Colvin and asked: "By the way, it would be just as well if you gave me a description of the missing necklace to work on."

"By Jove, yes," replied Colvin. "I'd forgotten you hadn't seen it closely. It's a rope of specimen diamonds, cinnamon and white, strung together alternately. There's a circular ornament of diamonds, blue, white, black, yellow—a unique collection, beautifully mixed—forming a pendant. The clasp is a small platinum lizard set with finest emeralds and rubies. There's not another necklace like it on this ship, anyway."

"From your description I'd have no difficulty in spotting it at once," said Vereker, and as Colvin stepped out into the alleyway he added, "Our slogan must be secrecy first. Leave everything to me, and I'll keep you posted with all important news."

"Mum's the word," agreed Colvin, placing a dramatic finger to his lips as he stood for a moment facing Vereker before he turned and hurried back to his own cabin.

"Well, I'm damned!" exclaimed Vereker to himself as soon as Colvin had disappeared. "This is mildly surprising to say the least

of it!" He stood for some moments fingering the stones of the
necklace with the emerald pendant and emerald butterfly clasp
which he was carrying in his left-hand trousers-pocket before
descending to the dining saloon on deck A for breakfast.

Chapter Six

I

When Vereker seated himself at the breakfast table neither the
captain nor Doctor Macpherson was present. The chief engineer,
a rubicund Scot with light shaggy eyebrows and a genial, hearty
manner, took the captain's place and was inclined to be talkative.
His conversation, however, turned on the subject of the belt of fog
which the "Mars" had run into the previous night, a topic in which
Vereker, occupied with the mystery of Mrs. Mesado's death, was
not deeply interested.

"I'd rather have a sixty mile an hour gale than a fog," remarked
the chief engineer.

"Give me the fog," replied Vereker with a smile. "I'm not a
good sailor and a gale fairly lays me out."

"Landsmen don't realise the danger of collisions in a fog. Did
you hear that vessel pass us shortly after two o'clock this morning?
She must have been less than a hundred yards off. She was
travelling much too fast. Possibly a cargo boat making up for lost
time reckless of consequences."

"What could her skipper be thinking of?" asked Vereker to
show he was listening to the engineer's conversation.

"Not always the skipper's fault. He has to answer to his
company's directors for monetary loss. Delay would probably have
been expensive. The truth seldom leaks out if there's a smash up.
A master's lot is not an easy one."

"I wonder where she was making for," said Vereker, pouring
milk over his porridge.

"God knows. Probably some French or Portuguese vessel heading for Lisbon."

At this point Ricardo appeared and sustained the conversation with the chief engineer until, having finished his breakfast, the officer departed.

"Well, mon brave, any further discoveries?" asked Manuel eagerly as soon as they were alone.

"An amazing one, Ricky. I ran into Colvin after leaving you this morning, and we had a confidential pow-wow. He's a slick sort of gent, as I told you, and I've decided on the 'helpful friend' approach as the best one to mask my real intentions."

"Unscrupulous hound! If you want to beat your man, take my tip and let the helpful friend stand unlimited drinks. What happened?"

"I think I managed to deceive him up to a point. He was guarded, however, and seems devilish eager not to have any trouble about the missing necklace. He's hiding something, and it strikes me that the necklace is a subsidiary factor in this business."

"It has nothing on a murder, anyway," replied Ricardo and asked the waiter to bring him some grilled bacon and fried eggs.

"I promised to exercise my powers as a private 'tec and restore the necklace without fuss or trouble, if possible. I could see he didn't want anything in the nature of an inquiry or search," continued Vereker.

"When you restore it without fuss or trouble your stock as a private 'tec ought to boom in his estimation. I'm beginning to think you're a hollow fraud, Algernon. I hope you didn't minimise the difficulties of recovering an article that was simply chucked at your head."

"It's not going to be as easy as you imagine, Ricky. I've struck a nasty snag already. The necklace that was chucked at my head is apparently not the necklace that's missing."

"It's certainly the one Mrs. Mesado wore," said Ricardo emphatically.

"Are you sure that this is not a good paste affair?"

"My dear Algernon, I'm not a fool. As part of your sleuth's equipment I suggest you learn a little more about precious stones. Did Colvin describe the missing necklace?"

"It's a rope of alternate cinnamon and white diamonds—all specimen stones. The pendant is a circular one studded with different coloured diamonds. The clasp is a platinum lizard set with the finest emeralds and rubies."

"Then where does the one you're cuddling in your pocket come in? It's one of Mrs. Mesado's and certainly not negligible."

"I've got to find a solution to that little puzzle, but I've a hazy notion how it all happened."

"Splendid, Algernon. You'd worm your way through armour plate. What's more, you've made me as keen on this business as a greyhound after an electric hare. I'm ready to start my side of the job instanter—no, not instanter, but after my second cup of coffee. Is there anything special you want me to find out?"

"Yes. If you can get into conversation with Gautier, Mrs. Mesado's maid, ask her all about her mistress's car smash, especially where it occurred. You're interested in motors, so it ought to be easy. Find out all about this man Miguel Dias from any source available. Miss Penteado will be most informative. Don't probe Colvin because there may be some secret bond between them. I'll investigate that line. Also question Gautier about the missing necklace and make certain whether Mrs. Mesado wore a signet ring or not on her left hand."

"Don't overload me, Algernon, or I shall explode and make a mess of things."

"Have you got clearly in your mind all I've asked you to find out?"

"Crystal clear. I don't feel equipped for the part without a revolver and a pair of darbies. Still, I can borrow a marline-spike and a bit of string from one of the crew. I shall be at the races with Miss Gautier, and at the swimming pool with Rosaura today. At least them's my intentions. To combine business with pleasure is nearly as profitable as combining it with religion."

"Don't be too scrupulous in your methods, Ricky. The art of detection, like all great art, is above moral criteria. Morals are the outcome of social limitations, and the true artist's outlook is unfettered. 'Find out at all costs' is the slogan of sleuthing."

"I'm a go-getter, Algernon, and I'm glad to hear you disregard costs. I shall be as amoral as a tiger and as expensive as counsel. I'll see you before lunch. Have an apéritif ready in your cabin and I'll then display my catch of news."

With these words Ricardo departed, and Vereker strolled out of the saloon and went up to the main promenade deck to sit and read in the sunshine.

The fog of overnight had vanished and the sea and sky were gloriously blue. As he hunted about for his deck chair he noticed that Mrs. Colvin was temporarily occupying it. This at once suggested an opening for conversation. She was seated with a rug wrapped about her, and on her lap lay a book which she was making a pretence of reading. Her soft, sweet face was drawn and pale and there were dark rings round her eyes. The tragedy of her sister's death had evidently been a great shock to her and had left its mark. At once she noticed that Vereker was in search of his deck chair and, sitting up, turned and glanced at the label pasted on the woodwork of the one she occupied. Vereker promptly seized the opportunity and approached her.

"Please don't rise. I can easily bag another chair," he remarked pleasantly.

"I'm sorry," she replied; "I thought I was sitting on my own. You're Mr. Vereker, I see. My name's Colvin. You've already met my husband, Mr. Vereker, and I was hoping I'd run into you before long."

"Nice of you to say so, Mrs. Colvin," said Vereker and, picking up the nearest vacant chair, seated himself beside her.

Anthony Vereker, in spite of his urbanity, was afflicted with that peculiar downright sincerity which finds it difficult to play the social humbug, and for some minutes his conversation, which was an expression of condolence, was halting and painful. He had, however, met in Mrs. Colvin a woman who had the gift of making the first steps of acquaintanceship easy and soon their talk drifted into a more natural freedom.

"It was the suddenness of the whole business that upset me," remarked Mrs. Colvin, referring to her sister's death.

"I can quite understand that," agreed Vereker, and added casually: "It wasn't long after you bade her good night."

"I left Beryl's cabin about one o'clock, and Dick, my husband, who had some business matter to discuss with her, followed later," replied Mrs. Colvin innocently.

"She wasn't ill at that time?" asked Vereker.

"As well as you or I."

"I can't understand her going out on deck at that time of night. It was miserably cold and foggy," said Vereker reflectively.

Mrs. Colvin was evidently disturbed by this remark. An uneasy look passed swiftly across her features. She hesitated a moment and then replied quickly:

"Doubtless she went up on deck for a breath of air. One of the symptoms of her trouble was a sense of suffocation. I believe it occurs in most heart cases."

"Of course," continued Vereker, "the shock she got in her accident didn't do her any good. Aftereffects so to speak."

"What accident?" asked Mrs. Colvin with a surprised air.

"I was inferring that she had met with some mishap to injure her hands so badly," said Vereker.

"Oh, yes, she had a motor smash on the road from London to Tilbury. It was a wonder she wasn't killed then. She was lucky to escape with minor injuries to her hands. Glass windscreens are awful things in an accident."

"Where did it happen, Mrs. Colvin?" asked Vereker casually.

"Oh—er—let me see. What's the name of the place?" said Mrs. Colvin, and puckered her brow in an effort to remember.

"I don't know the road very well," said Vereker, awaiting her answer with suppressed eagerness.

"Stifford—Stifford—that's the name," concluded Mrs. Colvin with an air of relief.

"Can't say I've heard of the place. She was motoring down to join the ship, I suppose."

"Yes. Skidded on a wet road and ran into a lamp standard. She had to leave her car in a local garage and hire for the remainder of the journey."

"That accident was the cause of all the trouble, I should say," remarked Vereker.

"It brought it to a head, anyway," agreed Mrs. Colvin, "but we were led to expect her death at any moment."

"Had she her maid with her at the time of the smash?" asked Vereker.

"Oh, yes. Gautier escaped without a scratch."

"She was lucky. No further news of Mrs. Mesado's missing necklace?"

"No. I'm afraid it's gone for good—probably stolen."

"It's the one with alternate cinnamon and white diamonds that's missing, isn't it?" asked Vereker, and turned to observe the effect of his words. He noted the air of perplexity that at once settled on Mrs. Colvin's face.

"Er—how d'you mean?" she asked hesitatingly, and her reply informed Vereker that he was dealing with a woman of charm rather than astuteness.

"I was under the impression that it was her other one, of pure white diamonds with an emerald clasp in the shape of a butterfly," said Vereker carelessly. Producing his cigarette case he opened it and offered it to Mrs. Colvin. A delicate scarlet flush had mounted to her cheeks, and her brow was knit in a frown of displeasure or distress.

"Oh, we have that one all right," she replied with false assurance.

"Fortunate that the thief didn't collar them both while he was about it," said Vereker.

"Well, you see, Beryl had locked that one safely away in her jewel-case. She had doubtless left the other lying on her cabin dressing table. She was terribly careless with her jewellery. She never seemed to realise the value of things," continued Mrs. Colvin with glib improvisation.

"One of the prerogatives of being rich," said Vereker and, feeling that he had gathered sufficient information for the moment from his interview, excused himself by saying that he had forgotten to bring the book he was reading with him and departed. He ascended leisurely to the upper promenade deck and was about to indulge in his usual morning exercise when he noticed Doctor Macpherson leaning over the taffrail, smoking his pipe and lost in a brown study. Vereker joined him and, after some adroit fencing on the part of the doctor, dragged the conversation round to the subject of Mrs. Mesado's death.

"D'you know, doctor, there's something about the whole affair that puzzles me," remarked Vereker.

"How d'you mean?" asked the doctor, turning a suddenly interested gaze on the speaker.

"There was a heated discussion and a scuffle in Mrs. Mesado's cabin only a quarter on an hour before Ricardo found her body on the deck."

"Is that so?" remarked the doctor distantly. The conversation had evidently entered forbidden territory as far as he was concerned.

"You see, I'm in the next cabin, and I heard the row," continued Vereker obstinately and not in the least disconcerted.

"H'm!" grunted the doctor, "even if there was, we can't interfere in the private quarrels of our passengers as long as they keep within certain bounds.

"I suppose not; but don't you think it had some connection with the lady's death?"

"Indirectly. Might have brought on the seizure."

"I'm referring to a more direct connection—say murder."

"Nonsense! You're being romantic, Mr. Vereker. There's not the slightest evidence to suggest such a thing."

"Did you notice that her hands were all cut and bruised, doctor?"

"Her sister said that she had met with those injuries in a car accident."

"There's something rather unsatisfactory about that explanation. Why didn't she get her hands bandaged as soon as possible after the accident?"

"I really can't say. It also struck me as unusual."

"Besides, I saw, or thought I saw, one of her hands the previous day, and there was no sign of injury on it."

"You probably made a mistake. We've got to accept her relatives' story as true as far as I can see."

"There's a further complication," continued Vereker.

"Oh, and what's that?" asked the doctor, his interest increasing.

"Of course this is strictly confidential. The dead lady had a very valuable diamond necklace, and it's missing."

"Good Lord!" exclaimed the doctor impatiently, "the skipper won't like to hear that news. This damned cruise seems to be bewitched."

"Being romantic, I coupled Mrs. Mesado's death with the loss of her necklace. Of course I may be utterly wrong. It may only be fancy," observed Vereker quietly.

"I don't think there's anything in it, Mr. Vereker. Sheer coincidence in my opinion."

"Possibly. I suppose rigor mortis has set in, doctor?"

"Oh, yes, I took particular notice of that when the body was being removed to the sick bay this morning."

"Then the flaccidity of the body when we came upon it wasn't secondary?"

"How could it possibly have been?" asked the doctor with a note of impatience. "Do you know what secondary flaccidity is?"

"Yes, the relaxed state of the muscles which sets in after the stiffness called rigor mortis has passed away."

"That's so, and in the light of your knowledge I can't see what you're driving at."

"Only theorising, doctor. I'm afraid it's a bad habit of mine. Your information about rigor mortis has temporarily upset one of my little fancies."

"I believe you're a keen amateur detective, Mr. Vereker?"

"I have that reputation, with an emphasis on the amateur."

"Then that accounts for your fancies. You can take it from me that there's nothing shady about this affair."

"You're trying to destroy one of my beliefs now, doctor, and I'm as obstinate as an ass," said Vereker with a disarming laugh.

"Tell me the reasons for your belief, Mr. Vereker. I'm interested in more ways than one. We've got to be jolly careful on board ship, as you know."

"Yes, I know, but you'll have to hear my story another time, say over a peg of whisky in my cabin. I suppose they'll bury the lady at sea?"

"Well, we can't keep the body for the duration of the cruise. You know the usual rule at sea?"

"Yes, but I thought the Colvins would cut their trip and take the body ashore at Lisbon. We put in at Lisbon tomorrow."

"That would suit the skipper, but the Colvins seem to be anxious for a burial at sea."

"You ought to persuade them to put ashore. There may be an unpleasant resurrection of the whole affair when I get back to England. I may leave the 'Mars' at Lisbon and return with one of the Blue Star homeward bound liners."

"Ah," said the doctor uneasily, "you're going to pursue the matter further."

"I shall see my friend Chief Inspector Heather of Scotland Yard immediately I get back, and we'll ferret out the whole business together if it's humanly possible. This mystery wasn't born on the 'Mars'."

For some minutes Doctor Macpherson was silent, and then said, "I'll see the skipper this evening. He may alter his plans, but for heaven's sake say nothing about this affair to anyone."

"D'you think he'd mind if I persuaded the Colvins to put ashore with the body at Lisbon? It would save him a lot of trouble."

"He'd be jolly glad."

"Then tell him definitely that they're going to do so and leave the rest to me. I'll be discretion itself."

"Very good. We'll leave it at that," replied the doctor. "You've roused my curiosity, Mr. Vereker, so much that I won't be satisfied until you let me into your secret theory."

"If I don't let you into it before I leave the ship tomorrow, doctor, I'll come aboard when you return from this trip and tell you my yarn. It'll cost you a dinner."

"I'll put the dinner on the company, but I'll foot the wine bill. Is it a bet?"

"Certainly, and in the meantime may I come and ask you seemingly irrelevant questions?"

"Do by all means. You know my cabin. Pop round any time after lunch or dinner. I'll be in."

II

At quarter-past eleven Vereker put in an appearance at the races held under the rules of "The Mars Turf Club". The course, marked out in chalk on the main promenade deck, was thronged with eager racegoers who, having backed their fancy with the totalisator, were excitedly watching the throwing of the dice that sent the six horses of the field forward at varying paces. Procuring a race-card from one of the stewards, Vereker learned that the first race on the flat was for the Mars Cup. Glancing down the list of horses and owners he found that the third horse, "Serial Rights," was owned by Mr. Manuel Ricardo. The owner's stakes were three pounds. The betting booth was doing a lively business in shilling tickets. As he wandered in the bright sunshine round the thronged deck with its happy faces, excited chatter and gay laughter, Vereker remembered that in a cabin above lay the body of a woman whom he felt certain had met her death by foul means, possibly for the very material gain which in a minor degree lent zest to the human play going on around him. His thoughts reverted to the book by Professor Dorsey that he had been reading. "Human hogs," said that writer, "are made not born. Greed is not part of our inheritance, not to the stuff we are made of has it biologic value." He was pondering on this statement. It appeared too sweeping an assertion. "Hunger," said the same writer, "is back of life, the primordial drive in life. Hunger has led to crime, suicide, cannibalism…" There seemed to Vereker some contradiction here, for greed was simply intensified hunger. Certainly hunger either for money or woman was the main incentive to murder. And a lively social instinct, the fear of and desire to avoid the censure of one's fellow beings, paradoxically another powerful motive. Hunger, an impulse for satisfaction, certainly was part of "our inheritance". He was musing on the subject, for the psychology of crime and the criminal interested him deeply, when he ran across Manuel Ricardo in company with Miss Renée Gautier. Ricky had evidently managed to make the acquaintance of that lady and was in animated conversation with her regarding the chance of his horse, "Serial Rights". He was laughingly persuading her to "put her camisole on it". Vereker strolled up to them leisurely and was informally introduced. He seized the opportunity during the ensuing conversation to have a good look at Mrs. Mesado's maid. She was undoubtedly a very fascinating specimen of young womanhood. Her figure was what is called svelte, one of those French terms that seem to express so much more than any equivalent English epithet. Vereker for some unknown reason disliked the word, but it instinctively rose to his mind. Her hair was dark, her eyebrows had been trimmed into a perfection of curve that lost the charming irregularity of nature and detracted from individuality. Her lips, well shaped but inclined to severity, had been loosened by art into curved bows. As she turned to greet Vereker she looked at him with disconcerting directness with a pair of very pale grey-blue eyes. There was a peculiar penetration and hardness in their glance which stole something from the attractiveness of the face, from the general feminine appeal of her whole person.

"Miss Gautier has plunged heavily on my gee, Algernon," said Ricky jovially. "Knowing that he's out of 'Royalties' by 'Best Seller,' I think she has invested her money well."

"I didn't know you owned a stable, Ricky," said Vereker banteringly.

"Your education has been sadly neglected, Algernon. We train on the high seas. You might say our nags are sea-horses. The only thing that worries me is that I stand to lose three quid on my own account, and several bob on Miss Gautier's."

"You're usually lucky, Ricky," commented Vereker.

"Great Scot, it looks like it! They've just put 'Serial Rights' two spaces—I might say instalments—backwards! I wish you'd go away, Algernon. You remind me of my car mascot. It was a skeleton, by the way, and the first day I fixed him up on my M.G. I ran into a fruit barrow and lost heavily on a pile of squashed grapes. I had several bones broken and the coster who picked me up remarked sympathetically to a pal, 'Blimey, if 'e ain't like a bag of walnuts, Alf!' You're a spectre on the course. Avaunt and have a Vichy water at my expense at the bar."

"I was thinking of backing a horse," replied Vereker.

"Then back 'Argent' for the next race. It belongs to Miguel Dias. I'll give you the stake knowing you'll ruin his chances."

"I hope Mr. Dias is not a particular friend of yours, Miss Gautier," he added, turning to his new acquaintance.

"Oh, no, not at all," said Miss Gautier. "He was a friend, but not a very great friend, of Mr. Mesado. I was Mrs. Mesado's companion and maid rolled into one, but I had to observe certain social distinctions. He has only known the Mesados for a few months. Do you dislike him?"

"He stole my dance partner from me last night. I was horribly jealous, but I hope I shall be able to console myself." Manuel Ricardo flung Miss Gautier an imploring glance with such facial grotesqueness that she burst into hearty laughter.

"Who was the lady, Mr. Ricardo?"

"Miss Penteado."

"Ah, very charming too," said Miss Gautier with an almost imperceptible frown which did not escape Vereker, who was admiring Manuel's skill in gathering information.

"Perhaps her wealth appeals to Mr. Dias," suggested Ricardo boldly.

"But Mr. Dias is enormously wealthy too," said Miss Gautier.

"Deep calling to deep. My means are slender, and Slender was cousin to Shallow, so I'm out of it," said Ricardo, and added, "You must pardon my puns, Miss Gautier; they're nearly as bad as Will Shakespeare's in the *Merry Wives of Windsor*."

"Doesn't wealth attract you, Mr. Ricardo?" asked Miss Gautier archly.

"Overwhelmingly, but the converse is the trouble. I can't attract wealth. In any case, for a pleasure cruise beauty is sufficient. Money only confuses the issue and makes the lady think you're suffering from double vision. By Jove, 'Serial Right' has advanced six spaces! That's because you weren't looking, Algernon. I wish you'd disperse."

"Well, I won't ruin your luck, Ricky. What's going to happen if you win?" asked Vereker as he was moving away.

"A miracle in the first place. Secondly, I'll stand you a bottle of your favourite claret. Thirdly and not least, Miss Gautier and I are going to paint the 'Mars' red tonight. There's a cinema show. The film is *Passion's Dupe*; it behoves me to attend. *Au revoir*. I'll see you ten minutes before lunch. Mine's a 'John Collins' as usual."

III

As Vereker passed through the garden lounge on his way to his cabin he noticed that Miguel Dias and Miss Penteado were seated at one of the small tables smoking and chatting. Dias every now and then glanced at her with that ludicrous ardour that only a Latin can conjure into his eyes, and Miss Penteado rewarded his efforts with a shining toothpaste smile. As he passed close to them he heard Dias remark:

"But, Miss Penteado, you are irresistible!"

"Please don't say that, Mr. Dias; you make me think I've said something rather silly," she replied with sudden reproach.

"But that would be impossible... fantastic, mysterious, but never silly. You are just being delightful..."

Vereker passed out of earshot, and reflected that Miguel Dias was making rather blatant advances to the wealthy Argentine. Perhaps, as Ricardo had put it, he was suffering from double vision in spite of his reputed wealth. He remembered distinctly the sudden frown that had passed over Miss Gautier's face when Manuel had told her that Dias had stolen his dance partner. Had she any interest in Dias's activities? In spite of her protestation that she was not at all friendly with him owing to a difference in social status, it might be possible. In the light of his own theories it was rather more than probable. He made a mental note that it was a matter into which he must probe discreetly when the opportunity arose. That opportunity came sooner than he expected. As he passed the bar situated at the foot of the companion leading up to D deck he ran into Colvin standing there with an appropriately gloomy countenance. On seeing Vereker his face brightened discreetly.

"What will you have, Vereker?" he asked cordially.

"A small whisky and soda," replied Vereker. "I've just attended the race meeting. My friend Ricardo is running a horse in one of the races and seems to be having a lively time with Miss Gautier."

"She's a jolly girl, well educated and up to snuff, to put it vulgarly."

"French, I suppose?"

"Some generations back. English to all intents and purposes. Beryl, that's Mrs. Mesado, treated her more as a companion than a maid. My wife doesn't cotton to her; thinks she isn't quite trustworthy."

"Been with Mrs. Mesado long?"

"About nine months. Beryl brought her back from Buenos Aires. Miguel Dias, who was a business acquaintance of Mesado's, recommended her very highly."

"Had she been in Dias's service?"

"No. He told us *sub rosa* that she was really distantly related to himself—umpteenth cousin—poor branch of the family. He seemed eager to help them in some way. She was too independent to take money and wanted to earn her own living."

"What d'you think of her yourself?"

"She's O.K. Knows her job inside out, and Beryl was delighted with her. Speaking confidentially, I should say she likes to exert her charms but thinks they have a high commodity value. From a man's point of view, too damned clever by half!"

"Do you think she's trustworthy?"

"Rationally rather than from moral principle. Most people are. It's the business instinct. Of course, Constance is biased against her. Constance is simple, tender-hearted and as straight as a gun-barrel, but with a curious spiritual rigidity. Not much 'play' in her somewhat mechanical philosophy."

"Some good people have an uncanny intuition at times. They see through studied charm to the unstudied reality. It's a disconcerting gift."

"She damn well sees through me all right!" exclaimed Colvin with a loud laugh, "and I can tell you it's often very disconcerting. That reminds me. I must join her; she'll be wondering where the devil I've got to."

"I think she'd know fairly definitely," remarked Vereker, a cheery smile blunting the pointedness of his remark.

"Any news?" asked Colvin mysteriously.

"You might look me up in my cabin after lunch. I should like to have a quiet talk with you."

"I'll be there without fail," replied Colvin and hurried away.

IV

Vereker had ordered a "John Collins", and the steward had just left when Manuel Ricardo burst unceremoniously into his friend's cabin.

"Algernon, old fruit, my horse won, won in a common canter, and brought home the dough!" he shouted, boisterously waving a bunch of pound notes in Vereker's face. "We must convert the dough into cakes, if not ale, as quickly as possible. Renée has retired to her bower staggering under a load of specie."

"You've got as far as calling her Renée?" asked Vereker quietly.

"She said I was a perfect darling when 'Serial Rights' romped home, so I promptly took the liberty of treating her as if I'd known her since she sucked her thumbs and was cocktailed with dill water. Ah, I see you've got my 'John Collins'! Racing always gives one a thirst. When you win you celebrate; when you lose you drown your woes."

"Will you be serious, Ricky, and tell me if you've found out anything?" said Vereker.

"Yes. Firstly, I'm a malicious brute. I was delighted when Dias's horse flattered and then faded away. Argent didn't shine. Ought to have run in the Eclipse Stakes or something of that sort. Dias turned up with Rosaura to see the finish of the race. When she saw that 'Argent' was last she appropriately gave a silvery little laugh. Dias laughed too. You know, the cackle that escapes from a man's throat when he's paying through the nose for the joke."

"I'm not interested in the turf history of the ship," remarked Vereker curtly. "Did Gautier know anything about the missing necklace?"

"She said Mrs. Colvin had merely mentioned the fact of its being missing. Renée was rather upset about it all. She knows Mrs. Colvin doesn't suspect her for a moment, but it made her feel very uncomfortable. I sympathised with her. Who could help it? I like Renée's cut, Algernon. She's built for speed."

"Fast enough even for you, Ricky, eh? Did she say anything about alternate cinnamon and white diamonds?"

"No. That's just the point. She referred to the one with the emerald butterfly clasp. What d'you make of it?"

"That's most significant. And did you get round to the subject of the signet ring on Mrs. Mesado's left hand?"

"Very dexterously, if you'll pardon the pun. Mrs. Mesado, it appears, never wore one. As I told you, Mrs. Colvin does, so you must have cleverly mixed the two women up."

"I don't think so, Ricky. I'm certain of my facts. Miss Gautier is simply not telling the truth."

"Then it's your fault, Algernon. Pretty women are born fibbers, but why push the darlings into it by asking them uncomfortable questions? Personally, I always pretend to believe what they say. They at once dub me a fool, and every one of them thinks it her mission in life to be a fool's salvation. It's the infant-rearing complex in terms of sex."

"Did you touch on Mrs. Mesado's motor smash?"

"Climbed up to it on top gear. Algernon, that motor smash is all bunk. Renée didn't know the make of Mrs. Mesado's car. I forgave her that with difficulty, because it's generally the only thing a woman knows about a car. She explained that she escaped injury because only the right portion of the windscreen hit a lamp standard. To convince me she became circumstantial. It's a dangerous form of lying. I always avoid it nowadays. I let her run on and found that the car skidded from the left centre of the road on to the left-hand kerb. This seemed strange, so I asked her if the car turned at all in its course. She had warmed up by now and stated very definitely that it kept its head straight forward. I didn't point out the silliness of this assertion, and casually remarked that the road must have been greasy. 'It was raining,' she remarked confidently. Now, Algernon, you know as well as I do that the 26th of March was a gloriously fine day. It didn't rain at Rainham or anywhere else in the district on that day."

"Why at Rainham, Ricky?"

"She said that the accident took place at Rainham, on the London-Tilbury road."

"Mrs. Colvin said it occurred at Stifford, which is well off that road. I think we may agree that it never took place at all."

"Then the yarn about her hands being cut by the windscreen is all poppycock?"

"Absolutely. Those hands were never cut and bruised in a motor smash. Besides, I found no mark of an accelerator on the soles of Mrs. Mesado's shoes, which I have carefully examined. The right shoe of a car driver invariably bears traces of the pressure on the accelerator. What does that convey to you, Ricky?"

"Simply that the injuries were received otherwise."

"Yes, we know; but why all these lies? First about the motor smash, and then about the necklace."

"To prevent us getting at the truth unless it's for the sheer joy of lying. Some people make a hobby of it. Outlet for an imagination that can't find a publisher, I suppose."

"If it's to prevent us getting at the truth, Ricky, the attempts have so far been decidedly feeble. Let us just review the facts. Mrs. Mesado and her maid are supposed to have travelled by car from London to Tilbury. The day was alleged to have been a wet one. The car skids on a greasy road and runs into a lamp standard, smashing the right side of the glass windscreen. Mrs. Mesado has her hands badly cut and bruised and two stones are knocked out of her marquise ring. Without troubling to bandage her injured hands she continues to wear a pair of chamois leather gauntlets which are too big for her and belong to her sister Constance."

"How do you know they belong to her sister, Algernon?"

"They have the initials C. C. in indelible pencil on the inside of the gauntlets. I presume those initials stand for Constance Colvin. The fact led me to deduce that the sisters wore the same size and type of glove. I found a pair of chamois leather gauntlets of exactly the same make and size in the drawer of Mrs. Mesado's cabin dressing table, and they were marked B. M. They must have got their gloves mixed up on some previous occasion and decided to initial them."

"But you said that Constance's gloves were much too big for Beryl," suddenly remarked Ricardo. "How could they get them mixed up?"

"That's a pertinent question, Ricky," replied Vereker. "I have a little theory up my sleeve on that score. In any case chamois leather gloves are washable and often shrink badly. Some women can't stand tight gloves for walking or exercise; others like them to fit very neatly, so that it makes the point a difficult one to theorise on. Still I'm glad you spotted the weakness. It's strange that the gloves in the drawer were of the same size as those on the dead woman's hands, but we'll leave the question of gloves for a moment and return to our review. Mrs. Mesado comes on board and never troubles to bandage the injured hands or get them properly dressed. She came down to dinner the other night with or without gloves, a fact which neither you nor I were able to observe. Now, about the lies. In the first place, I'm certain that Mrs. Mesado didn't drive a car from a scrutiny of her shoes. You find an impossible discrepancy in Gautier's description of the car skidding and smashing the right-hand side of the windscreen. Gautier says the accident took place at Rainham. Mrs. Colvin says at Stifford, which is not on the direct road from London to Tilbury. I am certain I saw Mrs. Mesado's left hand uninjured and wearing a signet ring on the little finger the day she arrived on the 'Mars' Gautier says she never wore a signet ring. You say I may have mistaken Mrs. Colvin for Mrs. Mesado. This is not likely, for Mrs. Colvin's hair is platinum and Mrs. Mesado's light golden. Still it's a minor point. There was a quarrel and scuffle in Mrs. Mesado's cabin between her and Colvin long after one o'clock. Colvin says he never saw his sister-in-law after ten. Mrs. Colvin contradicts this inadvertently in conversation with me by saying she left her sister's cabin at one o'clock, and that she left her husband there with Mrs. Mesado to discuss some business matter. Further, there is some extraordinary confusion about Mrs. Mesado's lost necklace. The one the Colvins say is missing consists of alternate cinnamon and white diamonds; the one Mrs. Mesado wore, which was flung into my cabin through the window, consists of white diamonds and has a completely different clasp. Gautier, her companion and maid, who ought to know, describes the one I have in my possession as missing. Mrs. Mesado is apparently well, say, at one-thirty, and is dead shortly after two o'clock. Altogether this is a pretty kettle of fish!"

"A basket of live eels, Algernon. What do you make of it?"

"Never mind that for the moment. Did you question Gautier about anyone called Maureen?"

"I trod very warily and brought the conversation round to Christian names. Said I liked Maureen best after Renée. Perhaps it was too blatant; she didn't bite greedily, but later remarked that personally she had never known anyone called Maureen. It wasn't a hearty statement. Reminded me of a cat treading on a wet pavement."

"Strange! As a matter of fact we know that Guillermo Mesado gave a certain Maureen a necklace which was the cause of some trouble unknown to us. From the conversation I overheard that necklace is also missing. Does that suggest anything to you, Ricky?"

"It seems to show clearly that two necklaces are missing, and I deduce—it's not often I condescend to deduce—that the one that belonged to Maureen was the cinnamon and white diamond affair."

"You're improving, Ricky," remarked Vereker, his face brightening with a smile.

"I'm glad you observe it, but I can't see that my brilliant inference leads us up to anything tangible. It doesn't solve the mystery of Mrs. Mesado's sudden death."

"It goes a long way to clearing up things. I want you to pump Miss Penteado about the Mesados' friends and relations and see if you can put your finger on Maureen. She possibly knows who this Maureen is. I may be leaving you tomorrow at Lisbon. There's no time to lose."

"What? You don't mean to say you're going to cut short your trip?"

"I've not quite decided, but it's probable. I want you to stay on the 'Mars' and carry on with the work of investigation."

"Investigation or no investigation, I'm going to stay on board the 'Mars'. I'm not going to cut short the only holiday I've had in ten years for a bit of detective enthusiasm on your part. I'm going to see Ceuta, smell Tangiers and die, emulate Chopin at Mallorca, dine at the Ritz in Barcelona, where there are nuts and nut-brown dancing girls. Strewth! who'd swap the sinuous grace of an Andalusian dancer for criminal investigation? Not Manuel Ricardo!"

"Don't get heated, Ricky."

"By comparison the game of detection leaves me cold, Algernon."

"I thought you were getting interested?"

"We'll say lukewarm; it's not a ruling passion."

"Are you going to see Miss Penteado tonight?"

"If I can out-manoeuvre Dias and detach myself from Renée with my usual grace. I'm going to pop into Renée's cabin this afternoon to see some of her photographs of Buenos Aires."

"By jingo, you're making giant strides with the lady. Keep your eyes wide open. Once you're in her cabin look round discreetly and try and pocket one or two of her photos of Buenos Aires."

"You mean pinch them?"

"If it's necessary."

"Algernon, you're dishonest in the cause of justice. I could only be so for the sake of gain. I might ask her for them."

"Do so, but keep your own fingers off the surfaces. I want the lady's finger prints if possible."

"And I'd like the impress of her lips," remarked Ricardo as together they repaired to the dining saloon.

Chapter Seven

I

After lunch Ricardo strolled up to the lounge for coffee, while Vereker retired to his cabin and rang for the steward. The day steward, Dyson, appeared a few minutes later.

"Oh, Dyson, I'd like a cup of coffee if you could get me one."

"Very good, sir," replied Dyson, and later on reappeared with a tray.

"I'm thinking of leaving the 'Mars' tomorrow night at Lisbon, Dyson. I believe we arrive just before dinner. I shall have my bag packed and ready, and I want to get off the ship immediately the gangway is fixed up," said Vereker.

"You're not going to complete the trip, sir?" asked Dyson with a pretence at interest.

"No, and I'd like you to have my bag in the vestibule so that I can be one of the first down the gangway. Time's rather important. Will you see to that?"

"Certainly, sir," replied Dyson and was about to leave the cabin.

"Just a minute, Dyson. I'm rather absentminded when I'm in a hurry and might forget to tip you at the last moment. I'll do so now."

Vereker drew a pound from his wallet and handed it to the steward, who thanked him profusely.

"I'm sorry you're not coming with us, sir," he said on a grateful note.

"Can't be helped, Dyson, I'm on business. Sad affair this in the next cabin."

"Shockin', sir, shockin'. I didn't know you were aware of it."

"Oh, yes, I happened to be on deck when a friend of mine discovered the body."

"That so, sir," commented Dyson. "Of course we're not supposed to talk about what happens on the ship."

"A necessary precaution; the affair doesn't concern the rest of the passengers. Did you see much of the dead lady?"

"Very little, sir. About twice, and only for a few minutes, in Mr. and Mrs. Colvin's cabin. She seemed to be a very nice party."

"Yes, I thought so too. By the way, did you notice if her hands were injured when you saw her first?"

"Not to my knowledge, sir. I think I'd have spotted it."

"She might have been wearing a pair of chamois leather gloves to keep the dirt out of her wounds."

"I'm sure she wasn't, sir. I'd bet on that."

"Good! And did you notice what kind of costume she wore?"

"Yes, sir, a black and white check. Very smart. I remember that because my missus got me to buy her a rig-out like that when I was ashore last. Got it at the Bon Marché in Brixton."

"I see you keep your eyes open, Dyson. Have you seen anybody enter her cabin during the day except her sister and brother-in-law?"

"Her maid's travelling with her, sir. She used to come and go when she pleased. Rather a stuck-up piece to my mind. The stewardess, Dibdin, would know more than me. I only cleaned out the lady's cabin."

"Have a quiet talk with Dibdin and find out what she knows. Be discreet and don't appear too inquisitive. I was very interested in the dead lady."

"We've already talked it over between us, sir. Dibdin says she got a terrible shock, because as far as she could see the lady was hale and hearty last night, and Martin, the night stewardess, was perfectly certain she saw Mrs. Mesado run up the companion and on to D deck about two o'clock in the morning. She was found dead a few minutes later. Now Fuller, the night steward, said he saw Mr. Colvin carry the lady up on deck in a dead faint half an hour before that."

"She may have recovered and gone up again later, Dyson."

"That's how we explained it, sir. But Fuller says, and rightly so, ''Ow about the lady's 'ands?' Dibdin says her hands were not cut when she came aboard. She noticed it particular because the lady varnished 'er nails bright red—a norrible thing in my opinion. I don't 'old with such fashions. My missus tried it on once, but I gave her a bit o' my mind. Makes even a real lady look like a fast baggage."

"Thanks, Dyson, that's all I wanted to know. You needn't trouble to question Dibdin. I'll possibly see Fuller tonight. I want to give him something for his trouble before I go."

"Thank you, sir," replied Dyson and, feeling that he was no longer needed, was about to depart.

"I suppose they've removed the body to the ship's hospital, Dyson?" asked Vereker suddenly.

"Took it up to the sick bay this morning, sir. If you'd like to see Fuller now, sir, I'll try and get 'old of him."

"Good. I may miss him otherwise. Send him along if possible."

Dyson vanished, and about a quarter of an hour later a knock sounded on Vereker's cabin door.

"Dyson told me you wanted to see me, sir."

"I'll be in a hurry tomorrow, Fuller; I'm going ashore at Lisbon. I'll give you your tip now," said Vereker and handed Fuller a note.

"Thank you, sir. Is there anything else?"

"There's a question I'd like to ask you, Fuller, and it concerns the lady whose body we carried down from D deck to her cabin last night, or rather just after two o'clock this morning. I know you've been told not to discuss the matter, so you needn't answer the question unless you like. But I'm interested in Mrs. Mesado; it's more idle curiosity than anything else."

"Depends upon the question, sir."

"Nothing like being discreet, Fuller, but it's not a very deadly question. Did you see Mrs. Mesado last night after you came on duty?"

"Only once, sir. I saw Mr. Colvin carry her up the companion in a dead faint at one-thirty."

"When did he return to his cabin?"

"Almost immediately. The lady must have come-to quickly and he left her, I should say, on deck to recover properly."

"You're fairly certain about the time?"

"Positive, sir. Three bells of the middle watch, that's one-thirty as you'd call it."

"Did you see Mrs. Mesado come down again?"

"No, sir, but Martin, the night stewardess, says she saw her run up again quickly just before two o'clock. Martin opines she must have thought she was going to take bad again and went up for air."

"It wasn't Mrs. Colvin she saw? The two sisters are not unlike one another. Her sister may have gone up to see how she was getting on?"

"Martin is positive it was Mrs. Mesado, because she was still wearing her diamond necklace."

"Was she in her evening gown?"

"No, sir; Martin says she had changed into her black and white check costume."

"She was found dead in her blue georgette evening dress, and was certainly not wearing her necklace."

"True, sir, and that's what makes me think Martin must have been half asleep and mistook Mrs. Colvin for Mrs. Mesado."

"Does Mrs. Colvin wear a diamond necklace?"

"I couldn't say, sir."

"Does Martin drink, Fuller?"

"She likes her drop of Guinness, perhaps two of three drops, but never one over the eight so to speak, sir. It wouldn't do aboard this ship."

"She might have had exactly eight drops last night?"

"That's not for me to say, sir."

"When you broke the news to the Colvins were they both up?"

"Yes, sir, up and dressed. They hadn't turned in."

"They were terribly upset, I suppose?"

"The gentleman kept his head; the lady was hysterical, half laughing, half crying."

"Was she still in her evening gown?"

For some moments Fuller was at a loss for a reply, apparently trying to recall to his memory the details of the scene. His brow was furrowed in thought, the forefinger and thumb of his right hand nervously rubbed his chin.

"I'm blessed if I can remember, sir. I was so hot and bothered I didn't look very carefully at either the lady or the gent."

"Was Mrs. Colvin wearing a necklace, Fuller? Try and recall."

"Ah now, sir, that reminds me; she was. They were crystal beads, because she tugged at them on hearing the news and they broke. She flung them on the bed and came along with her husband."

"Surely you can remember her dress, Fuller?"

"I wouldn't be positive, sir, but I think she had changed into a morning costume something like her sister's. That's how it strikes me now, but I wouldn't be positive."

"Has Martin or Dibdin seen Mrs. Mesado's body?"

"No, sir."

"Mr. Colvin was in evening kit?"

"Oh, yes, I remember that distinctly, sir. Dinner jacket."

"Thanks very much, Fuller. Don't say anything to anybody about my seeing you on this matter. My friend Mr. Ricardo, in No. 87, is going to be with you for the trip. I want you to look after him, and if he's inquisitive it'll pay you to answer his questions. I shall come on board the 'Mars' on her return to London and will make a point of asking for you then. That's all for the present."

II

It was not more than a quarter of an hour after Fuller had departed that Colvin knocked at Vereker's cabin door and entered. He was apparently still in a highly agitated state of mind, and even the whisky he had drunk during the morning had failed to steady his overwrought nerves. He looked to Vereker like a man who, having taken a desperate chance, is awaiting the result with a premonition of disaster. In his right-hand jacket pocket was a bottle of whisky, and in his left hand he carried a siphon of soda.

"You'll excuse my coming in with a little refreshment," he said on entering, "but I feel as if I'd been sponging on you. I thought of asking you into my cabin, but Constance might come in at any moment and interrupt our talk. I'm relying on you for glasses."

Vereker produced two tumblers, and as Colvin poured out the whisky he noticed that his hand was trembling violently. Vereker himself had been looking forward to this interview with some trepidation, for he in turn was going to make a hazardous throw in the game in which he was now deeply involved. That throw, if unsuccessful, might render the rest of his self-imposed task of investigation futile, but he had given it careful thought and was sanguine of success. He accepted Colvin's proffered drink with alacrity and asked his guest to be seated.

"You wanted to see me, Vereker, about that missing necklace, I presume. Any luck?"

"I might say yes and no," replied Vereker, handing his cigarette case to his companion. "But before I go into that matter I should like to know a little more about Miss Gautier, Mrs. Mesado's maid and companion."

"Fire away," said Colvin with evident relief. "I don't know too much about her myself, but I'll do my best to answer your questions."

"Mrs. Mesado trusted her, I believe?"

"Implicitly. Constance was always warning Beryl that she was too trustful."

"She was the only person permitted to enter Mrs. Mesado's cabin except the steward and stewardess?"

"That's so."

"Had she the key to Mrs. Mesado's jewel-case ever in her possession?"

"That's quite possible, but Beryl was usually careful to keep it on her person, seeing that her jewels were so valuable."

"Do you think it possible that she managed to steal Mrs. Mesado's necklace?"

"That would hardly be possible. You see, Gautier went to bed shortly after dinner last night and as far as we know never entered Beryl's cabin after she had helped her to dress."

"Did your sister-in-law wear her necklace last night at dinner? If so it must have gone astray after that."

"She dressed for dinner and put on her necklace, but didn't go to the dining saloon. Altered her mind suddenly and had dinner brought to her in her cabin."

"Did Mrs. Mesado always carry her key about with her, say even to dinner?"

"Oh, yes, in one of those tiny little evening bags."

"Who has the key now?"

"I have it here," replied Colvin, producing a small key from his waistcoat pocket and handing it to Vereker. The latter examined the key casually and returned it to Colvin without comment.

"I found it in her evening bag, which she had tucked under the pillow of her bed before she went up on deck last night."

"Mrs. Mesado apparently had more than one very valuable necklace with her?" asked Vereker quietly, and looked up at Colvin's face to see the effect of his words. He was wondering if Colvin and his wife had compared notes since his interview with the latter. Colvin's face, which was always unusually red, now went white, and the muscles of his cheek twitched nervously.

"Yes, she had two very valuable necklaces," he said, and his voice was hoarse with suppressed agitation.

"I don't want to pry too deeply into your personal affairs, Colvin, but there seems to be some misapprehension about the necklace that's missing. Your wife and you say it is composed of alternate cinnamon and white diamonds, and Mrs. Mesado's maid says it's a magnificent one of white diamonds that her mistress wore last night which cannot be found. If I'm going to help you I must be clear on this point."

"On looking into Beryl's jewel-case before I handed it over to the purser about midday I found, to my horror, that the one of white diamonds was also missing," replied Colvin.

"You didn't notice that when you went through her jewel-case early this morning in my presence?"

"No, I'm afraid not."

"Rather a bad oversight," remarked Vereker pointedly.

"I was too upset to think clearly or remember," replied Colvin weakly. "You see, I was searching for the cinnamon and white diamond necklace at the time, and it occupied my mind to the exclusion of everything else."

"I can quite understand. Anyone might do likewise in similar circumstances. Your wife must have made a mistake about the actual necklace that was missing when she told Gautier about the loss."

"It seems so," replied Colvin guardedly and poured himself out another stiff glass of whisky.

"Well, I've had one bit of luck in my quest, Colvin," remarked Vereker with a mysterious smile.

"And what's that?" asked Colvin, looking up quickly.

"I've recovered the necklace of white diamonds," replied Vereker and, drawing the jewel from his trousers' pocket, held it out to Colvin.

"My God! How did you manage to get it?" asked Colvin as he hesitatingly took the necklace from Vereker's outstretched hand. His face was ludicrous in its look of blank astonishment.

"I can't answer that question, Colvin. You remember our pact. I was to get the necklace back without fuss or trouble, and I've done so. You mustn't be too inquisitive at present."

"Well, Vereker, all I can say is that you're marvellous!" exclaimed Colvin.

"Not quite as marvellous as you think, Colvin. Still, I'm not going to divulge my secret at this juncture. I've got to try and recover the other necklace now, and I'm afraid the job's going to be a much tougher one."

A curiously uneasy look stole into Colvin's eyes. He glanced nervously up at Vereker, who was apparently lost in thought, and then stared with amazement at the necklace he held in his hand. Some anxious train of thought was evidently passing through his mind.

"By the way, did Gautier possess a key to Mrs. Mesado's large Saratoga trunk?" asked Vereker, waking suddenly from his reverie.

"Not to my knowledge, but why?" asked Colvin, starting with surprise.

"I was thinking Mrs. Mesado, in her careless way, might have left her cinnamon and white diamond necklace in it."

"Oh, no, she couldn't possibly have done that," said Colvin with over-hasty assurance. "Beryl always carried the key of that trunk about with her also. I have it here with the key to her jewel-case. I'm sure she only kept her clothes, shoes and odds and ends in that trunk."

"You have a similar trunk, haven't you?" asked Vereker, as if he was aware of some obscure reason for this coincidence.

"Yes. We bought them together at Martin's, in Bond Street."

"Didn't they give you two keys to each trunk?"

"They usually do," remarked Vereker.

"That's true; I have two on my chain."

"You can't say where the duplicate key to Mrs. Mesado's trunk is?"

"No, I'm afraid I don't know what she did with it. I hadn't thought of that. It's possible that Gautier has the duplicate in her possession," said Colvin excitedly, and a look of genuine surprise crossed his features.

"I'm almost certain she has," continued Vereker, "but we'll find out eventually. You say your sister-in-law was very fond of Gautier?"

"Yes, I think she was genuinely fond of her; she treated her more as a companion than a maid."

"Did Mrs. Mesado ever make a will?"

"Quite recently. About two months ago to be precise."

"Was Gautier a beneficiary?"

"Yes, I think she was to get about five hundred pounds. Beryl left all her property, real and personal, to my wife, Constance."

"She would leave a considerable amount, I presume?"

"About £100,000 altogether in personalty, and there's Firle House and effects at Jevington."

"Did she leave a duplicate of the will with her solicitor?"

"I really can't say."

"It's not very relevant, but I should like to know."

"Of course it has nothing to do with the missing necklace?" asked Colvin in a bewildered tone.

"Apparently not, but in my investigation a certain matter cropped up and I became interested in the question of a will. You see, Colvin, when I consulted Captain Partridge about this missing necklace affair a suspicion at once arose in his mind that there might be something not quite above board with regard to your sister-in-law's sudden death," said Vereker, putting as bold a front as he could on the falsehood.

"Good Lord!" gasped Colvin with acute distress, "how on earth could he think that?"

"People are naturally suspicious when they hear of missing valuables in connection with a sudden death. Of course, we know there's nothing in it, but we've got to convince them that there isn't. The doctor too now seems to have some doubt about Mrs.

Mesado's heart failure. He didn't actually say so, but I inferred from his remarks that he too was beginning to be influenced by the skipper's attitude. They're in a bit of a stew about it and may raise some difficulties about a burial at sea."

"This is damnable," exclaimed Colvin, wringing his hands in anguish, "utterly damnable!" Beads of perspiration had suddenly burst out on his brow.

"I'm afraid I took the matter into my own hands to save you and your wife from a nasty ordeal. I said you had changed your mind about a burial at sea and had decided to take the body ashore at Lisbon."

"Oh, thank God, Vereker, that was splendid of you!" exclaimed Colvin with heartfelt relief, and extended a hand which Vereker shook mechanically. "You've saved us from a heap of trouble. We must either bury Beryl at Lisbon or take her home to England."

"I think it'd be wise, Colvin. I'm afraid I acted rather rashly without consulting you, but I'm glad you agree with the course I adopted. I thought I'd put my foot in it immediately after I'd spoken."

"No, no, I'm glad you took a chance. After what we've gone through, Constance and I couldn't stand anything so beastly as an inquiry. I wish I'd said nothing about the missing jewellery."

"All's well that ends well, Colvin. The thing now is to disembark at Lisbon and carry out whatever programme you decide on with regard to the burial of Mrs. Mesado. I've recovered half the missing valuables, I may be able to lay hands on the other half. In the meantime don't discuss the matter with anyone. If you can trust me, I'll see things through for you."

"Do anything you think advisable," said Colvin readily; "I leave it entirely in your hands."

With these words he left Vereker's cabin and hurried into No. 90. On his departure Vereker poured himself out another whisky from the bottle which Colvin had left behind and lit a cigarette. He was laughing quietly to himself and there was a suspicion of triumph in his attitude. He was conscious that he had carried through a risky and difficult plan with complete success. So far things were going smoothly in the way he desired them to go.

"Very strange!" he soliloquised some minutes later. He was thinking of Fuller's statement that Colvin had carried his sister-in-law up on to D deck at one-thirty. It was palpable that Colvin had lied flagrantly about seeing Mrs. Mesado for the last time at ten o'clock. It was not difficult at times to discover falsehood, thought Vereker, but to a detective the motive behind a falsehood was of cardinal importance. What could be the motive, he asked himself, behind Colvin's persistent and unblushing mendacity?

III

Half an hour before dinner Ricardo entered Vereker's cabin. He was already dressed and held in his hand by their edges two or three photographic prints.

"Ah, you managed to get them!" exclaimed Vereker, turning round from the mirror in front of which he stood brushing his hair.

"Three. The glossy surfaces are simply engraved with Renée's finger prints. She had just been rubbing her hands with glycerine and lemon juice. I can see them with my naked eye. Nearly as beautiful as a bird's footprints in snow!"

"You're invaluable, Ricky," said Vereker, taking the photographs from Ricardo's hand and placing them very carefully in an empty collar box on his dressing table.

"I felt a priceless Judas at the moment she gave them to me," said Ricardo, "but I'm getting hardened in criminology. Some day I shall commit one murder to unravel another. You think those snaps'll do?"

"Admirably. I'm glad Gautier is used to doing a little hard work with her hands."

"Why?"

"The ridges are more pronounced in a manual worker's fingers."

"That's unfortunate; criminals generally fight shy of hard labour in more senses than one. Will those finger-prints last until you can get them photographed and developed?"

"I shall see to them as soon as I reach Lisbon. I know Mascarenhas, one of the Portuguese chiefs of police, and he'll get them done for me. As a matter of fact it's possible to develop a finger-print that's two or three years old. What arrangements have you made for tonight, Ricky?"

"A very pleasant programme. I asked Renée if she was going to see the cinema show at nine-fifteen, but she was non-committal, so I managed to fade out mistily. I had tea with Rosaura and simulated jealousy of Miguel Dias with excellent results. To salve my wounded feelings she has consented to have a special dinner with me and accompany me to the cinema show. Criminal investigation seems to be as expensive as keeping a fashionable mistress, Algernon."

"But it has the advantage of being exciting," remarked Vereker, smiling. "Did you learn anything of Maureen?"

"Not yet. I shall bombard that position tonight. I find that the Penteados don't know the Mesados very well. Both derive their wealth from cold meat. Mesado is a bit of an expert in refrigeration. What he doesn't know about freezing the devil couldn't utilise for his own comfort."

"Have the Penteados and Dias viewed the body yet? It's going ashore at Lisbon tomorrow."

"Certainly not; this is a pleasure cruise, not a coroner's inquest. They've just heard the sad news, and offered tactful condolences to the Colvins."

"I see," remarked Vereker thoughtfully, and asked: "Did you keep your eyes skinned while you were in Gautier's cabin?"

"You bet, and the gods helped me. Just as I was about to enter the lady's bower a stewardess came out carrying a note in her hand. She was repeating the name 'Dias' audibly as she passed me, probably to prevent herself from forgetting it. I inferred that the note was for Dias. This interested me, because Renée had already told me that she was only slightly acquainted with Dias. I said nothing, however, and once in Renée's cabin I was promptly handed a photograph album and a score of loose prints to look at."

"With your usual charm, Ricky, I suppose you simulated great interest in Buenos Aires and district?"

"As if the place belonged to me, Algernon. I even called it B.A. after the manner born. Renée lounged and smoked languorously in a wicker chair, and I'm afraid a perfectly moulded leg in a silk stocking was an overwhelming counter-attraction to the beauties of B.A. The latter weakened sadly: it was an unequal contest. One of these days I shall write a profound article for a stodgy monthly on the significance of legs in human courtship."

"Never mind your leg theories, Ricky. What else did you see?"

"Very little until Renée was suddenly called away. Mrs. Colvin wanted to see her for a few minutes, and she asked me to wait until she returned."

"You promptly nosed round, I hope."

"I spotted a writing pad of bank paper—you know the thin stuff it is—on her table. Beside it was one of those silverpoint stylos I've seen you use for sketching at times."

"That's interesting, but a silverpoint has to be used on a specially prepared chalk paper. It's useless on ordinary paper."

"I know, and that's what intrigued me. I was about to try the silverpoint out on her pad when I noticed that the business end was still wet with a colourless fluid."

"Secret writing. Did you root about for the liquid?"

"Like a pig after truffles. I couldn't find any trace of a bottle anywhere."

"Disappointing! She may have used ordinary saliva. It works fairly well and can be made visible by washing the paper with a thin wash of ink and water when the writing's dry."

"By Jove, fancy getting one's information straight from the mare's mouth so to speak. The process explains the phrase 'spitting it out' and makes x's a fair approximation to kisses. Anyhow, finding no bottle of fluid, I picked up the stylo to see if the paper was in any way prepared. I was at once surprised to find that the pressure of the stylo had gone through and left a perfectly legible impression on the leaf underneath."

"Ricky, that's splendid. Did you detach the leaf?"

"Thought it was too risky, but I read the note after painful hesitation. Posterity will always be able to say of me: He was a detective and a gentleman."

"Never mind posterity. What did the note say?"

"Very little. Simply: Dearest. Sit next me at cinema performance. Renée."

"She used the word dearest?"

"Legitimately, I should say. The superlative implies a host of comparatives and positives."

"You must have got a cold douche, Ricky!"

"Positively, but it didn't deter me from another scratch round. I saw nothing more of importance, unless a phial labelled 'Nembutal' fits into our scheme of things."

"You've surpassed yourself, Ricky. I must inquire into nembutal; it's a drug I've never heard of before."

"The phial was empty."

"Where was it, Ricky?"

"In an attaché case from which Renée had taken the album of photographs. On her return to the cabin after her interview with Mrs. Colvin she happened to notice the phial as she was putting back the photographs. She looked startled, picked it up and hastily threw it out of the porthole."

"It may be vital and it may mean nothing at all. This is one of the most complicated cases I've ever dealt with. I'm simply enmeshed in a tangle of clues," said Vereker wearily.

"After further polite conversation Renée wriggled out of her half-promise to accompany me to the cinema performance and, knowing the reason for her withdrawal, I didn't press the matter.

I promptly retaliated by inviting Rosaura to take her place at dinner and the show. 'Pon my soul, Algernon, flirtation's nearly as spiteful a game as croquet."

Ricardo, having glanced at the clock on the cabin mantelpiece, suddenly jumped from his chair.

"Hell's bells, but I'm late! So long, Algernon. See you before I turn in," he shouted as he vanished through the door.

"Good hunting, Ricky!"

Chapter Eight

I

The dining saloon of the "Mars" had been rapidly converted into a temporary cinema theatre, and the orchestra, seated in a gallery, were playing Strauss's march, "Radetzky". The audience were slowly filtering into their seats, and were composed for the major part of elderly passengers; the youthful section evidently preferring to spend their time in more exciting forms of recreation. Even the title, *Passion's Dupe*, failed to appeal to the general company, the more modern of whom probably thought that passion precluded duping and was its own reward. Perhaps the very thought of "pictures" made them anxious to avoid the stale routine of their lives ashore. The attendance was surprisingly low, and here and there half a row of seats was unoccupied. Vereker was one of the first to enter the theatre, and took up his position in a secluded corner by the door in order to have a good view of the arriving audience. He had not been seated long when Renée Gautier entered alone and took a seat in the third row from the back. Shortly afterwards Manuel Ricardo appeared with Miss Penteado, the latter every now and then laughing gaily at some bright flippancy flung off by her vivacious companion. They took their seats in the centre row of the auditorium, and as they edged their way between the closely arranged rows of chairs Vereker noticed that Ricardo had observed Miss Gautier and given her an exaggerated bow. She had returned the salutation with a bright nod and smile and, seeing that Miss Penteado was exchanging greetings with a gentleman in front of her, had pursed her lips in a moue which was doubtless intended to be coquettish rather than impertinent. Close on their heels followed Ferguson, Vereker's Scots acquaintance with a penchant for theological discussion, and his appearance caused Algernon to make himself momentarily less obtrusive behind one of the support stanchions close to his own chair. Ferguson had hardly attached himself to another of his fellow passengers when Miguel Dias descended the steps into the dining saloon and posed statuesquely as he surveyed the room with his dark, flashing eyes. Renée Gautier's glance met his without a hint of recognition, and at that moment the lights were extinguished for the commencement of the performance. Vereker waited till Dias had vanished in the dusk. Then, rising from his seat, he silently and unobtrusively made his way to the rear of the auditorium, where he slipped into a chair just behind and to the right of Miss Gautier and Dias. From this coign he could easily overhear their conversation even if whispered, and was fairly safe from recognition by Miss Gautier until the close of the film and the switching on of the lights for the interval.

Passion's Dupe was an American production, in which sentimentality made a travesty of any rational morality, and the commercial insertion of sexual suggestiveness turned natural human love into an obscenity. Vereker, however, was not interested in its illogical perversities and was sitting with ears alert and his attention fixed on the couple in front of him. For a considerable time they sat as if they were complete strangers to one another, simulating an absorption in the screen play, and then Renée Gautier, turning to Dias, whispered:

"The Colvins are going to leave the ship tomorrow."

"At Lisbon? Why?" asked Dias, with evident surprise in his tone.

"I don't know. There's not going to be a burial at sea after all."

"Haven't you any idea?"

"Not the vaguest. Sudden change of plan. Something unusual about the whole business."

"Are they going to take the body back to England?"

"I don't know definitely."

"Very strange. I can't understand their change of plan."

"Neither can I."

"I shouldn't worry. Did you get the stuff?"

"I have it here."

"You'd better give it to me now. Safer."

Some moments of silence ensued, during which Miss Gautier handed a small packet to her companion, who swiftly thrust it into an inside pocket of his dinner jacket. After this transaction both either became absorbed in the story of *Passion's Dupe* or were lost in their own thoughts. Neither spoke for about a quarter of an hour.

"You're paying a lot of attention to the young Penteado woman, Miguel," remarked Miss Gautier in a querulous voice at length.

"What of it?"

"Oh, nothing. She's very beautiful."

"Jealous?"

"A little. I can't help it, Miguel."

"Don't be childish. Purely a business matter."

Renée Gautier here made some remark which escaped Vereker's preternaturally acute hearing owing to a burst of laughter which accompanied some absurdity of the film story.

"I've managed that all right."

"Good! I shall be glad if it comes off."

"You deserve it, Renée. I'm indebted to you, and if anything nasty happens I'll stand the racket willingly for your sake. Who is this young fellow Ricardo?"

"Charming boy—frivolous, witty and thinks himself no end of a success. Quite an innocent flirtation; it amuses me."

"Doubtless, but you must be very careful."

"Don't get scared. I'm perfectly safe."

"Fond of him?"

"Don't be ridiculous. He's very ingenuous."

"Are you piqued?"

"He's young and good-looking. Has he money?"

"He writes stories for a living."

"*Suffit, cela suffit!* He has a travelling companion?"

"Yes, a painter, who seems comfortably off."

"Otherwise he wouldn't paint. I've not spoken to him, but he looks a cunning fellow. Instinctively I'm afraid of him. His eyes see everything."

"A dreamer and a bit of a prig. Nothing to fear."

"I'm not so sure. My judgment is not often at fault."

Again there followed an interval of silence, which was at length broken by Renée Gautier.

"Fancy the two of us being together for the rest of the trip! Aren't you glad, Miguel?"

"I'm not going further than Lisbon, Renée."

"What do you mean?"

The question was asked in a sharp tone in which surprise was mingled with anger, and could be heard distinctly by other people some seats distant.

"Shut up, you fool. You're attracting attention. I mean what I say."

"But, Miguel, you promised me..."

"I know, but this is business, not amusement. Do you want the whole affair to end in disaster?"

"But why are you leaving at Lisbon?"

"Don't ask silly questions. Can't you see that I must get clear of this ship at the first opportunity? The Colvins are getting dangerous."

"But we have them safely in our hands."

"I'm not so sure. Nothing is ever absolutely safe."

"Then I am to travel alone?"

"You must go on. I shall cross Spain later and meet you at Barcelona. Then we can run up to Paris and get married."

"What are the Penteados doing?"

"Why ask me?"

"I want to know."

"I believe they are thinking of landing at Lisbon and catching a Blue Star liner to B.A. in a couple of days. The old lady is sick of the trip already. Nothing has been definitely settled."

"You are not altering you plans to suit Miss Penteado, are you?"

"Look here, Renée, if you're going to be stupidly jealous like this we had better part now for good."

"Don't be angry with me, Miguel. I'll try hard not to be jealous, but I wouldn't be jealous if I didn't love you madly."

"That's better. Now everything is settled. We mustn't be seen together again on the 'Mars'. It's too risky. You understand?"

"I shall be glad when we reach Paris..."

Shortly after this the film story concluded and the lights were switched on. Vereker was about to move away discreetly and leave the theatre when Dias turned and flung an inquisitive glance round him. Vereker looked in his direction to see if he had been recognised, and noticed an expression of alarm and suspicion cross Dias's features. The next moment Renée Gautier swung quickly round in her seat, but Vereker was gazing blankly at the cinema screen in front of him as if he were eagerly awaiting the second item on the programme. He sat thus for some minutes and noticed that the pair were evidently uneasy that he had been so close to them during their conversation. The lights were once more lowered, and the second film had not proceeded far in its story before Dias rose from his seat and quietly left the theatre. Vereker sat patiently till the end of the performance. The orchestra played the National Anthem and the company began to disperse. Renée Gautier turned, looked directly at him and smiled. Vereker simulated surprise with complete success.

"Good evening, Miss Gautier," he said. "I didn't know you were sitting so close to me. When did you come in?"

"I have been here all the time. I didn't see you."

"What do you think of the show?"

"Very good... so remarkable to be able to go to the cinema on board ship. What a pity they were silent films!"

"I prefer them myself. I believe there are so many Board of Trade restrictions with regard to fire that the company can't give us a really up-to-date film."

"I didn't know that. Where is your friend Mr. Ricardo?"

"I'm sure I don't know. He said something about attending the performance with you, and I was surprised to find that you were unaccompanied. I had arranged to come with him, but we altered our plans. I only decided to put in an appearance at the last minute because I was at a loose end."

On reaching the vestibule outside the dining saloon Miss Gautier, saying she was going to retire, bade Vereker good night and disappeared down one of the alleyways running off that antechamber. Vereker made his way up to the smoking room on the next deck and passed out of it on to the promenade, which was deserted. He was about to patrol the deck when Doctor Macpherson turned round a corner walking at a brisk pace.

"Good evening, doctor. Taking a little exercise before turning in?" said Vereker, joining him.

"My sleeping draught I call it," replied Macpherson.

For some time they marched along together, chatting generally, when the doctor, glancing at his watch, came to a halt.

"Will you come to my cabin and join me in a peg before you get into your hammock?" he asked.

Vereker accepted the invitation with alacrity, and together they made their way to the doctor's cabin. When seated over their drinks the doctor became confidential and asked:

"You managed your point all right with the Colvins?"

"Certainly."

"Because we've made all arrangements for putting the body ashore at Lisbon to-morrow."

"That's satisfactory. The Colvins agreed with me that it was the best thing to do."

"Any more news about the missing necklace?"

"I recovered the property and returned it to them."

"Splendid. How the devil did you work the miracle?"

"It was a simple matter. But we'll keep to our agreement. I'll tell you all about it when the 'Mars' reaches London again."

"Very good. Any irrelevant questions to ask?"

"Only one. What kind of a drug is nembutal, doctor?"

"Ah, I can tell you very little about it, because I've never had occasion to prescribe it. It belongs to the barbituric group of hypnotic drugs, such as veronal, medinal, luminal and others. It's a new drug, and even experts have not finally determined the dosage. It evidently has toxic effects, and in a recent inquest Sir William Willcox, the Home Office analyst, was reported in the Press to have said that in his opinion it was a dangerous drug. That's as much as I can tell you about it."

"Would it produce prolonged unconsciousness?"

"An overdose certainly would, I should say. There might be a considerable period of coma before death."

"That's extremely interesting; it fits in so aptly with one of my theories."

"Still puddling in romance, Mr. Vereker?"

"No, doctor, only piecing together deadly realities."

At this point the conversation turned on other topics, and an hour later Vereker rose, thanked the doctor for his hospitality and was about to leave.

"I'd like to ask you one question before you go, Mr. Vereker," said Macpherson.

"Out with it, doctor."

"What was your idea in getting the Colvins to disembark at Lisbon with Mrs. Mesado's body?"

"That's not sticking to our agreement, doctor. You must wait and see. In detective work one has to leave nothing to chance. Every possible line of inquiry must be explored. Many of these lines only end in culs-de-sac and are a deadly waste of time, but none of them can be ignored."

"I'll bet you have the idea of an exhumation later on. You can't hoodwink me," said the doctor pertinently.

"Good night, doctor," replied Vereker with a laugh and closed the door behind him.

II

When Vereker entered his cabin he found Ricardo lounging in a comfortable chair smoking a cigarette.

"You're late, Algernon. I believe you've made a conquest. I saw you in earnest conversation today with that silver-haired grandame who affects a monocle and wears buttoned boots. I believe you've been helping her to take off her bottines, you cunning old bambocheur!"

"You mean Lady Hildenborough? Charming woman of the old school, Ricky. Victorian and as fragrant as lavender!"

"She reminds me of a hansom cab. I can't explain why, Algernon."

"I saw you at the show with Miss Penteado. Did you gather any information?"

"I've learned a good deal of the history of the Diss sisters."

"And who are they?"

"Beryl and Constance, or, if you prefer it, Mrs. Mesado and Mrs. Colvin."

"That's useful. How many sisters were there?"

"Three. Beryl, whose body lies in the ship's hospital; Constance, alive on board; and Amy, who died when she was a girl of seventeen. They come from Fakenham, in Norfolk. Their father was rather well off once upon a time, but got through most of his money. Constance married Colvin, who once had a bailiff's job on a large Norfolk estate, but lost it down his throat. Beryl went on the stage, into the ballet, and was on the way to becoming a premiere danseuse when she made the acquaintance of Mesado, the meat millionaire. Strange how these monsters of modern industrialism succumb to the delicate enchantment of a fine body inspired with rhythm! He married her. Colvin, as I've told you before, got a parasitic job from his brother-in-law and has lived the life of a country gentleman ever since."

"And did you get any other information about Amy?"

"None whatever, except that there was some mystery about her death."

"That's not very helpful. Are the Penteados old friends of the Mesados?"

"I can't quite get at the truth from Rosaura on this point. She equivocates, and I think there's a minor mystery hidden there. Père Penteado and Mesado were warm friends through chilled meat. The former died about a year ago and left his millions to his wife for life, and in reversion to his daughter. Rosaura got on very well with Beryl up to a point. Says Beryl was a jealous, temperamental woman with the very devil of a temper and most difficult to live with. Guillermo she thinks a most charming man, but very fond of the fair sex."

"Was that the cause of the recent trouble with his wife?"

"Presumably. There was a woman in the case, but Rosaura doesn't know who. Beryl believed in Romantic Love and, like many people, thought marriage put a full stop to amatory diversion."

"I'm old-fashioned enough to think it ought to," remarked Vereker gravely.

"I'm old enough to know that it frequently doesn't, Algernon. I wouldn't be surprised if in the near future jealousy is considered a crime punishable with seven years' 'hard'. You must admit it's an unsocial trait in human nature."

"Had they separated?"

"Guillermo has presumably gone back to the Argentine. Beryl, before leaving England, put up the house and furniture in Sussex, which is her property, for sale."

"Was there going to be a divorce?"

"No mention of it. The fight had just commenced. Opening bombardment, so to speak."

"What does Miss Penteado know of Miguel Dias?"

"Not very much, but is certain he's an adventurer."

"Give any reasons for her conviction?"

"Only that her father always said so and warned her against him. Old Penteado evidently knew more of Dias than he ever cared to disclose."

"She seems to be very thick with Dias in spite of paternal warnings."

"Merely an oceanic flirtation—watery waste affair. Dias pays her marked attention probably with an eye on her reversion, and you can't blame a pretty woman for exercising her charms for Art's sake. Might as well try and stop a cat from sticking her claws into a ball of wool."

"I saw you were present at *Passion's Dupe*."

"Yes; it was unintentionally a delightful farce. We both ached with laughter, much to the annoyance of a reverend gentleman and his wife sitting in front, who doubtless thought us promising candidates for damnation. Where were you hiding?"

"Just behind Renée Gautier, who was seated next to Dias and in earnest conversation with him throughout the play. She's evidently very much in love with him."

"But he's leaving the 'Mars' at Lisbon tomorrow, and is going to stay at the Hotel do Parque, Estoril. He's been doing his best to persuade the Penteados to do the same."

"They've refused?"

"Definitely. Is Renée going ashore with the Colvins?"

"No, she's going on further, and I want you to carry on the work of investigation. Dance attendance on the lady. You won't find that difficult, but you must be on the qui vive. In speaking to Dias she said you were an ingenuous youth and thought yourself a great success."

"Good I won't be stupid enough to let her find out that I really am one. What did she say about you?"

"Called me a bit of a prig!" replied Vereker, smiling.

"You got off lightly. After all, a prig is a fellow whose perfect equilibrium is intensely annoying to wobblers. Do you think Renée's implicated in this Mesado death mystery?"

"She knows something about it, and so does Dias. From a fragment of their conversation that I overheard it appears they have a strangle-hold over the Colvins in the matter. You must try and find out what she knows."

"I'll do my best, Algernon. How far is she going?"

"Dias is going to meet her at Barcelona, and they're travelling to Paris to get married. At least that's his story. She seemed disappointed at his leaving her, but apparently agreed that it was advisable owing to some danger that threatens him."

"She's another of Passion's dupes. What d'you think is the danger? Is he responsible for Mrs. Mesado's death?"

"I can't say, but he's capable of anything, and we must treat them both as suspects in the meantime."

"How long will you stay in Lisbon?"

"Only a few days. I shall try and keep an eye on Dias and the Colvins, and then I must get back to England by the Blue Star liner *Avila Star*. She's a pet boat of mine and is on her way back from Buenos Aires. If Dias turns up at Barcelona you might leave the 'Mars' and follow him up. I'll go to London on my return and get Heather on the job. He may know something of our friend Dias. There'll be a little history of the gentleman in the records at Scotland Yard, if I'm not mistaken."

"This is all very exciting, Algernon. I see that I'm going to enjoy myself."

"I'm sure you will. The only danger is Miss Penteado. If she condescends to pay any attention to your advances you'll promptly throw up the whole business for another maudlin love affair. I know you pretty well by now, Ricky."

"You can dismiss that danger from your mind, Algernon. Miss Penteado has confessed to me that she's in love. With whom do you think?"

"How should I know, Ricky?"

"Guillermo Mesado."

"Good Lord, this is startling news! Was she the cause of the Mesado estrangement?"

"She didn't say. Good night. I'm going to in. I've given you something fresh to think about. Don't let it keep you awake. As for my falling in love, well:

'Out upon it I have loved
Three whole days together,
And am like to love three more
If it prove fair weather.'"

Chapter Nine

I

Next morning Vereker rose early and wandered out on to the upper promenade deck. The air was warm, the sea calm and here and there in a blue sky sailed rounded masses of sun-steeped clouds. Only two or three of the more energetic passengers were up enjoying this sudden mergence of winter into summer. At breakfast Vereker met Ricardo. They were the only two who sat down to the meal at the captain's table, and Vereker seized the opportunity to give Manuel final instructions with regard to the work of investigation into the Pleasure Cruise Mystery. He was, if possible, to ingratiate himself with Renée Gautier and obtain any further information he could from her. He was not to be too disappointed if the results were meagre, for the task was going to be a formidable one seeing that that young lady was already on her guard. She might, however, be inveigled into shedding some light on the relations existing between Miss Penteado and Guillermo Mesado and disclosing if they had any bearing on the estrangement that had taken place between Mesado and his wife prior to the latter's death. He was also to follow up Dias and Gautier when they met at Barcelona and took train to Paris for their proposed marriage. Having settled these matters definitely and arranged a code for communications the two friends agreed to part provisionally.

During the remainder of the day Vereker kept aloof as much as possible from his fellow passengers. He looked in at the wireless office on the starboard side of the games deck and despatched a coded wireless message to his old friend Chief Inspector Heather of Scotland Yard. The message was a request to put Tankerton, a trusted private inquiry agent, to discover all he could about the Diss family of Fakenham, in Norfolk, and have his report ready on Vereker's return to London. Now that he was eager on the trail he chafed at every moment of unnecessary delay and found an idle day on board ship particularly exacerbating to his restless and impatient mood. He was frankly delighted when after lunch two massive and sullen rocks, the first glimpse of Portugal, rose up forbiddingly on the eastern horizon. Towards evening the range of mountains, the Sierra da Estrella, that runs parallel to the western coast, appeared, and their sharp-cut pinnacles, caught in the late sunshine and standing out dramatically against the deep azure of the sky, were almost fantastic in their rugged beauty. By some trick of association they reminded Vereker of bandits and grand opera, and then more prosaically that he must pack his trunk. This done, he exchanged his English money at the purser's office for escudos notes and was returning to his cabin when he ran into Colvin. The latter, in case they did not meet again before his disembarkation, wished Vereker good-bye and handed him his card bearing his English address.

"You must run down and see us when you come back from this cruise, Vereker," he said cordially. "We'll do our best to make you comfortable. We are indebted to you for your kindness to us. Constance, as you know, is sole beneficiary under Beryl's will, and we shall be glad to entertain our friends at Firle House, Jevington."

Vereker, after thanking him and promising to look him up as soon as he could seize an opportunity, asked: "Have you fixed on your hotel in Lisbon?"

"Yes, we are going to stay at Carcano's."

"I know it—a very comfortable place. Staying long?"

"After the funeral we shall go on to Madrid, put up there for a few weeks and return overland."

They parted with a handshake, and Vereker turned off the alleyway into his cabin. He glanced again at Colvin's card, which he still held in his hand, and stood lost in thought before placing it in his pocket book. He was thinking that Colvin was either playing a daring game of bluff or was satisfied that he had nothing to fear from any further meeting with him. On the face of it the man was either over-confident or innocent in the matter of the mysterious death of Mrs. Mesado, and in the light of his discoveries Vereker was inclined to think that willingly or unwillingly he was gravely implicated. For some moments his confidence in his deductions was shaken. Had he himself been too cocksure in drawing conclusions from the data he had collected, or would his theorising prove correct when he had probed deeper into this baffling tragedy? With swiftly returning assurance he dismissed the subject from his mind and picked up his book to return it to the library.

Just before dinner the "Mars" moved smoothly into the wide mouth of the Tagus as the sun was flooding the western sky with gold and crimson. Lisbon rose up from the darkening sea a chequered pattern of pink and white formed by the shingled roofs and light-coloured walls of so many of its buildings. Vereker, gazing at its terraces of houses of Moorish aspect, gilded by the mellow light, found it inexpressibly beautiful. For some time his thoughts wandered away dreamily from his grim occupation with the Pleasure Cruise Mystery and slipped back into the happier region of painting, which he had for the time being deserted in favour of his exacting hobby of detection.

II

The "Mars" berthed at the quay at Alcantara-Mar and a large number of the passengers went ashore to spend the evening in Lisbon. Immediately the gangways were in position for disembarkation Vereker hurried on to the quay, quickly satisfied the Portuguese Customs with regard to his trunk and hailed a taxi. Seated in this car (it was quite unlike the regulation English conveyance), he asked the driver to take up a position from which he could see the other passengers emerge. Eventually Miguel Dias came through the throng that had gathered to welcome the arrival of the ship, and quickly disappeared into another car after giving the driver hurried instructions. Ricardo had learned from Miss Penteado that Dias was going to stay at the Hotel do Parque, near the Casino gardens at Estoril, but Vereker was not going to take anything for granted. The Penteados' evasion of his invitation to leave the ship at Lisbon might in any case have caused Dias to change his plans. No sooner had he boarded the car and it had moved off than Vereker instructed his driver to follow at a discreet distance behind. The foremost car travelled at a reckless pace, taking the road which lies parallel with the electric railway skirting the shore. Vereker had frequently travelled by that electric railway on former visits, and knew that the line ended in the little fishing village of Cascaes, a mile or so beyond Mont Estoril, this charming section of the coast being known as the Portuguese Riviera. It was evident that Dias was making for Estoril, and after about half an hour's drive his car came to a halt in the centre of that residential district about two miles beyond the Hotel do Parque and the Casino, with its palm-bordered walks and geometrically planned beds and borders of flowers. His conveyance pulled up before the Hotel da Pena, where he alighted and, having paid his fare, disappeared quickly into the reception clerk's office in the entrance hall. Vereker ordered his chauffeur to drive on to the market place at Cascaes, where he entered a small and stuffy wine shop. He shared a bottle of Collares with his driver, smoked a cigarette and was driven back to the Hotel da Pena. He had thus given Dias time to settle in before he himself made an appearance. He was greeted as he entered by the manager, Julio Roca, who had once been a waiter in Soho and who had known Vereker as a frequent diner at the little restaurant in Greek Street where he was employed.

"Still here, Julio?" remarked Vereker as he shook hands with his old acquaintance.

"Sim, senhor, always here now," replied Julio.

"A gentleman called Miguel Dias has just arrived, I believe?"

"You know him, sir?"

"No, but I'm interested in his movements, Julio."

"Ah, I see, I see, he is wanted at Scotland Yard?"

"Not at the present moment as far as I know. He may be wanted by them later. Keep an eye on him. Has he booked his room?"

"Yes, sir; No. 17 on the first floor."

"Good. Is No. 16 vacant?"

"Yes, sir. You want No. 16?"

"Have my bag sent up there, Julio, and if I leave your hotel hurriedly send it down to the Blue Star agents, 10 Travesso do Corpo Santo, and ask them to put it on board the 'Avila Star' immediately she arrives in Lisbon. I'm going to return to England by that boat if possible, and I'll leave enough money with you now to settle my debt to the hotel in case I depart without further notice."

"That will be all right, sir. Have you dined?"

"No. I had something to eat before I came ashore and will turn in early. See that I'm wakened at seven o'clock."

"All right, sir."

"Is Mr. Dias going to dine, Julio?"

"Yes, sir. A gentleman has been waiting for his arrival, and a table has been reserved for them."

"Thanks, Julio," said Vereker and straightway went up to his room. He could hear movements in No 17, and presumed that Dias was dressing for dinner. A porter had brought up his trunk, deposited it and vanished. Vereker walked listlessly round his room, pondering over Julio's statement that Dias's arrival had been expected. Evidently Dias had had no intention of completing the pleasure cruise on the "Mars" before he started or had altered his plans during the voyage and communicated with his friend by wireless. Vereker had a shrewd suspicion as to the cause of this sudden disembarkation and visit to Estoril. There was nothing to do but to shadow Dias and get some confirmation. He quickly unpacked his bag, placed his belongings in a chest of drawers and hung his clothes in a wardrobe. Then he walked over to the wide-open window, quietly pushed one of the jalousies ajar and stepped silently on to the wooden balcony outside. Cautiously approaching Dias's window, he crouched down and peered through a crack at the bottom of the closed jalousies. Dias was dressed for dinner and was lounging in an easy chair smoking a cigar. Suddenly a knock sounded on his door and, jumping to his feet, he crossed the room, admitted a man and carefully locked the door. The two men greeted one another briefly in Portuguese and then advanced together till they stood directly under the electric chandelier in the centre of the room. Dias fumbled in his pocket and immediately produced something which he handed to his friend. Vereker was unable to see what this object was owing to the fact that Dias presented a back view to the window; but a few moments later the stranger altered his position and examined the object lying in his left hand under a more direct light. In his right hand he held a jeweller's magnifying glass. He laughed and nodded with evident appreciation and then extended his left hand. As he did so a ripple of dazzling light formed a loop in the air and swung scintillating from his finger. It was a magnificent cinnamon and white diamond necklace.

"Maureen's necklace at last, whoever Maureen may be!" thought Vereker, and as he crouched peering fixedly through the tiny interstice at the bottom of the wooden venetian blind, waiting for developments, a gust of wind rattled the blind noisily. Instantly both men turned towards the window and the necklace swiftly disappeared into the stranger's pocket. Guessing the cause of the noise, they both smiled sheepishly at one another, their alarm vanished and they resumed their conversation. Dias, however, was apparently one of those men who through experience or temperament leave as little to chance as possible. As they conversed he turned once more uneasily towards the blind and, determined to satisfy himself that they were not being spied on, quickly approached the window. In a flash Vereker retreated along the balcony and disappeared through his own window into his room, quietly closing the green jalousie behind him. He heard Dias fling open his jalousies, which swung outwards on hinges like a casement window, close them firmly and adjust the hooked catch.

Satisfied with his important discovery, Vereker lit a cigarette and listened to see if he could pick up any of the conversation proceeding in the next room. Owing, however, to the thickness of the walls and the lowered voices of the speakers, he could only hear a subdued murmur without gathering its purport. Seating himself in an easy chair, he decided to finish his cigarette, read a book and then turn in. He had hardly settled himself in his chair when the door was brusquely opened and Dias stepped briskly into the room. He glanced at Vereker without the faintest show of recognition.

"I'm very sorry, sir," he exclaimed immediately in Portuguese. "I have made a mistake. I thought in my hurry that this was my apartment."

"Il n'y a pas de quoi, monsieur!" replied Vereker, calmly resuming his reading, and Dias, with a "Sinto muito, senhor," withdrew and closed the door behind him.

"So now you know!" soliloquised Vereker, smiling to himself, "and I think my French was about as stupid a bit of camouflage as your Portuguese, Mr. Dias!"

He immediately rose and, thrusting on his hat, was about to leave his room. The sound of voices still in conversation in the adjoining apartment made him decide to wait until Dias and his companion went down to dinner. He switched off his light and stood quietly at the door with ears alert for any indication of their movements. The two men had now ceased talking and utter silence reigned. Several minutes passed, and Vereker was beginning to wonder if the confederates had made a noiseless exit when his quick hearing detected the sound of a stealthy footfall on the balcony outside. He was now glad that he had closed his jalousies and switched off the light, for by so doing he had rendered it impossible for anyone to detect his presence in the darkened room from the balcony without. Very cautiously making his way to the window, he thrust open the wooden blinds with a swift movement and sprang lightly out. A full moon was high in the heaven, flooding the façade of the hotel with a pale light, which was intensified by the light coloured paint of the walls. In its radiance the whole length of the ornate wooden balcony could be clearly seen, but it was deserted and the blinds of Dias's room were closed. That room, moreover, was in darkness. The discovery gave Vereker a lively shock. Surely his ears had not deceived him? He paced the length of the balcony and peered into the garden below. The high enclosing walls of the hotel grounds, however, had converted that restricted and shrub-covered area into a well of gloom and it was impossible to detect the presence of a human being in the heavy, confusing shadows lurking there. Without further delay he returned to his room and descended quickly to the entrance vestibule. There he met Julio Roca standing with his hands behind his back as if expecting new arrivals.

"Ah, Julio, just the man I wanted to see. Did Mr. Dias and his friend go into the dining saloon?"

"No, sir, they have just gone out. They seemed in a hurry."

"They didn't say where they were going?"

"No, sir."

"Thanks, Julio," replied Vereker and ran down the flight of steps into the front parterre of the hotel with its lawn and trimly tended flower beds. Passing rapidly out on to the white road he glanced round. A group of villagers stood gossiping together, silhouetted against the moonlit gable of an adjacent house; a mongrel lazily crossed the road and vanished down a dark, shadowy alley; a car whirled past on the main thoroughfare, sounding its horn with unnecessary vehemence, but he could see no sign of Dias and his companion. He hurried down the road leading to the station, passing a plantation of graceful eucalyptus trees on his right. The night air was laden with the spiced fragrance of these trees, with the odour of stocks and carnations and the haunting perfume of the long silver trumpets of the datura blossoms. The scene was magical. Here the villas standing in their own grounds with enclosing stone walls, down which fell cascades of pink roses and pelargoniums, flung mysterious little towers and minarets and cupolas against the dark blue of the sky, their walls adorned with faience plaques and friezes clearly visible in the light of the moon. Palms lazily waved their long, dark fronds caught in a warm breeze from the sea, which lay sparkling mistily below. An electric train rolled out of Estoril station and rattled away along the sweep of the coast, a gliding cordon of yellow fire. Vereker knew his way about and, having nothing particular to do, entered a little shop which sold sweets, tobacco and refreshments. He ordered a whisky and soda, chatted for a while with the proprietor and then, lighting a cigarette, sauntered up one of the main thoroughfares leading inland from the coast road. He had decided to walk for an hour or two before returning to his hotel. He soon passed out of the closely inhabited area into a region of isolated villas with extensive grounds. He was stepping briskly along, preoccupied with the bewildering features of the case on which he was engaged, when he stopped to admire the singular lines of a villa's architecture which stood out boldly above its palm clusters against the sky. As he did so he happened to glance backwards and notice a man, who had apparently been walking some twenty yards behind him, suddenly step off the pavement into the recess of a gateway and remain motionless under the cover of a tree shadow. The action, stealthy and swift, arrested his attention, and he came to the immediate conclusion that he was being followed. At once he experienced a thrill of excitement and a curious smile crossed his lean, alert face. Was the follower Dias or one of his emissaries? From the gait and build of the man which he had temporarily glimpsed he felt certain that it was Dias himself. If he were being shadowed he would lead the shadower a puckish dance. The change from hunting to being hunted was a new and stimulating experience. Proceeding a few hundred yards further, Vereker came to the open rolling country lying to the north and west of Estoril and, leaving the road, descended into a shrub-covered and rock-strewn dell. Glancing upwards he noticed the lonely pursuer coming swiftly along the road. There was no mistaking his figure; it was that of Dias himself. At that moment the latter halted, left the road and began to descend the slope into the dell, moving rapidly from clump to clump of thickly growing shrubs as if advancing to an attack and taking advantage of every piece of cover. The procedure at once informed Vereker of his folly in taking to this stretch of lonely downland. He was unarmed, and it flashed upon him that Dias was probably armed. Vereker had, however, roamed these hills and valleys often before and knew every inch of them. Even in the moonlight he could distinguish the clumped masses of Spanish iris growing only a few inches out of the hard, rocky soil and covered with blue blossoms. Here he had gathered bee-orchids, periwinkle, borage, asphodel, sorrel and numberless other wild flowers in his tramps with easel and canvas, but it was no occasion for reminiscence. Dias was swiftly approaching. Rising from his crouching position, Vereker dashed

on to a boulder-strewn mule path and hurried up the next incline.
Looking back he became aware that Dias was only fifty yards
behind him and advancing rapidly. He broke into a steady trot
and swung round a projecting hillock into a still wilder stretch of
country. Here the slopes above the mule path were strewn with
massive boulders and covered with a dense growth of shrubs,
chief among which was a dwarf sharp-spined dog-rose. Not a
dwelling or a human being was in sight. A small herd of goats
grazing on the fine grass bordering the path disappeared into a
tangle of briar, startled by his sudden approach. He stood for a few
seconds wondering whether he should take cover or keep straight
on. At that moment he felt a stinging pain in his left forearm and
simultaneously heard the sharp crack of an automatic pistol.
Simulating an agonised cry, he pretended to stagger into the dense
growth at the side of the mule path and plunged forward with the
skill of an acrobat. At once he began to scramble under cover up
the slope, and when he had progressed some fifty yards he peered
back to see if Dias was going to follow. In the clear light he saw his
pursuer stand for a few moments, hesitate and then, turning, run
back along the mule path till he disappeared round the projecting
shoulder of the hillock. Either he thought he had settled accounts
with his quarry or had suddenly realised the danger of standing
in the open as a mark for his opponent, who had taken cover and
might be stealthily approaching him. Vereker at once continued
his ascent of the hill, and on reaching its summit caught a glimpse
of Dias away down in the valley below the main road. He was
returning to that road at a steady jog-trot. It was clear that for the
moment all danger had passed, and Vereker immediately made his
way back to the mule path from which he had ascended. There he
pulled off his jacket and found, to his relief, that Dias's bullet had
merely grazed the flesh of his left forearm. Binding it up with his
handkerchief he slipped on his jacket again and pressed forward.
A mile further ahead he saw above him the stone dyke bordering
the secondary road which led down again towards Cascaes and

the sea. Increasing his pace, he reached the dyke and followed it along till he came to an opening where a jet of water fell from the dyke into a stone trough beneath, for along the top of the dyke ran a covered-in water conduit. Thirsty from his exertion and excitement, he cupped his hands and drank. Resting until he felt thoroughly refreshed, he tramped at an easy pace down into Cascaes. Here he caught an electric train into Estoril and hurried up to his hotel. Julio was still presiding in the vestibule and, on seeing Vereker enter, rose from his chair and approached him. He was obviously excited.

"I know what you're going to tell me, Julio," said Vereker quietly.

"But how can you, sir?" asked Julio, bewildered.

"It would take too long to explain, but you were going to say that Mr. Dias had suddenly left the hotel with his baggage."

"That is so. He told you?"

"No. I guessed it, Julio. Do you know where he has gone?"

"He hired a car and told the driver to drive like hell—depressa—depressa—to Lisbon."

"Thanks, Julio. I'm hungry. Give me something to eat in the dining-room, and I'll have a bottle of Bucellas with it. Then I'm going to turn in."

Chapter Ten

I

Vereker rose early next morning, breakfasted on the usual rolls, butter, honey and coffee supplied by the Hotel da Pena and took the electric train from Estoril into Cais do Sodre, Lisbon. From the station he walked into the town and called on his friend Mascarenhas, of the Portuguese police. Mascarenhas greeted him with the dignified geniality of his race and soon they were busy talking "shop". Vereker related to him in detail the story of Mrs. Mesado's death, and of how he had managed that her body should not be buried at sea. Something in this narration amused Mascarenhas to such an extent that several minutes elapsed before he could control his laughter and listen to the rest of Vereker's story. Alert to the significance of every incident, the Portuguese at once formulated his own theory and explained his deductions step by step with vivacious gesticulation. It was not in accord with Vereker's own solution of the mystery, but such an ingenious conjecture that he clapped his friend heartily on the back, a gesture which the Portuguese accepted as appreciatively English but destructive of his own lofty dignity as a police official.

"You ought to have collected some fingerprints as further corroboration," he said at length.

"It wasn't purely friendship that brought me to see you, Mascarenhas," remarked Vereker, smiling. "I have here some photographs bearing the prints of Renée Gautier's fingers, a comb which was used by Mrs. Mesado and two other photographs bearing the imprints of the dead woman's fingers."

"I see you work as thoroughly as ever, Vereker. You want me to develop them and give you photo-micrographs of the impressions?"

"Exactly."

"You shall have them this evening if you will call again," said Mascarenhas, "and after that we will dine together and continue our talk."

Thanking him for his courtesy, Vereker took his leave and called at the Blue Star offices in the Travesso do Corpo Santo, where he learned that the "Avila Star" was leaving for London on the following day. This was gratifying news, because he felt that any further stay in Lisbon would be unproductive from his own point of view. To kill time he visited the sub-tropical garden for which Lisbon is famous, searched for and found the monument to Chiado, the drunken bohemian monk, lunched at the Hotel de l'Europe and drank coffee and a Portuguese liqueur at a coffee house memorialising Bocaze, a native poet. In the evening he called on Mascarenhas, whom he found in a state of considerable excitement about the photo-micrographs obtained from the articles he had left with him in the morning. Handing one of them to Vereker, he exclaimed:

"Now this is an extraordinary find, Vereker. You see this finger-print? It was obtained from one of the photographs of the Palacio del Congreso in Buenos Aires."

"Yes, I managed to get that photograph through a friend from Miss Renée Gautier, Mrs. Mesado's maid."

"Yes, yes, we have Miss Gautier's finger-prints on another photo, but this one belongs to a man known to us. We have applied the test of counting the sweat pores on a given area—you know the System?"

"Yes; discovered by Doctor Locard of the police lab at Lyons."

"Good. Well, that print belongs to a man called Cardozo. He is a most expert jewel thief, or rather he has been the principal in some daring jewel robberies. His system consists of making love to ladies' maids who are the servants of wealthy mistresses. He is a very handsome man and generally manages to engage the affections of his dupes. Then he gradually unfolds his plan of marrying the dupe if she will relieve her mistress of some valuable article of jewellery, on the sale of which they can live happily ever afterwards. It is an idyllic story, and he is a most persuasive conversationalist. He is, moreover, a reckless man at times and does not hesitate to kill. We suspect him of being the culprit in a murder on the Riviera last year. A wealthy American woman was shot in her villa at Nice, but the mystery was never solved. It was thought that the woman's maid knew something about the business, but she would divulge nothing, for she was doubtless in love with Cardozo if our suspicions had any foundation in truth."

"He never marries the dupe?" asked Vereker, deeply interested.

"It would be unreasonable to expect him to do so," said Mascarenhas, with such gravity that Vereker was obliged to smile.

"I think I know your man," said Vereker.

"Where is he?" asked the police officer eagerly.

"In Lisbon if I'm not mistaken. Of course he has changed his name?"

"Several times. The last time we heard of him he was in Buenos Aires, but he slipped the authorities there and we haven't heard of him since."

"I saw him and spoke to him last night in the Hotel da Pena, in Estoril."

"Is he there now?" asked Mascarenhas, rising and seizing a telephone on his table.

"No, he left hurriedly last night," replied Vereker, and gave the officer a detailed account of his adventure of the previous evening with Miguel Dias.

"He seems fond of the name of Miguel Dias, because that's the name he assumed when he brought off a coup in Madrid two years ago."

"Well, he has managed to bring off another coup under the same name on board the Green Star liner 'Mars'. The procedure was the same. He made love to Renée Gautier, Mrs. Mesado's maid, and managed to secure possession of the very valuable necklace of cinnamon and white diamonds which I saw last night, and which I've told you about. He has promised to meet her at Barcelona and take her to Paris, where they are to be married."

"The old story once more. He will not be there, but if he is in Lisbon we shall have a good search for him. I feel sure I know his confederate. He's a notoriously clever fence. There's just a chance we can get back the necklace without making any arrests."

Mascarenhas disappeared from his room to give instructions to his subordinates to keep a sharp look out for Cardozo, and then returned.

"Now we can dine without troubling ourselves further about our friend," he said, and together the two men left the building and repaired to a restaurant which Mascarenhas always patronised. They continued their criminological reminiscences throughout their meal, and when the time came to part Mascarenhas suddenly remembered the subject of the photomicrograph that he had developed and printed for Vereker.

"I nearly forgot to tell you, Vereker. The fingerprints found on Mrs. Mesado's comb are not the same as those on the photographs you pressed against the dead woman's fingers. Somebody else must have used that comb."

"Not her maid, I hope?"

"No. Renée Gautier's prints are quite different. It must have been some other lady. You say her sister, Mrs. Colvin, was travelling with her?"

"Yes."

"Ah, she may have been the last person to use the comb."

"I don't think that's likely," said Vereker with suppressed excitement, "though of course it's possible."

"Or the stewardess, if her hair became disarranged while she was tidying up the lady's cabin."

"That too is feasible. In any case it's very interesting," continued Vereker, and after taking leave of his friend his thoughts reverted to the subject. "It's more than interesting," he soliloquised, "it's simply apocalyptic!"

Taking the train at Cais do Sodre, he travelled back to Estoril in a highly self-satisfied humour.

II

Next morning, just after Vereker had breakfasted and was smoking a cigarette in the lounge, Julio came and informed him that he was wanted on the telephone.

"Who is it, Julio?" asked Vereker.

"He would not give his name, senhor," replied the manager.

Wondering who his caller might be, Vereker disappeared into the telephone box in the entrance vestibule and picked up the instrument.

"Ah, you, Mascarenhas! Any news?"

"Come along to the Plaz do Pillhourino at once. I have something important to tell you."

Vereker at once ordered a car and had his bag brought down from his bedroom. Having settled his account and said good-bye to Julio Roca, he told the chauffeur to proceed straight to Lisbon. After depositing his luggage on the "Avila Star", which lay at Alcantara-Mar and was due to sail in the afternoon, he was driven to the Plaz do Pillhourino. He waited there for some minutes and then espied Mascarenhas near the strange monolith in the middle of the spacious square. At the same moment Mascarenhas saw him. They met and at once turned into a wine shop and seated themselves at a small table where they could talk without being overheard by the other occupants.

"We have managed it," said Mascarenhas after sipping his wine and lighting a cigarette.

"You have got Dias?"

"Oh, no, not Dias. He has completely vanished. We have hunted Lisbon for him and found no trace of the devil, but we have laid hands on Ribeiro, his confederate."

"That was quick work. Any news of the necklace?"

"It will be returned to the Colvins if no further questions are asked. Do you think they'll agree to that?"

"I'm certain of it."

"Otherwise we may never see it again. If Ribeiro suffers they will certainly lose the necklace. We must compromise sometimes if we wish to achieve satisfactory results. It's illogical to exact the penalty of the law if that course entails the defeat of one's aims, and it's our aim to restore the stolen property."

"I can tell them that the necklace will be returned?"

"Certainly. Where are the Colvins staying in Lisbon?"

"At Carcano's Hotel."

"It will be there at midday. I can guarantee that!"

"Excellent, Mascarenhas. I am going to see the Colvins before I sail this afternoon. I presume the person returning it won't object to a small reward?"

"It is usual in such cases."

"Very good. I'll see that £100 is sent on to you, and you can arrange for its disposal to the person or persons concerned."

Having finished their wine and arranged to meet in London later in the year, the two men parted, and Vereker at once took a taxi to Carcano's Hotel. He found Colvin seated in the lounge smoking and trying to gather the news from a Portuguese newspaper. Mrs. Colvin had gone out to do some shopping and would not return till lunch. On Vereker's entry he rose and, in spite of his effort to appear delighted, an uneasy look stole into his eyes and his brow contracted unpleasantly.

"This is unexpected, Vereker," he said as he extended his hand. "I thought you had gone on with the 'Mars'."

"I changed my mind at the last moment, Colvin," replied Vereker, "and decided to spend a day or two in Lisbon."

"Important business?"

"Well, it concerned your lost necklace of cinnamon and white diamonds."

The statement made Colvin start visibly.

"Good Lord!" he exclaimed, "we had given that up as lost for good."

"I hadn't. It will be returned to you at midday today. I pledged myself that no questions would be asked and no legal action taken in the matter."

"As long as we get the necklace back we shall certainly not bother to take any proceedings," agreed Colvin with a surprising lack of interest.

"That's satisfactory. I felt that a small reward would not be out of place, and arranged that £100 should be sent to a police friend of mine to be handed over to the person responsible for the restitution. I hope that I wasn't extravagant considering the value of the jewellery."

"I'll write you out a cheque at once," said Colvin and, producing a cheque book, wrote a cheque for the amount and handed it to Vereker. After heartily thanking Vereker for the trouble he had taken on his behalf he asked casually: "And when are you returning to England?"

"This afternoon, by the 'Avila Star'; and you?"

"Constance and I are going on to Madrid in a few days' time, and after a week, or perhaps two, we shall get back as quickly as possible."

"To Firle House, Jevington?"

"Yes, for a while. I'm afraid we shan't be able to keep Firle House up. Beryl had already put it on the market before leaving England. It's a big place and will probably remain unsold for some time."

"I know the place well and should like to have a look over it before you part with it. On my return I'm going to make Jevington my headquarters for a painting holiday. The downs in the vicinity are a favourite subject of mine."

"Please put up at Firle House, Vereker. I'll write and give Dobbs and his wife, Beryl's butler and housekeeper, who have been left in charge of the place, instructions to do everything to make you comfortable. We'll join you there later if you are still in residence."

Vereker accepted the invitation readily, for it was part of his plan to secure an entrée to Firle House as soon as possible, either through the proper channels or by subterfuge. Having achieved his object with unexpected ease, and seeing that Colvin was in an expansive mood, due possibly to his recent escape from money troubles, he suddenly decided on a bold move. All along in his investigations he had been anxious to discover the identity of the mysterious Maureen whose name had been used in connection with the necklace of cinnamon and white diamonds. Every attempt he had made towards that end had either been deliberately foiled or had ended in failure. He pulled out his watch and glanced at it. He felt that the identity of Maureen was one of the key-pieces to the solution of the Mesado mystery.

"I shall leave in a few minutes, Colvin," he remarked, "and in less than half an hour you ought to be in possession of Maureen's necklace."

With these words he looked straight into Colvin's face. The latter promptly lowered his eyes, and a greyish pallor swiftly tinged his cheeks. He was about to speak, hesitated and then coughed uneasily.

"Your methods achieve remarkable results, Vereker," he stammered at length and passed a trembling hand across his brow. An unpleasant pause ensued, and Vereker came to the conclusion that the truth about Maureen was once more about to slip from him by a studied evasion on Colvin's part. That element of combativeness in him which never admitted defeat in a difficult task steeled him to a direct inquiry. He was rather dubious about the wisdom of such a line of action, but at the moment he could think of no other plan. Afterwards too he was obliged to admit that he had allowed himself to be nettled into an indiscreet boldness.

"By the way, who is Maureen, Colvin?" he asked bluntly, and to cover the seeming impertinence of his inquiry added: "Miss Gautier referred to the cinnamon and white diamond necklace as Maureen's when I happened to speak to her about it."

"Oh, you questioned Gautier?" asked Colvin, with a look of surprise and some annoyance.

"Not directly. I happened to enter into conversation with her on board the 'Mars' and the subject cropped up. I can't for the life of me recollect what led up to it, but you needn't worry on that score; I was discretion itself. I was fairly confident she had something to do with the loss of that necklace and I had to 'gang warily'."

"Had she a hand in the pie?" asked Colvin eagerly.

"We'll call it a finger, but she was not altogether to blame. She was acting under the influence of Miguel Dias."

"Good heavens! Constance always said he was a crook."

"Your wife has a shrewd insight into character. He is a crook. But to return to our subject, if I'm not being impertinent, who is Maureen?"

By this time Colvin had recovered from his discomposure, and the digression had given him time to think.

"Oh, Maureen!" he exclaimed, smiling. "Funny you should mention that. Maureen O'Connor was the name Beryl assumed when she was on the stage before she was married to Guillermo Mesado. We sometimes called her Maureen to the last."

During this explanation Colvin busied himself lighting a cigarette, and his eyes carefully avoided Vereker's cold scrutiny. There was something in the tone of his voice and a studied precision in his action which convinced Vereker that he was not telling the truth. Feeling that it was useless to pursue the subject further, perhaps even imprudent, for his inquisitiveness might rouse the man's suspicion, Vereker turned the conversation deftly by asking in a casual tone:

"Miss Gautier will return to Firle House at the end of the cruise, I suppose, Colvin?"

"Oh, yes, for a time, anyway. Constance doesn't like her, but we haven't had time to settle anything definitely about the girl's future."

"Her present intention is to meet Dias at Barcelona and travel with him to Paris, where they are going to be married," said Vereker.

"Oh, is that so? First we've heard of it. Still, that would suit us admirably," remarked Colvin readily, but the statement gave him pause. After a moment's reflection he added, almost in soliloquy, "Yes, that would suit us admirably. We shall have no further need of her services."

"I wouldn't count on it if I were you," continued Vereker. "I'm pretty sure Dias hasn't the slightest intention of marrying Gautier, and I doubt whether he'll turn up at Barcelona. In the circumstances she may think it prudent to return to Jevington and keep her little love tragedy a secret."

"I'm glad you've put us on our guard," said Colvin. "We shall be prepared to discuss business from a proper angle when she arrives."

After a few minutes' further conversation, which turned on general topics, Vereker took his leave of Colvin and promised him that if very urgent matters did not prevent him he would accept his invitation to Firle House and be there when he and his wife returned from their holiday in Spain.

Having lunched at the Hotel de L' Europe, Vereker took a taxi down to Alcantara-Mar and went on board the "Avila Star." He had journeyed on a previous occasion to Buenos Aires on this comfortable vessel, and felt very much at home on it. By a piece of good fortune he managed to secure his old cabin on D deck and, having settled in, produced his case book and set down all the salient features of the Pleasure Cruise Mystery that he had collected up to date. In doing so he was following one of his invariable customs. A detailed account written in code seemed to clarify his point of view and helped to put events in proper perspective. Incidents which appeared too significant during the stress and excitement following their occurrence fell into their proper place, and seemingly unimportant data adjusted themselves until they acquired their true values and disclosed themselves as vital to a successful issue of his undertaking.

Chapter Eleven

On his return to his flat in Fenton Street, Vereker rang up Inspector Heather.

"Has Tankerton done that little job for me, Heather?" he asked.

"Yes, I have his report with me, Mr. Vereker. Are you in a hurry for it?"

"I'd like it as soon as possible. Bring it round like a good fellow."

"Tomorrow I'll be with you. I'm busy at the moment about a young London lady who's missing, and we don't know where to find her. Possibly a lot of trouble for nothing. Still it's all in a day's work. You know I don't drink wine or whisky."

"What's that got to do with missing ladies or Tankerton's report?"

"I'm coming round to you with Tankerton's report tomorrow evening. D'you take me? A nine-gallon cask of Burton won't be out of place. Reports are dry things and missing ladies give me the hump, so I'm not being unreasonable. Did you enjoy the trip?"

"Found it dull at first, and then I ran head on into a mystery. One of the most puzzling I've struck so far. At the moment I can't get the hang of things."

"Never mind, I'll help you out," laughed the inspector; "in the right way. What's it all about?"

"A murder, Heather."

"Dear, dear, I wonder you don't stick to your painting. Painting's a smelly kind of job, but it doesn't harm anyone. Has the murder anything to do with the Diss family, whose history seems to interest you?"

"You'll hear all the details tomorrow. As for the cask of Burton I'm not so sure. It's an occasion for some deep thinking, Heather."

"Then I'm your man for the occasion, Mr. Vereker. You said deep drinking, didn't you?"

"No. Deep thinking."

"Still I always hold that four pints clear the head remarkable. After that one gets a bit too brilliant for ordinary detective work and feels like a commissioner or a chief constable. Tomorrow evening for certain at eight o'clock."

"Make it seven and we'll have a meal together."

"Better and better. Good-bye."

Next evening the inspector called sharp at seven o'clock, and the two men repaired to their old haunt, Jacques' Restaurant, in Soho. During dinner Vereker related the story of his strange adventure on board the "Mars", giving every detail of his discoveries in connection with the mystery of Mrs. Mesado's death and allowing Heather to draw his own conclusions. The two men, when working on former occasions as friendly rivals or in close cooperation, had found this method of discussing a case very useful, for Heather looked at a problem with the matter-of-fact and experienced eye of the hardened police officer, while Vereker approached it from the imaginative and more elastic standpoint of an enthusiastic amateur. After dinner they returned to Vereker's flat and made themselves comfortable before a cheery fire over their pipes and coffee. Albert, who had been Vereker's batman during the war and was now his trusted factotum, was responsible for the coffee. Having brought in the steaming pot with the necessary equipage, he invariably waited for his master's opinion of the brew.

"Albert, you've surpassed yourself," said Vereker, "and I'm sure Inspector Heather will agree with me."

"Best cup of coffee I've ever tasted," agreed Heather generously. "Learned the trick when you were in France, Albert?"

"That's so, sir," replied Albert gloomily, for he was never known to smile, "from Mademoiselle from Armentieres."

Satisfied with the verdict, Albert "dismissed" and left the room as if he were the principal mourner at a funeral.

"Now you've got the chief facts of the case, Heather, clearly and succinctly," said Vereker. "You can see that I was hampered by the environment. I couldn't wander at will into other people's cabins. The captain and the doctor were naturally in a difficult position and somewhat aloof. They adopted an ultra diplomatic attitude which tied my hands, or rather my tongue. I didn't envy them their position; it was a singularly difficult one. Ricardo was invaluable in digging out vital information and I couldn't have done without him. What do you make of it?"

The inspector, who had listened to the story with rapt attention, sat puffing at his pipe in silence for some minutes.

"Rum business. At first glance looks like a brilliant idea very badly bungled," he commented, raising his shaggy eyebrows and giving his pointed moustache a ruminative twist between his right forefinger and thumb. Then he looked shrewdly at Vereker.

"The lady was actually dead when you joined Ricardo after his discovery of the body on D deck?" he asked.

"That's a vital question, Heather. Neither Ricardo nor I could detect any sign of life, but as you know it's a difficult and delicate job to make certain of such a fact when you've neither the time nor the opportunity to do so.

"It's easy to make a mistake," agreed Heather. "You're of the opinion that she was dead?"

"Yes. And the doctor said rigor mortis set in some time after we had carried the lady down to her cabin."

The inspector grunted and his brow furrowed in thought. "I wonder if his statement was correct," he remarked.

"I think we can take that for granted. Macpherson was not unfriendly, and I should say he had the Scots characteristics of thoroughness and accuracy. I have an inkling of what's in your mind, Heather, and it seems to be working on similar lines to my own. I asked him if the flaccid state of the body when we found it was secondary, and he simply scouted my suggestion."

"Knocks my theory a bit askew, Mr. Vereker, but I'll give the problem a good examination before I make any definite statement as to my conclusions. Rigor mortis is a tricky sort of thing when you come to reckon on it in conjunction with a question of time."

"I agree," commented Vereker, and a smile of amusement spread over his features. "I've been boggling over that point ever since the game began and I haven't settled it yet."

"We'll leave it for the moment," continued Heather, "and look at Tankerton's report. Before doing so, what d'you make of the necklace being thrown in at your window?"

"I'm certain Mrs. Mesado hurled that necklace into my cabin. In her state of mind, which we can assume was not too clear, she mistook the window of my cabin for her own, which was next to it."

"Good. I had come to the same conclusion," said Heather and drew from his pocket Tankerton's report of his discoveries with regard to the history of the Diss family of Fakenham, in Norfolk. He tapped the paper with his forefinger before handing it to Vereker. "I'll give you the gist of this now and you can digest it properly later. You will learn from it that the Diss family is an old and honourable one and has been held in high esteem in Norfolk for some two hundred years. They were farmers, and proud of it. Later on they moved upward in the social scale, if that's possible, and were considered country gentry. This arose out of a family knack of managing money and hanging on to it with their toe-nails. They bought up property, made good investments and became landlords instead of tenants. Their lads went into the army, navy, law and the Church. From the fighting Disses came Colonel Diss, the father of Beryl, Constance and Amy Diss, with whom you are particularly concerned. Comely girls according to all accounts and all well hunted by the males for miles around. But a family, Mr. Vereker, always reminds me of a wave at sea; it's born, hangs together, pushes forward in a solid mass, gathers speed and then there comes a point when it loses cohesion and breaks into spume. With the Diss girls the family began to get light and sprightly. Beryl, the sparkiest of the lot, ran away from home and went on the stage. This was a shock to the outlook of the family. Not long ago, even in my young days, the stage was a sort of ante-room to hell in most proper people's opinions. Even when she got on and made a bit of a name as a dancer, she wasn't accepted by the family, especially the section that fished for bread from a pulpit. The family atmosphere improved when she went to Buenos Aires on a world tour and was married to Mesado, the meat millionaire. Even a social outlook can't stand up for six rounds and beat a moneybag; it's not human. The family had begun to forgive Beryl her sins when Constance secretly married Colvin, a bailiff on a neighbouring estate, who drank hard and needed reforming. Constance was born to save sinners and has had her work cut out keeping Colvin from the wrath of the Lord. This was another blow to the ageing parents, whose fortunes were beginning to wilt a bit under the colonel's notion of his own importance as a soldier and a gentleman. Then came the final disaster. Amy, the youngest, fell in love with one of their grooms and, to the horror of her parents, thought she'd perpetuate her lover's likeness by getting into what is politely called 'a certain condition.' She was promptly kicked out of the house, and disappeared with the groom. They went to London. The groom later joined a racing stable and, learning from horses how to run, ran away and left young Amy to look after herself. Being extravagant in her tastes and a very beautiful young woman, she quickly saw the commercial value of her charms and became the mistress of a young blood who had little use for the marriage tie in his relations with the fair sex. He was the first of a series of his kind who found the beautiful Amy a great comfort in hours of need. Tankerton followed up Amy as far as her fourth experiment in the companionate business and then lost all trace of her. She had changed her name several times of course and was living on the last occasion under the name of Maureen O'Connor."

"Great Scott! The very woman I've been looking for!" exclaimed Vereker, jumping from his easy chair and bringing his hand down on the table with a crash.

"I didn't think you were that soft, Mr. Vereker," said the inspector, with a sly twinkle in his eye.

"No, no, Heather! She's the woman in the case!" stammered Vereker in his eagerness.

"So I gathered from your yarn this evening. She was living about a year ago at Percy Street, near Victoria Station. She must have come down a bit in the world. You'll understand my meaning. Rum how a big railway station has a subtle connection with the oldest trade in the female world, but sellable stuff must find a market. Fish go to Billingsgate; meat to Smithfield, and so on. Terrible but true!"

"Well I'm damned!" interrupted Vereker. "I must get a move on and start the hunt from Percy Street. This is getting exciting, Heather."

"Wait a jiff, Mr. Vereker. My best bit of news I've kept to the last. Miss Maureen O'Connor has just been reported to the police as missing from a flat in Sussex Gardens. I found she had a very sumptuous place there. Her stock had evidently boomed of late and, apart from possessing a considerable bank balance, a nice car and a staff of servants, she left a considerable amount of jewellery in her flat. Her maid says that for some time she has been very excitable and queer in her actions. One day she said she was going into the country for a rest and, packing her bag, set out alone. From that moment she vanished and hasn't been heard of since. The maid reported the matter to the local police, and now the affair is in our hands. We've been trying to trace her whereabouts. So far we've been unsuccessful. Now, Mr. Vereker, I've given you a start and you've got to put a jerk into it. Get busy!"

"Heather, this is great. The annoying bits of my puzzle are beginning to tumble into position."

"I had an idea I'd gathered the vital pieces together and put them into your hands. What are you going to do next?"

"I'm going to start on a painting holiday tomorrow, Heather. Colvin has put Firle House, his place in Sussex, at my disposal. I intend to make myself comfortable there until he returns. Those Sussex Downs are the very devil to paint. Serene, imperturbably serene, they whisper to you of the slowly unfolding destiny of man, of his past, his fretful, uncertain, tentative struggle against the stubborn resistance of Nature—of themselves in fact. It's only a murmurous whisper, hardly audible when a soft sou'wester sweeps and sighs in summer over their suavely rounded backs. I've heard that voice; its calm, persuasive tones give me strength and courage in moments of despair. I begin to experience some of their philosophical indifference to the nervous agitation of modern life. What do money and love and fame and wars matter? You've only to see a Baby Austin climbing one of their slopes to gather their attitude to the cosmos. All that's left to us is beauty, and beauty is all... beauty is..."

"Did you get that nine gallon of Burton in as I instructed you, Mr. Vereker?" asked Heather after coughing noisily.

"Yes. Albert has been taking care of it. He says it's in nice condition now."

"Albert'll be in a nice condition if we leave him alone with it much longer. I'll sample it before I go."

Heather rose from his chair, pressed the electric bell at his side and a few minutes later Albert appeared with a tray on which were a foaming quart jug and two pewter tankards.

"By jingo, Albert, you're a thought reader!" exclaimed Heather on his entry.

"Middlin good guesser, sir, that's all. Nice drop of Button that, if I may take the liberty of sayin' so. Reminds me o' mother's milk with a flavour of 'oney. It's a good companion to any lonesome soul."

"You've sampled it, I'll bet," replied Heather, smiling.

"Just a heggcupful now and then to see 'ow it was getting on, sir. You can't muzzle the hox as treads the corn. It's as near perfection now as our young Prince of Wales. God bless 'im!"

With this solemn benediction Albert left the room, and Heather, filling his tankard, emptied it at a draught.

"I feel a better man already," he breathed noisily and, fumbling in his pocket, produced a photograph and handed it to Vereker. "That's Miss Maureen O'Connor, a recent portrait," he added.

Vereker took the print and scrutinised it eagerly for some seconds. He was bubbling over with excitement.

"She's a captivating creature," he remarked.

"Now, now, come off the captivation business, Mr. Vereker. You're not interested in her that way. The vital question is, is she like her sisters, Beryl and Constance?"

"They're all very much alike," replied Vereker, smiling.

"I thought so," continued Heather and, rising from his chair, prepared to leave. "Before you go down to Firle House and start listening to what the Sussex Downs whisper about beauty, I would run round to Sussex Gardens and listen to what Miss O'Connor's maid has to say. You're not a police officer, and though I'm a bit of a success with women I think you'd get more out of her than I did."

"Not a bad idea, Heather. Did she give you the frosty paw?"

"No, no," said Heather, glancing at himself in a mirror and twirling his moustaches, "but the words 'Scotland Yard' make a girl forget a chap's handsome and human. You'd better be Miss O'Connor's long lost brother or cousin or faithful lover. Perhaps a faithful lover who has been jilted would be best. Romance is a good worm when you're fishing for information. Most girls snap at it without thinking about barbed hooks and all that."

"Detection's a heartless game at times, Heather," remarked Vereker reflectively.

"Yes, I sometimes go home and sob myself to sleep thinking what a cruel, cruel man I am. Burglars and murderers don't know that side of my nature or they'd like me better. Perhaps they weep bitterly themselves when they think how badly they treat me. Life's a rum show without the Sussex Downs whispering about it and letting the cat out of the bag, Mr. Vereker."

"I'll run round to Sussex Gardens tomorrow, Heather, and if I find out anything important I'll ring you up. Then I'll go down to Firle House."

"Good. Keep in touch with me. I like to give a trier like yourself a helping hand. When I'm with you I always feel like a great painter encouraging a promising young pupil in a difficult career."

With these words, spoken with inimitable smugness, Heather took his leave, and Vereker, picking up the photograph of Maureen O'Connor from the table where he had temporarily laid it, looked at it very carefully and then slipped it into his pocket book.

"Came the dawn!" he soliloquised with a smile and prepared to turn in.

Chapter Twelve

I

You are Miss Maureen O'Connor's maid?" asked Vereker as he stood on the threshold of Maureen's flat in Sussex Gardens.

"Yes, sir, but Miss O'Connor's not at home," replied the girl, looking at her visitor with anxiety and suspicion in her glance.

"I'm quite aware of that. That's just why I called," replied Vereker.

"Are you from Scotland Yard, sir?" came the question.

"God forbid. I'm a friend, a great friend, of Miss O'Connor's. My name is Vereker. I was informed by Scotland Yard that she was missing. How they found out my address I don't know, unless some one here told them."

"Nobody here told them as far as I know."

"Strange how they discover things at Scotland Yard. May I come in? I should like to have a private talk with you, Miss..."

"Marchant," supplied the maid.

"Miss Marchant," concluded Vereker, and was promptly shown into a beautifully furnished sitting-room.

"Would you mind closing the door, Miss Marchant?" asked Vereker when he had taken a seat. "I want to talk very confidentially to you."

Miss Marchant, with some show of apprehension, closed the door and took a seat facing her caller.

"Are you a relative of Miss O'Connor's?" asked the maid when she had come to the conclusion that Vereker was not a police official.

"No, I am no relation at all. I heard she was missing, and as I'm—well, shall I say deeply interested in Maureen, I came to see if I could get any information at all about her."

Miss Marchant, evidently from the country and gifted with that ingenuous shrewdness which is a peculiar trait of those who have lived a rural life, at once jumped to conclusions on Vereker's use of her mistress's Christian name. She promptly assumed that it hinted at some affair of the heart and that this Mr. Vereker, clever as he might think himself, was unable to conceal it from her. He was without doubt one of Miss O'Connor's admirers, and from the solemnity of his face probably one whose affection was not adequately returned. She had seen that hungry look before. There were several others in the same sad plight. She knew their general symptoms and had sympathised with them on many occasions.

"I'm terribly sorry to hear of her disappearance like this. I can't make it out. Was she very unhappy?" asked Vereker, instilling a world of sadness into his voice.

"Of late she's been acting very queer, sir. I didn't know what to make of her."

"Poor Maureen! A man in the case as usual!" remarked Vereker, his whole bearing drooping with grief.

"Two," admitted Miss Marchant, shaking her head at the admission. "I told her no good would come of one of them. I never liked the look of him, and she seemed afraid of him, like a rabbit with a stoat. Whenever he came to the flat she was all at sixes and sevens, and he nearly always bullied her and left her in tears."

"I think I know the man by sight. Dark fellow," essayed Vereker.

"Yes, that's him. Dark, with flashing eyes. Very handsome, but he looked wicked—one of Satan's own. She called him Mig or Miggie. I don't know his surname, but it sounded something like 'dice'. He was a foreigner. The other was a real gentleman; always remembered to leave me something. His name was Mesado. Though I don't hold with foreigners and usually can't abide them, I must say I liked him. He was kind and thoughtful and was very good to Miss O'Connor until they quarrelled over something or other and he went away and left her."

"I know them both," said Vereker, "especially Mr. Dias. He's a scoundrel if I'm any judge of character. Was the quarrel with Mr. Mesado the cause of Maureen suddenly going away and not returning?"

"I couldn't say exactly. Miss O'Connor didn't tell me all about her private affairs, or bedroom secrets as she always called them, but I gathered that Mr. Mesado warned her to have nothing to do with Mr. Mig. She must have refused, and so Mr. Mesado never called again.

"Jealousy, I suppose?" remarked Vereker reflectively.

"Mebbe, but Mr. Mesado always treated her more like an uncle than er—you know. He used to bring her flowers and chocolates and all that sort of thing and always behaved most polite. She told me he was a relation, a distant relation."

"He's her brother-in-law," said Vereker.

"Well I never! She never let on about that. Very close in some things she is," exclaimed Miss Marchant with unconcealed surprise.

"Did Mr. Mesado help her financially?" asked Vereker.

"He was always making her presents and paying off her debts. I used to tell her it wouldn't last and that she ought to put most of it by, but she wouldn't listen to me. As for Mr. Mig, he used to sponge on her for everything—money, clothes, food—fairly bled her white. At last Mr. Mesado refused to help her any more until she got rid of Mr. Mig."

"Was Mr. Dias the cause of their final quarrel?" asked Vereker.

"Indirectly, I should say."

"Looks very much as if Mr. Mesado was in love with Miss Maureen," remarked Vereker.

"Love or no love, I advised her to stick to Mr. Mesado. He had the money and was real generous. It's all very well talking about love, but you can't quarrel with your bread and butter. What's the use of being in love with a sponger without a bean?"

"Did Mr. Mesado give her a regular allowance as well as presents?"

"Oh, yes, a thousand a year, bought her a lovely car and paid the rent of her flat here. He was a fairy godfather, so to speak. She was a fool not to get rid of Mr. Mig. He was no earthly good to her, but I know she was very fond of him. Used to sit on his knee and make a fuss of him and call him 'Mig darling'. Some women have no sense when they get sweet on a man. She fair went crackers on Mig!"

"Did Mr. Mig, as you call him, know Mr. Mesado before the latter called on Maureen?"

"Oh, yes, he brought him here. They had evidently become acquainted with one another when they were in the Argentine. They often spoke of a Miss Penteado and others as their mutual friends."

"I see," said Vereker, lost in thought. It was now clear to him that Dias had ferreted out the Diss family history and become acquainted with Miss Maureen O'Connor with a very definite purpose.

"When exactly did Miss Maureen leave here?" he asked.

"On Friday the 23rd of March. She said she was fed up with London and all lovers and was going into the country for a week-end, but I'm sure that Mr. Mig was at the back of her going. I heard him telling her that she must go or he would finish with her. I think he wanted her to make it up with Mr. Mesado because he found the money getting tight."

"Did she give you any idea where she was going?" asked Vereker, deeply interested.

"Not definitely. She simply said she was going into the country, somewhere in Sussex, for the week-end."

"Take much luggage with her?"

"Only just what she would need. A tweed costume which she was wearing, an evening dress, dress shoes and a few other things she would need. She left all her jewellery here in my charge except a very valuable diamond necklace."

"I remember that necklace. Cinnamon and white diamonds."

"Fancy you remembering it! It was a real beauty and the one piece of jewellery I envied her. The rest of her stuff was a bit too flash for me. No lady would wear it."

"Was the necklace a present from Mr. Mig?"

"Not on your life! He never gave her anything you couldn't buy in Woolworth's. It was a present from Mr. Mesado on her birthday, and Mr. Mig used to quarrel with her often because she wouldn't pawn it when he was short of dough."

"She used to take drugs at times to sooth her nerves, didn't she?" asked Vereker.

"Drugs? Oh, no, sir, nothing of that sort. She was hysterical at times, and once when a lover had had a row with her she went into a trance. I thought she was dead, but the doctor said no. He said it was a cataleptic state due to hysteria. It seems as if she had these fits at times, but she has only had one since I've been in her service. Though she never took drugs, on the other hand she was very fond of a bottle of Guinness with a drop of port in it. She always said it was strengthening and good for one."

"I suppose you don't know where Mr. Mesado is?" asked Vereker with suppressed excitement, for Miss Marchant was proving a mine of vital information.

"No. He said good-bye, and I'm sure he was crying when he left her, but he never said where he was going. Miss O'Connor told me his home was somewhere in South America, but I never can remember these outlandish names. Somewhere in the Argentine is all I know about it."

"Thanks, Miss Marchant. I think that's all I want to know. I have an idea where Miss Maureen has gone. In the meantime what are you going to do about her flat here?"

"Well, I can't stay on here without money to carry on with. She left me enough to run the place for a little while in case she stayed longer than the week-end. I didn't know what to do about it when she didn't return, so I informed the police that she was missing. A very nice man from Scotland Yard came down and said he would look into things and see if he could trace her."

"Was it Inspector Heather?" asked Vereker quietly.

"That's him. Big handsome man. Patted me on the back and told me not to cry, and spoke so kind to me that I could hardly believe that he was in the police force. Still, I don't like the police. Fair to your face they are, and foul behind your back. They're too inquisitive, and I didn't let him pump me about Miss O'Connor's private affairs. None of his business. As I told him straight, his job was to find her somehow and not ask so many questions about things that didn't concern him. They broadcasted about her being missing on the wireless, but nothing came of it."

"Did Mr. Mig call again after Miss O'Connor left?" asked Vereker.

"No, I haven't seen him, and if he turns up he'll get marching orders from me. I may get blamed for it afterwards, but I'm taking no risks where that gent is concerned. After he'd been in the house for five minutes something would go missing for certain sure."

"I'll back you up, Miss Marchant, so don't be afraid to show him the door. In the meantime I'll leave some money with you so that you can carry on. When you need some more just phone me up at my flat in Fenton Street. My name is Anthony Vereker."

"Thank you very much, sir. If it's a fair question, were you very fond of Miss O'Connor?" asked Miss Marchant boldly.

"No, well, I wasn't in love with her, if that's what you mean," stammered Vereker, rather abashed by the directness of the question. "More like a brother, if you can understand."

"I'm glad to hear that," replied Miss Marchant with unexpected emphasis.

"Why, Miss Marchant?" asked Vereker, nonplussed.

"Well, Mr. Vereker, it's this way. Some women seem to get more lovers than they want, and it's always the fast ones that men run after. They're not faithful to their men. Those women who could be good and true to a man never seem to get a chance. It don't seem fair somehow. It's not as if we were made any different. None of us has got more than two legs in any case. I said I was glad to hear that you weren't in love with her because she'd only break your heart if you were, and you seem to be a real nice gentleman."

"Too nice to have my heart broken?" asked Vereker with amusement.

"I'm certain of it, sir, and I'm a good judge of character too," replied Miss Marchant, blushing becomingly.

"It's nice of you to say so, Miss Marchant. I'm sure we shall be good friends. Now I would never break a man's heart," said Miss Marchant confidently.

"I'm convinced you wouldn't," agreed Vereker, and hastily added, "In the meantime if Mr. Dias turns up you'll know what to do with him. I don't think he will, because I feel sure he's abroad. If Mr. Heather from Scotland Yard calls, just tell him that he's a Nosey Parker and that Mr. Vereker told you he was hardly worth his beer money as a detective. You might add that, although he's big and handsome, Mr. Vereker thinks he ought to shave off his spikey moustache. Good-bye for the present, Miss Marchant."

"Good-bye, sir, and I'll tell Mr. Heather what you've said. If I hear anything more of Miss O'Connor shall I ring you up?"

That's the idea. I feel sure I'm on her track already, and I won't rest till I find her."

With these words Vereker took his leave, and was given such an arch glance by Miss Marchant that he began to feel that he really was too nice a gentleman to have his heart broken.

II

Next day Vereker packed his bag, his easel, canvas and paints and made his way down to Jevington, in Sussex. Taking a conveyance at Polegate Station, he drove up to Firle House, where he was expected. Dobbs, the butler, and his wife, the housekeeper, made him welcome, and on Vereker expressing a wish to have a look around Dobbs escorted him over the whole mansion. Much to his satisfaction he found the butler a garrulous man in spite of his pompous air and reserved mien. Dobbs soon disclosed that he had been a butler to the "quality" nearly all his life and that though the Mesados were wealthy there was an unbridgable gulf between trade and birth.

"A very nice man to work with, you know, sir, but still a furriner and a noover rish. Now Mrs. Mesado was the goods. Came from a good old Norfolk family. Sad business her dying at sea and being buried among a lot of Portuguese cutthroats, but what's going to happen's going to happen. This place is up for sale, and as I've no instructions to the contrary from Mrs. Colvin I suppose it's still on the market."

"It will be Mrs. Colvin's property now?" asked Vereker, anxious to know how much Dobbs knew of Mrs. Mesado's testamentary dispositions.

"Oh, yes, sir. Mrs. Mesado has often told me that if anything happened to her she was leaving everything she possessed to her sister."

"It was common knowledge?"

"I think so, sir. Mrs. Colvin often used to joke and say she had a good mind to poison off her sister so that she could be well off."

"The two sisters were fond of one another?"

"They were like Siamese twins, sir, they hung so well together, and yet Mrs. Colvin was as different from Mrs. Mesado as chalk from cheese. Nevertheless I don't remember ever hearing one snap at the other."

"What kind of a lady was Mrs. Mesado?" asked Vereker.

"Very changeable, sir. Sometimes as sweet as honey, and next moment a regular spitfire. You never knew when you had her. She led Mr. Mesado a dance at times—regular hornpipe he had to dance too. But I liked madam; she always treated me fair, and you can't wish for more than that.

"And Mrs. Colvin?"

"A perfect saint, sir. Never put out by anything, sir, and always doing a good turn to somebody. But she was very churchy and was dead nuts on atheists and their kidney. Always said they ought to be burned at the stake, though I couldn't see the young lady burning a cockroach. Now Mrs. Mesado, when she lost her temper she was dangerous. She'd pull her enemies to bits with red-hot pincers. I never seen a woman with such a fiery temper."

"Mr. Colvin used to live with the Mesados too?"

"Yes, sir. He was a sort of companion to Mr. Mesado, doing this, that and t'other thing for him. But he's a toff, sir, a regular toff. Liked a drop of drink, sometimes a drop too much, but he's as good as gold. I don't want a better master than Mr. Colvin, and I'm glad Mrs. Dobbs and me are going with them when they leave. They told us that definite in their letter to us from Portugal."

"Have you been in Mr. Mesado's service long, Dobbs?"

"Some three years now. Ever since they came to Firle House. I was with Sir Henry and Lady Waterton up in Fakenham, Norfolk, before that, and the Disses and Watertons were great friends always. I've known the Diss sisters ever since they was so high." Dobbs accompanied his words with an explanatory gesture as to stature.

"There were three of them, I believe? What happened to the youngest, Amy?"

"There was a bit of a scandal about young Miss Amy," said Dobbs, lowering his voice discreetly. "Got up to mischief with one of their grooms when she was in her teens, and the colonel kicked her out neck and crop. She went up to London, and some say she went all to pieces with men and drink. It's not for me to say, because I don't know. She was the prettiest of the three sisters, and they were all oil paintings fit to marry dooks and as like as triplets to look at."

"Have you ever seen Miss Amy since then, Dobbs?" asked Vereker casually.

For some moments Dobbs hesitated and then replied: "Only once, sir, for a few minutes. Just before madam went on this cruise Miss Amy came down here for a week-end. Mrs. Mesado sent me and Mrs. Dobbs up to town that Friday she arrived and told us we could have the week-end off to see our friends in London. Paid all our expenses for the trip. She was real good like that at times. All the house servants except Gautier had been discharged because madam said she was giving up Firle House and wouldn't live in it again. When we returned on Monday morning Miss Amy had gone. Madam said she left suddenly on Sunday night."

"Had there been a quarrel?"

"Gautier hinted at something of the sort, but she and I never got on well together. She was closer than an oyster when she liked. Fancied her luck with the men too."

"Did Mrs. Mesado and Mrs. Colvin call their sister by the name Amy?" asked Vereker.

"No, sir. When they spoke of her, and that was seldom in my hearing, they called her Maureen. Her real name was Mrs. O'Connor, because she married the groom she fell in love with. He was a handsome Irishman, but as tricky as a monkey. They say he went off with another woman some years later. If it's true he ought to have his skin peeled off him. Leading a young lady astray and then deserting her."

"Had they any children, Dobbs?"

"Only one, I believe. The cause of all the barney, and it was born dead. Merciful I call it."

"Mrs. Mesado and the Colvins left for Tilbury on Monday morning, the 26th, to join the cruising liner 'Mars'?"

"Yes, sir, just after we arrived. When they'd had breakfast they set off."

"Do you know which room Miss Maureen occupied, Dobbs?"

"Yes, sir, the nicest of the guest rooms, and the one we've got ready for you. There's a cupboard in it with some clothes and two pairs of shoes she left behind, but as we were told not to touch her things we have left them there. They won't be in your way, sir, as there's a gentleman's wardrobe in the same room, which has been cleared for your use."

"Thanks very much, Dobbs. Please don't disturb anything on my account. I may be here for a few days only, so I have brought very little with me."

"Very good, sir; and there's one drawer in the chest of drawers with some of Miss Maureen's odds and ends in it. Mrs. Mesado left that locked up and said it was not to be disturbed on any account."

"That won't trouble me, Dobbs. By the way, when did Mr. Mesado leave Firle House? Was it long before his wife went on this cruise?"

"About a fortnight before, sir."

"Do you know where he has gone?"

"We don't know for certain, but his valet, who went with him, told me on the quiet that he was going back to Buenos Aires. That's his home."

"Did he stay very much at Firle House?"

"No, sir; he only came down occasionally, and nearly always spent all his time at his flat near Hyde Park Corner. He didn't like the country very much, and madam didn't like the town, which wasn't a very happy business. For a little while after he took this place he was as keen as mustard on it, planning and altering and furnishing, and then he took a sudden dislike to the place. The gentry round here gave him the cold shoulder, and he couldn't stand that. The gentry are very conservative with furriners."

"Wasn't there some sort of tiff between him and Mrs. Mesado?"

"Well, yes, I suppose there was, but we never knew the cause of it. Probably Mrs. Mesado's fault. Her temper would upset the angel Gabriel at times. Mr. Mesado was one of the easiest men to get on with and every one liked him. Some say he was a bit of a hairy lad with the ladies, but you can't always blame a man for that. It's born in some of them and they can't help theirselves. And it ain't always the man who's to blame, sir," said Dobbs, turning to Vereker and fixing him impressively with his round grey eyes.

"I suppose not," remarked Vereker innocently.

"As for Mr. Mesado, whatever he did in that direction he did like a gentleman, and nobody ever knew or heard about it."

Vereker was obliged to smile at Dobbs's peculiar moral point of view, and the butler's statement shed a confirmatory light on the information he had gathered from Miss Marchant. He was now convinced that there must have been some guilty liaison between Mesado and Miss Maureen O'Connor.

"Did a Mr. Miguel Dias ever come down here, Dobbs?" he asked after a pause.

"Only once, sir. He called to see Mr. Mesado. Said he was a business acquaintance. The master was out, so he stayed to tea with madam and Mr. and Mrs. Colvin and then went back to town. When Mr. Mesado heard of it he was very angry. When the master was angry he always went as white as a sheet and shut himself up in his room. He gave orders that if Mr. Dias ever called again he was not to be admitted, but he never came again to my knowledge. I didn't like the look of the gent. Flashy, handsome man like a cardsharper. The week-end Mrs. Mesado and the Colvins left for their cruise there were only themselves, Miss Maureen and Gautier, the maid, in the house. That's all, sir."

"Miss Maureen arrived on Friday night and left on Sunday night?"

"Yes, sir. She must have had a nasty row with madam or she wouldn't have left her case and clothes here."

"It looks like it, Dobbs. At what time is lunch?"

"One o'clock, sir. You'll just have time to have a look at our refrigerating plant and room before the gong goes."

"Anything special about it?" asked Vereker without enthusiasm.

"Oh, yes, sir, one of the finest refrigerating rooms I've ever seen. We're very proud of it and show it off to all our guests. It was a particular hobby of Mr. Mesado's, because he was in the frozen meat trade and knew all about cold storage. It cost him a mint of money to install."

"What principle docs it work on, Dobbs? Brine circulation or carbon dioxide?"

"Neither, sir. Mr. Mesado always said the ammonia compression method was the best and most economical. Direct expansion of liquid ammonia," replied Dobbs with an air of technical superiority.

"Not dangerous, is it?"

"Well, no, sir, but we have special ammonia helmets ready in case of accident by bursting of portions of the plant. That, I'm led to believe, is not a likely affair."

"I'm very much interested, Dobbs. If you'll just show me where the freezing room is I'll have a good look at it on my own after lunch. Is it working?"

"Not at present, sir. Mrs. Mesado had the machinery stopped before she left. We have no use for it at the moment. You see, sir, when Mr. Mesado came down here he used to entertain on a large scale and we had very big house parties. Then the cold room was essential for keeping fish, meat, game and foodstuffs, and it was always full. Still, it's in working order and can be switched on if we want it."

After being shown the location of the refrigerating room and the beautiful equipment of the kitchen, scullery, pantry, etc., Vereker went upstairs to the dining-room for lunch. During the meal he told Dobbs, who waited on him, that after having a look at the cold storage he would retire to his own room for the afternoon and get his painting materials ready for his first excursion on to the Downs. He impressed upon the butler that he did not wish to be disturbed until dinner, which he would like at seven o'clock. After lunch he rested for half an hour and then went downstairs to make a careful inspection of the refrigerating room. He was at first not intensely interested, but as he had never been in a modern cold storage room before he felt that he must not let slip an occasion for widening his general knowledge. It might come in useful some day.

He approached the room through a small airlock or ante-chamber, and was at once struck by the construction of the heavy insulated door. With his usual meticulousness he examined this door and found, to his surprise, that it could not be opened from inside. This seemed a dangerous oversight to his calculating appreciation of mishap, and his searching eye wandered over the inside of the massive door. He was standing in this act

of examination when he noticed on the light painted surface
several dark smudges and three clearly defined finger-prints.
Immediately he was struck by the smallness of these finger-prints
and concluded that they were those of a female hand, From his
study of criminology the very fact that they were finger-prints gave
his mind an inquisitive bias, and he promptly assumed that they
had been left by one of the maids or the cook pushing open the
door with soiled fingers. A moment of reflection shook this theory,
for maids and cooks who handled food would hardly have soiled
hands to such an extent as to leave well-defined finger-prints.
Could they be blood? More than likely where meat and game and
fish were being touched and carried. Pulling out a magnifying
glass which he always carried with him, he examined them more
closely. Doubtless they were blood, though even an expert, as he
knew, could not dogmatise on that point without microscopic aid.
The stains were dark brown as if made of congealed blood, but
then he was aware that congealed blood could assume strange
hues, from black to a vivid green, according to the material on
which it had dried. As he was pondering on this he was all at
once struck by the fact that the stains were on the surface of the
door nearest the hinges. This discovery came with the thrill of
an electric shock. A cook or maid pushing open the door when
leaving the room would have left her finger impressions on
the side farthest away from the hinges. This was startling, and
now, thoroughly alive to possibilities, he made a most careful
examination of the fingerprints and smudges. Those clots and
smudges were intriguing; they were certainly never caused by
anyone pushing the door open for purposes of ordinary egress.
Leaving the door, he switched on the electric light and made a
careful survey of the whole plant. He found nothing further of
interest and was returning to the door when a spot of brilliant
green light on the floor near the exit caught his eye. He stood for
a moment looking at it and, shifting his position, discovered that
it was immediately eclipsed but that only a few inches from that

point another starry speck of burning red burst into view. At first he thought they must be tiny fragments of mica or other silicate forming shining particles of the stone or concrete floor. Drawing his electric torch from his pocket, he switched it on and ran it over the area from which those gems of light had shone. He found that they were caused by two small particles of what at first glance appeared to be glass. He picked up these fragments, examined them on the palm of his hand and to his amazement discovered that they were a small emerald and a ruby of similar dimensions.

"By Jove, what a find!" he exclaimed, and for the moment he was so overwhelmed by its importance that he stood as if stupefied, gazing at the diminutive stones glittering in his hand. Carefully wrapping them up in the tissue paper torn from the inside of a packet of Gold Flake cigarettes, he stowed them in his waistcoat pocket and made a further search on the floor. This search proving fruitless, he once more examined the door of the refrigerating room and, satisfied with his scrutiny, ascended to his bedroom and picked up the telephone from the table beside his bed. Giving Inspector Heather's private number, he was at once put in communication with him.

"Ah, you, Mr. Vereker! Where are you?" came the familiar voice.

"Firle House, Jevington. You know Jevington?"

"You bet I do. It's famous; I was born in the neighbourhood."

"Can you come along tomorrow?"

"You're excited. Anything important?"

"Hot scent. You know all about photography?"

"Not half! Want me to come down with the apparatus?"

"Yes, and bring your usual equipment. Can't say whether the prints are sanguine or merely dirt. We may also want a precipitin test later," explained Vereker, speaking as cryptically as he could in case he might be overheard.

"I'll be down by car first thing in the morning. What's the name of that pub at Jevington, Mr. Vereker?"

"Never mind pubs, Heather. Beer's the only thing you can think about."

"It's the only thing worth thinking about when you're thirsty, and I feel the symptoms coming on. Good-bye. First thing in the morning."

Putting down the telephone instrument, Vereker sank into an easy chair, and for over half an hour he remained there, his eyes closed as if in sleep; but a curious nervous compression of the masseter muscles of his cheek declared that he was not only wide awake, but very much excited. The Pleasure Cruise Mystery which had proved so baffling was beginning to move rapidly towards a solution. The various puzzling incidents, apparently so refractory at first, now seemed to be gliding into position, and after a little further investigation he felt he would be in possession of the truth and have unravelled one of the most amazing criminal cases in his career as an amateur detective.

Rising at length from his chair, he glanced round his bedroom and at once remembered Dobbs's information about Maureen's clothes being in one of the cupboards. Crossing over to the cupboard he tried the door, but found it locked. Next he turned his attention to a walnut chest of drawers standing on the opposite side of the room. All the drawers had been emptied and newly relined with paper for the reception of his clothes with the exception of the small right-hand top drawer, which was locked. The contents of that cupboard and drawer might prove informative, and he began to ponder on some method of opening them. He tried all the keys on his own bunch, but none of them fitted either lock. He could procure skeleton keys from Heather, but that would take time, and time was important. He could pretend that he had left the key of his case behind and get a further selection from Dobbs, but that might rouse the butler's suspicions without attaining a successful result. He was busy thinking of some way out of this difficulty when he noticed on the mantelpiece a beautiful Satsuma vase. At once he forgot all about keys and cupboards and went over to the ornament to admire it more closely. Picking it up to examine the bottom, he turned it over and two keys rattled against the porcelain mouth of the vase and fell on the floor.

"Looks as if I possessed Aladdin's lamp for the time being," he exclaimed and rescued the keys. Gratified with this piece of good fortune—for he was certain they were the keys of the locked receptacles—he picked them up and tried them. His surmise proved correct. The first key he tried was that of the cupboard, and with a sensation of breathless excitement he felt it turn and next moment the door stood open. From a decorated coat-hanger hung a tweed costume and jumper, and on the floor lay two pairs of shoes, one pair for evening wear and the other for ordinary morning use. Beside the shoes was a carelessly tied brown paper parcel. Walking over to his bedroom door, he locked it and returned to the cupboard. He then picked up the brown paper parcel and laid it on a small table at his bedside. A few moments sufficed to untie the loose knots of the string and lay out the contents. To his astonishment they consisted of undergarments and a pale green georgette evening gown. This gown, ostensibly new, had been rolled into a bundle in such a manner that it was clearly an act performed in the utmost haste and without any thought as to the ruin of the garment. He unrolled it carefully and found it stained in several places with ominously dark stains.

"Blood without any doubt!" he soliloquised and, rolling up the garments, once more parcelled and tied them up in their original covering. After replacing this bundle he withdrew the two pairs of shoes. He examined them and an involuntary exclamation of satisfaction escaped him on finding that they were size four. Maureen evidently took a size smaller than her sister Beryl. Replacing the shoes he locked the cupboard and dropped the key into the Satsuma vase. The small right-hand drawer of the chest next engaged his attention. It contained hair-brushes, cosmetics and an oval jewel-case bound in morocco. He picked up the jewel-case, pressed the catch and flung up the lid. On the black velvet interior of the receptacle lay a necklace of cinnamon and white diamonds exactly similar to the one he had seen in Dias's possession at Estoril.

"Well, I'm damned!" he exclaimed and, taking the ornament from its box, stepped over to the window to examine it carefully. At first he thought it was a fine paste imitation, but on further scrutiny concluded that it must consist of genuine stones so brilliant was their sheen and so beautiful the setting. At that moment he remembered Ricardo's jibe about enlarging his education as to precious stones, and bitterly regretted his insufficient knowledge. He must either take them to Dupont the jeweller, of Bond Street, whose name was on the white satin lining of the lid, or get Heather's opinion. Of course Heather would know good paste imitations from genuine stones at a glance. He must wait for the inspector and see. Rummaging through the remaining contents of the drawer, he found nothing further of importance except a letter from Mrs. Mesado to her sister Maureen, inviting her to Firle House for the weekend. An examination of this letter surrendered an unexpected clue. The envelope had been sealed, and in sealing it Mrs. Mesado had pressed a wet thumb into the cooling wax. This was to Vereker a discovery of vital significance, and slipping the letter into his pocket he locked the drawer. Highly satisfied with his afternoon's work he fixed up his easel and began to prepare a canvas for a sketch, but his thoughts were not in paint and canvas. He was busy with his hands on his task, but his mind was trying to find some explanation of the existence of two similar necklaces of white and cinnamon diamonds. In the midst of this occupation he suddenly rose from his chair, unlocked his bedroom door and stepped out on to the thickly carpeted corridor. Hearing no sounds of movement anywhere, he advanced noiselessly along to the door of the adjoining room, which opened on to the suite used by Guillermo Mesado when he stayed at Firle House. He found this room tidy as if ready for immediate occupation. A glance round declared that there was little to be discovered there which might help him in his investigation, and he was about to leave when his eye fell on a small silver-mounted photograph on the dressing table. Standing in the shadow cast by a large mirror on the table it had escaped his first hasty observation. He strode noiselessly across to the dressing table and picked up the photograph. Producing from his pocket the photograph of Miss Maureen O'Connor which Heather had managed to procure from Miss Marchant, he compared the two portraits very carefully. The sisters had the same cast of countenance, the same finely chiselled features and the same eyes, but one could not easily be mistaken for the other. In fact, Maureen resembled her sister, Constance Colvin, much more closely than she did Beryl Mesado. As he replaced the silver-mounted photograph of the last on the dressing table he reminded himself that he had never clearly seen that lady's face in the flesh and alive. It had been a cardinal factor in the difficulties he had encountered in his investigation, but now that he was no longer in any doubt as to her facial appearance a very formidable obstacle to the validity of his theory of the crime was swept away, and he left the room with a feeling of redoubled satisfaction. Tomorrow he would see Heather and unfold the story of his amazing discoveries. He looked forward to that hour with unrestrained eagerness, for he knew Heather would be appreciative, and a master's appreciation was a satisfactory reward to an enthusiast like Anthony Vereker. He spent the remainder of the afternoon in the library, and just before dinner was informed by Dobbs that he was wanted on the telephone. The caller was Albert, his batman, who had rung up from Fenton Street. He had received an urgent message from a Miss Marchant for his master, who was to be told that a Mr. Mig had called at Sussex Gardens the previous night and had been sent about his business. Mr. Mig had been inclined to aggression, but a phone call to the police station had made him depart with unceremonious haste.

"Forewarned is forearmed," thought Vereker, but to make doubly sure he drew an automatic pistol from its box in his case, slipped it into the pocket of his dinner jacket and went down to the dining-room.

Chapter Thirteen

Next morning Heather arrived just after Vereker had breakfasted and, having sent Dobbs into Eastbourne for a supply of a special tobacco sold only by a tobacconist in the Terminus Road, a ruse suggested by the resourceful inspector, the two men descended to the refrigerating chamber. There Heather took the necessary photographs of the finger-prints on the insulated door and scraped off sufficient of the clots and smudges to enable him to have the precipitin test for human blood applied. They then went up to the library to have what Heather called "a special board meeting" on the whole case.

"Now, Mr. Vereker," said the inspector when they were both seated at the library table, "I have been thinking a great deal about your murder mystery since I left you, but for the life of me I can't come to any definite conclusions. I'd have solved the problem long ago if I'd been on the spot, but I want more facts. Facts are my strong point. I'm not Sherlock Holmes's brother, who could sit in his armchair and give you a satisfactory answer to your questions by sheer imaginative reasoning. I'm only a poor C.I.D. man, and we're not quite as bright as that. Before we go any further, however, and from the facts you've given me, I make one startling deduction."

"Out with it, Heather!"

"You've struck one great difficulty in your investigation, and that is the identity of the body found on the deck and which has been accepted by nearly all concerned as that of Mrs. Mesado. You're right, Heather, but I think I've decided that point."

"Well, what's your conclusion?"

"My conclusion is that the body found on D deck of the liner 'Mars' was not the body of Mrs. Mesado at all, but that of her sister, Amy Diss, or Maureen O'Connor as she afterwards called herself," said Vereker quietly.

"I'd like to hear how you arrived at it, Mr. Vereker."

"I'll give you my reasons. The first factors which made me scent that there was some mystery about the Colvins and Mrs. Mesado was a conversation which I overheard in my cabin. Mrs. Mesado's cabin was next to mine. She and her brother-in-law were having a heated discussion, and Mrs. Mesado warned him that he would have to 'do the job as soon as possible'. He was on the defensive and hinted at the risks. A missing necklace was mentioned, and was called Maureen's necklace. This necklace has given me endless trouble, because it has run all along in harness with the story of a very strange murder, and I have had some difficulty in disentangling them and keeping the two threads apart. But for the present we'll keep strictly to the murder. The night following the one on which I overheard this discussion in Mrs. Mesado's cabin there was a scream from the lady, and high words between her and Richard Colvin. Mrs. Mesado said, 'Dick, it's all up,' and he replied, 'You're not going to leave this cabin, Beryl.' Mrs. Mesado replied, 'Remember it's murder. Damn you, get out of my way!' There were sounds of a brief struggle, a door slammed and all was silence. Now this occurred just after half-past one, say between one-thirty and a quarter to two. The time is most important, Heather, as it frequently is in such cases."

"One-thirty and a quarter to two," repeated Heather and jotted the note down on a sheet of paper.

"I immediately jumped from my bed and was wondering what action I should take in a very difficult business when I heard something rattle on the floor behind me. I was under the impression that something had fallen off my dressing table, but on examination found I was mistaken."

"That was the necklace which it's certain Mrs. Mesado flung into your window in the belief that it was the window of her own cabin. We can assume that she must have been alive and on the starboard side of D deck at that hour."

"Exactly, Heather. I found the necklace later on in the morning, but at the moment the necklace is an irrelevant intrusion beyond the fact that it possibly clears up the point of Mrs. Mesado being alive and active at quarter to two."

"She vanished from that moment, anyhow, and that's significant enough!" remarked the inspector.

"Don't interrupt me for a moment, Heather; I want to make my story absolutely clear. At two o'clock Ricardo rapped on my window, and after some hesitation I went out to see what he wanted. I found him standing over the body of a woman. Dressed in Mrs. Mesado's blue georgette evening gown and evening shoes and very much like her facially, except for the strange difference caused in the appearance of a human face by death, I hastily assumed, as Ricardo had done, that it was Mrs. Mesado. You must remember—and this is a cardinal point with me—that I had never seen the lady absolutely face to face. My error was excusable to a certain extent, but a bad error from a detective's point of view."

"We'll forgive you provisionally. Go on, Mr. Vereker."

"I sent Ricardo for the ship's doctor and made a very hasty examination of the body. I came to the conclusion that the lady was dead or on the point of death. If she was not dead, life was so nearly extinct that it was undiscernible under such a cursory inspection by a layman. Two very interesting facts I gathered, however. First, though the lady was in evening dress she was wearing a pair of ordinary chamois leather gauntlets. I pulled these off and found both hands terribly cut and bruised. The flesh was sticking to the gloves owing to the congealing of the blood of her wounds."

"She was alive at quarter to two, and this was at two o'clock. Where were your wits, Mr. Vereker?" asked Heather.

"Wool gathering. I was working at a big disadvantage. The whole business was too sudden and fantastic for me to think coldly. Never mind. Secondly, on the right forefinger was a marquise ring out of which two stones, an emerald and a ruby, were missing. There was, moreover, no signet ring on her left hand. Still a woman changes her rings as readily as her mind, so I couldn't make much of this point. I noted her blue satin shoes, and on feeling them remarked that they were certainly a size too large for her. Few women, even for comfort, wear dress shoes that are too easy, and the fact made me ponder."

"It ought to have hit you in the face like a straight left," remarked Heather with a malicious smile.

"I felt it as a mere flick at the moment. The doctor, Ricardo and Fuller, the night steward, immediately appeared on the scene. Fuller and I carried the body down to Mrs. Mesado's cabin, where the doctor solemnly announced that the lady was dead. I could see Macpherson was worrying about how the whole business affected the ship's point of view rather than anything else. He tactfully got rid of Ricardo and me and sent for the dead woman's sister and brother-in-law. I missed seeing their psychological reaction to the dreadful news and was terribly disappointed and handicapped."

"That psychology stunt will be the ruin of you as a 'tec, Mr. Vereker. Stick to facts; they never let you down too badly," remarked Heather, lighting his pipe with slow satisfaction.

"When Ricky and I were alone together in my cabin I got from him the story of his discovery of the body," continued Vereker, heedless of the inspector's sarcasm. "Just prior to his find he had made a detour of the promenade deck and near the window of my cabin saw what he thought to be a man and woman in a lovers' embrace, or, as he put it, in the conventional osculatory pose.

"What's the English for that?" asked Heather.

"He thought the man was bending over the woman and kissing her."

"That young man's thoughts will land him in trouble yet if his language doesn't."

"By this time," continued Vereker, "I was already beginning to make contact with reality. I jumped wildly at a theory and presumed on the strength of it that the 'lovers' had been Colvin with Mrs. Mesado's body. I concluded that he had been about to heave the body overboard when he was surprised by Ricardo's sudden appearance and, being a man whose nerves were sadly on edge through drink, got the wind up badly, dropped the lady and rushed back to his cabin."

"Not bad for a wild guess," suggested Heather, shoving a thick forefinger into the bowl of his pipe.

"Funnily enough it was correct up to a point," laughed Vereker. "To proceed with my yarn, I asked Ricardo if he had noticed anything strange about the dead woman's appearance. He simply remarked that her face was considerably altered in death, that her clothes looked as if they had been pulled about and that she was wearing ordinary chamois leather gauntlets with evening dress. You see, Ricky was observant but not acutely observant. He ought to have spotted the fact that, though the body was dressed in Mrs. Mesado's evening gown and shoes, it was not the body of Mrs. Mesado, even though they were very much alike. He had seen Mrs. Mesado face to face."

"His lack of trained observation helped to mislead you, Mr. Vereker," agreed Heather.

"Yes, in spite of my dawning suspicion that there was something very strange about the whole business. Eventually Ricardo left my cabin, and I was about to turn in when Colvin knocked on my door and I admitted him. He was, as I expected him to be, in a highly nervous state, but after a drink he pulled himself together and said he had come to thank Ricky and me on behalf of his wife and himself for the trouble we had taken and the help we had given over the sad matter of his sister-in-law's death. He then told me Mrs. Mesado had suffered from serious heart trouble and that they had been led by her medical adviser to expect her sudden collapse and death at any moment. He added that she had apparently been quite well when he saw her last, which was at ten p.m. I knew this statement to be a deliberate lie as far as time was concerned, but I applied my knowledge in the wrong direction in drawing an inference from it. I promptly accepted the fact that the dead woman must be Mrs. Mesado; indeed, up to this point I hadn't seriously questioned the identity of the body, but I leapt to the conclusion that he was lying about the time in order to cover his own guilt. Provisionally I mentally jotted him down as a suspect of the murder of Mrs. Mesado, and concluded that he had only paid me this visit to find out whether I'd overheard him quarrelling with her as late as one forty-five."

"You were a bit hasty, Mr. Vereker, but I can see the circumstances were extraordinarily complicated and difficult. I don't think I'd have fallen into the identity error so easily," remarked Heather gravely.

"I'm not so sure, Heather. Let me repeat that I had never seen the lady face to face myself. Neither Fuller nor the doctor had taken the slightest notice of the lady prior to her death even if they had seen her. The stewardesses, who might have shed a light on the matter, never saw the body after death. Ricardo overlooked any difference in appearance, and finally her own sister and brother-in-law offered not the slightest hint that the body was not Mrs. Mesado's. This act of theirs completely deceived me at first. By suggestion the human mind slips into the grossest errors with fatal ease, Heather. I stress this point very emphatically. Suggestion permeates and works miracles in the whole realm of human psychology. Immediately you depart from concrete facts you enter into the dominion of its strange power. Suggestion is at the heart's core of all advertisement and propaganda; it lurks, dangerous, in a rhetorical outburst, in a polemic, in soft persuasion. It rings in the melody of a poem, in the yearning of a lover's voice; it snarls in a maniac's threat!"

"You're trying it on me now," remarked Heather with a bland smile.

"That's irrelevant, Heather. Let me proceed. I accepted the tacit admission of the Colvins that the body was that of Beryl Mesado without objection. The very absence of any protestation on their part, their silence, swept me on to acceptance with the force of a mighty current. I was completely at the mercy of the working of my own mind—of the human mind in general. It instinctively responded to suggestion, was temporarily hypnotised. I was under the power of an idea, and an idea once formed is almost infrangible. It was only the subsequent persistence of glaring discrepancies and the critical elasticity of my own brain that freed me from my complete domination by that idea."

"Tell us how you performed this little miracle, Mr. Vereker. I like to know how you do these bright things," said Heather calmly.

"The very first inkling I had that I'd made some error in identity was given me by the question of the dead lady's jewellery. I've told you the story of the two missing necklaces; and the fact that Mrs. Mesado had called one of these Maureen's necklace introduced a mysterious Maureen among the *dramatis personae*. I openly asked Colvin at a later date who Maureen was, and he lied and told me it was a name Beryl Mesado had assumed when she was a ballet dancer. Since then we've found out who Maureen is. But prior to this I was assailed by continuous glaring discrepancies. I'll detail them for your future guidance in investigation. The gloves on the hands of the dead woman were too big for her and were initialled C. C., clearly showing they belonged to Constance Colvin. Mrs. Mesado's gloves, of an exactly similar make, were marked B.M., and it was evident that the two sisters wore the same size of glove, and as they lived together they had taken the precaution to initial them to prevent confusion as to ownership. I found a pair of Mrs. Mesado's chamois leather gauntlets in her cabin drawer, and found that my assumption was correct. Yet the lady whose dead hands were encased in Constance's gloves was wearing gloves much too large for her. Her hands were more than a size smaller! I did not stress the importance of this point at the time, owing to the fact that chamois leather gloves shrink after being washed and might be purchased a size too large for preliminary wear. It was splitting hairs, but I'm over cautious at times. Later in the morning, when I accompanied Colvin into Mrs. Mesado's cabin and had a good look at the body once more, I made a startling discovery. The dead lady parted her hair on the right side of her head, and I knew from the one clear view I'd had of Mrs. Mesado's hair that hers was parted on the left. The colour of the hair was fair in both cases, but Beryl's was a good deal lighter than that of the deceased. The dress shoes on the dead lady's feet were a size too large for her, her dress too ample in the girth. She had evidently taken off a wedding ring and a signet ring from her left hand and wore a marquise ring on her right forefinger. Two of the stones of this ring were missing. The injuries on her hands which the Colvins said had been caused by a car smash troubled me, for I was certain that Mrs. Mesado's left hand, which I had seen just after we had set sail, was uninjured when I saw it. Ricardo rather confused me on this point by suggesting I had seen Constance Colvin in Beryl's cabin. Now Constance wore a signet ring on her left hand, but she parted her hair on the right side like Maureen, the dead lady. Moreover, when Colvin went through Mrs. Mesado's jewel-case in search of a necklace I noted the fact that there was no signet ring and no wedding ring among her effects. I naturally asked myself where they had gone. I was now smelling a rat very strongly. I picked up Mrs. Mesado's passport, and though the accompanying portrait was certainly something like the lady whose body lay on the cabin bed I concluded it was not *her* portrait. The hair parting was again the vital difference. I then opened the cabin wardrobe and, though Mrs. Mesado had worn a black and white check costume for morning wear, there was no such costume among all her clothes! This was a revelation, Heather!"

"Naturally the costume went with the lady when she vanished," remarked Heather.

"I agree, but where had the lady vanished to?" asked Vereker pertinently.

"Overboard, of course. She committed suicide, I should say, but why, Mr. Vereker, why? That's what I want to know."

"Now, Heather, you're looking at the answer before working out the sum. We'll get at the answer by a logical process, please. The next step in the direction of a solution came from my discovery in my cabin of a very valuable diamond necklace which, as I've suggested to you, must have been flung in at my window. I could think of no person as the thrower of that necklace except the owner. At this juncture Colvin drew a nasty red herring across the scent by telling me that Mrs. Mesado's necklace of alternate cinnamon and white diamonds was missing. Now Ricky satisfactorily identified the necklace which had so unexpectedly come into my possession as the one Mrs. Mesado had worn at dinner one night. He even distinctly remembered the emerald butterfly clasp, a point which was firmly imbedded in my own mind. I was temporarily bewildered but, to fit the circumstances together in a rational scheme, assumed that there must be two necklaces. I had heard of 'Maureen's' necklace and for the sake of a working hypothesis called the cinnamon and white diamond one 'Maureen's' necklace without knowing who this mysterious Maureen might be. By a curious association of ideas I now began to think not only of two distinct necklaces, but two distinct owners. It was a happy psychological accident. I tried hard through my friend Ricky to discover the identity of Maureen. Miss Renée Gautier, whom he questioned, denied all knowledge of a Maureen, but made the fatal mistake of saying that the necklace which Colvin was searching for was one of pure white diamonds. At once I jumped to the conclusion that there was a conspiracy among Colvin, Mrs. Colvin and Gautier and that they had not definitely agreed on the minor details of their

story for public consumption. Once I had firmly grasped the idea
of conspiracy things began to assume a clearer shape. My mind
travelled backwards and the discrepancy in the story of where the
car smash had occurred became significant. I soon proved to my
satisfaction that there had been no car smash; ergo, Mrs. Mesado
could not have injured her hands in a car smash, and yet from
the state of the wounds they had certainly been injured prior to
her arrival on board. As I was now convinced that Mrs. Mesado's
hands had not been injured at all it was conclusive that the body
with the injured hands was not that of Beryl Mesado. The fog was
beginning to clear, Heather, but it was still pretty thick, I returned
to the circumstances of the fatal night. I had positively heard Mrs.
Mesado's voice talking to Colvin at one-thirty, or between that
time and one-forty-five a.m. She was dead on deck at two o'clock.
This was rather difficult to swallow easily, and I questioned the
night steward, Fuller. Now Fuller, as I've told you before, made
the remarkable statement that he had seen Colvin carry up Mrs.
Mesado on deck at one-thirty a.m. in a dead faint and return
almost immediately to his cabin. He was very precise about the
time. Dyson, the day steward, told me that Martin, the night
stewardess, saw Mrs. Mesado run up the companion on to D deck
about two o'clock. She was sure that it was Mrs. Mesado because
she was wearing her diamond necklace and her black and white
check morning costume. It was of course possible that Martin had
taken Mrs. Colvin for Mrs. Mesado, but she would hardly make
a mistake about a diamond necklace. She would almost certainly
know the difference between it and the string of crystal beads
that Mrs. Colvin wore. I took it for proven that Martin was right
and that Mrs. Mesado was alive just before two o'clock. There
was now no doubt in my mind that the body found by Ricardo at
two o'clock on the starboard side of D deck was not that of Mrs.
Mesado. As I have said it's difficult to remove a fixed idea, but I
had at last managed to do so. Being now positive that the body was

not that of Mrs. Mesado, I had to find out whose it was and how it had come there."

"I might have done the job quicker, but I couldn't have done it better, Mr. Vereker," said Heather, reaching for his glass. There followed a silence broken only by a grunt of satisfaction emitted by the inspector as he stuffed his handkerchief up his sleeve after wiping his mouth.

"This astounding discovery forced me to alter my whole mental attitude to the case. It was as disturbing as removing from one flat to another. I was so obsessed with the idea of Mrs. Mesado being murdered on account of her wealth that I felt quite depressed. There were so many lovely motives for murdering Mrs. Mesado. Her necklace was worth several thousand pounds. Her sister Constance benefited to the tune of £100,000 and the mansion at Jevington. Colvin was always hard up through his drunkenness. Renée Gautier was left £500 under the will. Mrs. Mesado's husband had quarrelled with her and might be glad to get rid of her. Miss Penteado was in love with her husband and would certainly marry him if he were free. She was such a likely subject for murder that I could almost have done the job myself!"

"The next step was to find out who the murdered lady was," suggested Heather.

"No, strangely enough, I was at first more concerned about how the body had got there. It was at once fairly clear that Colvin had carried it up from Mrs. Mesado's cabin with the intention of disposing of it by an unorthodox burial at sea. It was the body that the steward had mistaken for Mrs. Mesado in a dead faint, being taken up on deck by her brother-in-law at one-thirty a.m. The next question was how had it come aboard, and why. After very little reflection it was evident that it must have been packed in a large trunk, and both the Colvins and Mrs. Mesado came on the 'Mars' with identically similar Saratoga trunks of unusual dimensions. A dismembered human body can be packed into a small compass as you know, Heather."

"Yes, the dimensions of the Charing Cross Murder trunk were only 31 inches by 19 inches by 23 inches."

"Dismemberment was impossible in this case, probably due to a vital matter of time, but we'll get to that point later. I was sure that the body had been packed in one of those trunks, and from the conversation I'd overheard between Colvin and Mrs. Mesado, when she said, 'You'll have to do the job as soon as possible, Dick,' I inferred that it was Mrs. Mesado's trunk. I have a theory why there were two trunks, but it's unimportant at the moment."

"I see the reason for the chamois leather gloves, Mr. Vereker."

"Good, Heather; let's have it!"

"To prevent her injured hands from leaving incriminating traces of blood on the interior lining of the Saratoga."

"I agree. Now, working backwards once more we come to the question of conspiracy. From the facts I've already enumerated it's evident that the Colvins and Mrs. Mesado were involved in the business, and as Gautier was more a companion than a maid to her mistress it's reasonable to assume that she was in the know. But here's an important point: she was also in league with Dias. It was under Dias's impulsion that she managed to filch Maureen's necklace or, to be explicit, the necklace of cinnamon and white diamonds. Dias, whose lover, perhaps mistress, Maureen had been, had long coveted that necklace, which we know was given to her by Guillermo Mesado. Gautier stole that necklace from Maureen's body when it was in Beryl's trunk on the 'Mars'; this fact accounted for Mrs. Mesado's most significant remark, 'Maureen's necklace has gone!' Gautier was fairly safe in stealing the jewel, because she had the Colvins and Mrs. Mesado in her power through her share in the conspiracy. She could blackmail them if necessary. I saw her pass a package to Dias during a cinema performance on board, and I had an idea what that package contained. Later on, at Estoril, I saw Dias hand a cinnamon and white diamond necklace to his confederate, Ribeiro, probably for the purpose of sale, and was at last sure of my facts. I nearly lost my life through my eagerness in the pursuit. Dias had discovered that I was on his tracks and tried to bump me off."

"Now, Mr. Vereker, we're clear upon some points. First and most important, that the murdered lady whose body has caused all the trouble was Maureen O'Connor. Before we discuss who murdered her, and how, I'm going to ask you a very nasty question."

"I can guess the question, Heather, but fire away."

"Let us assume that the lady was murdered on land and her body put in a trunk and brought on board the 'Mars'."

"You must assume it, Heather," interrupted Vereker. "You know that the one great difficulty in a case of murder is for the murderer to dispose of the body. It's the crucial thing that has brought every other murderer who has been caught to the gallows. Crippen, Landru, Wainwright, Mahon—I could go on enumerating them, but you know them all better than I do. Now in this Mesado mystery whoever committed the murder had the bright idea of disposing of the body by throwing it in the sea. However badly the thing was bungled the conception was original and brilliant. To get rid of the incriminating carcase from a liner making a pleasure cruise seems at first sight a plan bold to the point of madness. But you've only to look at the matter calmly for a few minutes and you see there was more method than madness. The very idea of carrying out the job on a pleasure cruise is so unorthodox that it at once becomes a bulwark against suspicion. Anyone who has travelled on board a liner knows how absolutely deserted a ship's decks can be at certain hours, and instances of travellers having vanished from vessels carrying hundreds of passengers without anyone having seen them disappear or knowing how they went are innumerable. In my journey to Lisbon on the 'Mars' I could easily have jumped overboard at night without the remotest fear of being seen. Correspondingly easy would it be to heave a body overboard. Once the body of the murdered person is in the sea the chances of it being recovered are extremely small, and I'm surprised that this method of disposing of a murdered body has not been tried frequently. At the moment I cannot recall a single case. Doubtless there have been innumerable instances, and they have all proved successful!"

"All very true, Mr. Vereker, but now for my nasty question. If the lady in our case was murdered on land and carried in a trunk for so many hours, say forty-eight, how is it that rigor mortis did not set in before. It usually sets in from five to six hours after death. You have led me to believe that Doctor Macpherson was of the opinion that life had just petered out when he was called on the scene."

"That's so, and as I've said before Macpherson is an accurate and thorough Scot. I couldn't very well satisfy myself that he was wrong, Heather. Rigor mortis is not a thing you can be positive about, but it's a fairly good basis to work on with regard to the time of death. I found this point an almost insuperable stumbling block, for Macpherson said that rigor mortis had set in before the body was moved from Mrs. Mesado's cabin to the sick bay. This was quite normal if we assume that the lady died at two o'clock in the morning and was removed just before breakfast."

"As far as Macpherson was concerned she died of heart disease?" asked Heather.

"Yes, he accepted the statement of her relatives, whatever doubts he may have had in his own mind. By a piece of finesse I managed to get the Colvins to bury the body in Lisbon, so that if it becomes necessary we can subsequently get an exhumation."

"A wise precaution, Mr. Vereker, but I don't think it'll be necessary now," said Heather, rubbing his chin thoughtfully.

"I'm not out of the wood yet, Heather, but to revert to this question of rigor mortis, the only explanation I could offer myself was that the lady died from the effects of some hypnotic drug which caused prolonged unconsciousness prior to death. I conjectured that she had been poisoned and was really in a comatose state during transit in the trunk. She only expired after she had been taken out and carried up on deck. Yet those injured hands had to be accounted for. Poisoning and violence rarely go together. It was a peculiarly puzzling obstacle to my theoretical reasoning. But in conversation with Miss Marchant I made another extraordinary discovery. I found that Maureen O'Connor suffered from hysteria, and as you know hysterical subjects are liable to go into trances or cataleptic states which to an ordinary man are difficult to distinguish from death."

"By heck, but I never knew that!" exclaimed Heather.

"I knew of it all right, but until Miss Marchant told me Maureen O'Connor had had one of these trances during the time she had been in her service I never thought of considering such a phenomenon applicable to my case."

"How did you make it fit in?" asked Heather eagerly.

"I haven't been able to make it fit in yet, Heather, and that's the rub. With regard to the manner of death, I want a few more facts before I can feel I'm on a sure thing. Those finger-prints you've just photographed and a test of the blood on the refrigerator door are two things I'd like to know a little more about. Is it human blood and whose are the finger-prints?"

"But you'll want other finger-prints in order to make a comparison, Mr. Vereker. Aha! there's something you've been hiding from your old colleague all the time!"

"You're so damned smart, Heather, that I had to do something to make the problem interesting and worthy of your talent," laughed Vereker and, opening a large attaché case he had with him, produced the photo-micrographs made for him by Mascarenhas of the Portuguese police. "Here are some nice little pictures for you, Heather. Number one is a finger-print of the man Dias taken from a glossy-surfaced snap belonging to Miss Gautier. His real name is Cardozo and he is wanted in France, Spain, Portugal and the Argentine for daring jewel robberies."

"I'm sure we've got a dossier concerning that gentleman filed away in our archives, but I'll have it looked up and refresh my memory," said Heather, puckering his brow in an effort to recollect.

"Numbers two and three are finger-prints which I took from the dead woman's hands. Number four is one secured from a celluloid comb used by Mrs. Mesado. Naturally I expected it to tally with one of the prints of the dead woman's fingers. You'll observe they are utterly different. It's quite possible that the finger-prints on the celluloid comb are not Mrs. Mesado's. I didn't overlook that contingency, but it's no use hunting for trouble, and I think we can safely assume for our purposes that the impressions were left by Mrs. Mesado. The discovery that there was a discrepancy was illuminating. Number four is Renée Gautier's hall-mark."

"But the principal question in this business, Mr. Vereker, is, who killed Maureen O'Connor?"

"We've come to that vital stage in our board meeting at last, Heather. But even now I feel that the moment hasn't arrived for me to answer the question with any degree of certainty. I want you to let me have the photo-micrographs of the fingerprints on the refrigerator door and the result of the blood test as soon as possible. Now I'll ask you to come up to my room, where I have some more bits of evidence that may prove important."

The two men went upstairs, and after showing Heather Maureen's blood-stained evening gown, her tweed costume and shoes, Vereker asked him what he thought of them.

"They fairly give the show away!" exclaimed Heather. "Miss Marchant said that these were all the wearing apparel and shoes Maureen took with her for the week-end. If she disappeared from this house she disappeared in her naked pelt and bare feet."

"Just so, Heather. I think we can assume that her body was stripped of clothes and shoes and packed in Mrs. Mesado's Saratoga."

"Good. Anything else?"

Vereker drew from his pocket Mrs. Mesado's letter of invitation to Maureen and, crossing to the chest of drawers, extracted the jewel box containing the cinnamon and white diamond necklace.

"Lord above, another necklace!" exclaimed Heather after reading the letter. "Enough necklaces in this case to hang a regiment of mutineers."

"Are the stones genuine, Heather? I'm not an expert."

"They are, and worth a chief inspector's ransom."

"Well I'm hanged!" said Vereker with astonishment. "Either there are two similar necklaces of genuine stones or the one which Gautier stole from Maureen's body is a paste one."

"I'll bet my last bob the latter necklace was a very good paste one," remarked Heather, "and that's why our friend Cardozo was so easily persuaded by the Portuguese police to return it to the Colvins in Lisbon. What's your next move, Mr. Vereker?"

"In the first place, Heather, you might take this seal from Mrs. Mesado's letter and give me a photo-micrograph of the thumb-print on the sealing wax. It ought to tally with the one I've got from her celluloid comb."

"You're improving wonderfully, Mr. Vereker," said the inspector and, tearing the seal off the envelope, placed it carefully in an empty matchbox and stowed it away in his pocket.

"I shall stay here until the Colvins return. I want to see Richard Colvin badly. In the meantime I'm waiting on you, Heather."

"I must return to town immediately. I'll come back with the photo-micrographs of the fingerprints on the refrigerator and on the sealing wax and let you know the result of the precipitin test. That ought to enable you to put the last turn on your screw, and you'll then have to act. Ring me up at any time if you want assistance. You may, for you're nearing the danger line. It'll cost you something of course..."

"More beer, I presume," interrupted Vereker; "and, by the way, Cardozo or Dias is in England. Miss Marchant got a telephone message through to me last night warning me he had called at Sussex Gardens."

"Good. We'll keep him under observation if we can trace his whereabouts. Got a gun handy, I hope."

"Yes; it's not often I carry one, but I'm taking no chances."

"Don't hesitate to use it. I don't want to lose a talented pupil. In the interval of waiting to hear from me you might just jot down in your notebook all that the Sussex Downs have got to say about beauty and all that. Good day."

Chapter Fourteen

Shortly after Inspector Heather's departure the afternoon turned wet and chilly, and Vereker spent it in an easy chair in the library before a roaring fire. He had taken down John Langdon Davies' *Man and His Universe* from one of the shelves and, absorbed in that book, soon forgot all about the Pleasure Cruise Mystery. Soon, however, he came across the passage: "So, too, with our attitude towards the criminal. Evolution encouraged the idea that he was one of Nature's failures, doomed to extinction and artificially kept alive to the great danger of the human future; that the main problem with regard to him is how to protect the community from his depredations. Relativity lays the emphasis on the cause of his conduct being his environment. Given all the factors of the case he had to act as he did, and whether or not society has to be protected from him, nevertheless it must treat him with consideration due to his having acted on compulsion." The passage and its context awakened in him a train of reflection bearing on his own attitude to the criminal, and he was obliged to admit that his interest in criminal investigation, though it possibly had its birth in some vague traditional idea of protecting the community, had long since lost tangible connection with social morality as a motive. He even doubted whether Heather was now actuated by such a motive, and Heather was a paid servant of the community, paid for its protection. No, his own attitude to criminal investigation had arisen out of his artistic impulses apart from an innate bent for ratiocination; of his love of culture, and he smiled with keen appreciation when he remembered a phrase used by one of Aldous Huxley's characters on the subject of culture: That's the definition of culture, knowing and thinking about things that have absolutely nothing to do with us. Absorbed in his thoughts, he sat smoking until the dinner gong sounded. He ate sparingly, drank some of the best claret he had ever drunk and about ten o'clock decided to go to bed.

Though gifted with artistic imagination, Vereker was peculiarly practical in his outlook on life and seldom surrendered to any fears of the unknown. Yet on retiring that night he became peculiarly sensitive to the atmosphere of his room, to the dismal sound of the wind driving the cold rain in gusts against the window panes, to the silence and gloom of the large almost untenanted mansion. The very presence in a near-by wardrobe of a dead woman's blood-stained evening gown, of her dress shoes and morning suit, affected him with a force he had never felt before. Had these ordinary articles any tangible connection with the human spirit that had so recently left its material body? He strove to reason away these imaginings, but his perusal of Langdon Davies' book had loosened his mind from its practical and mechanical attitude to life. His thoughts began to wander into the vague and hesitating outlook that even modern science has adopted towards the mystery of the universe and man's existence. Our knowledge seemed to him so superficial and in a desperate state of flux; it was proving a poor bulwark against inherent superstition and that dread of the unknown which lies at the core of the human soul. Gradually he fell into a disturbed sleep and unpleasant dreaming, from which he was suddenly wakened by the light creaking of his bedroom door on its hinges. Having left his window partially open, he was certain that he had closed his door firmly before getting into bed in order to prevent its being swung to and fro on a gusty cross-current of air. The realisation of this fact roused him to immediate and alert wakefulness. He lay still, listening intently, and, raising his head, tried to pierce the gloom with his eyes. The night, however, was intensely dark and he could discern nothing. At that moment a spot of light suddenly appeared on the wall beyond the foot of his bed and flitted jerkily about the room like a large luminous moth. For some seconds he experienced a sharp insurgence of fear; his brain was still moving nervously in a world of phantoms, vague, monstrous, terror-instilling. Pulling himself together with an effort of will, he soon realised that this eerie, dancing spot was the circular disc of illumination cast by a tiny electric pocket torch, and in the faint light issuing from the ray he clearly descried the outline of a man's body. Recovering from his surprise he slipped his hand under his pillow and, gripping his automatic Colt, pushed down the safety catch. For a few breathless seconds he waited, and saw the intruder move swiftly and noiselessly over to the chest of drawers, the right-hand top drawer of which contained the valuable necklace of cinnamon and white diamonds. Some moments of silence followed, and then he heard the almost noiseless turning of a key in a lock. At that instant he pushed the electric light switch above him through its pendant knob and, sitting up, covered the intruder with his weapon.

"Hands up!" he shouted, and without a moment's hesitation the figure obeyed. "Keep them up, Dias," said Vereker firmly, "or I'll fire!"

"All right," replied Dias, and the look of alarm and anger which had held his features slipped into a sheepish grin. Vereker noted the change and realised that the man, whatever his other characteristics might be, possessed a sense of humour. Springing from his bed and thrusting his feet into his slippers, all the while keeping Dias covered with his automatic, Vereker approached him.

"Any weapons on you?" he asked.

"I never carry them in England; it doesn't pay," replied Dias coolly.

His words were convincing, but Vereker was not taking anything for granted and, pressing the muzzle of the Colt against

Dias, swiftly searched him with his free hand. Satisfied that he had told the truth he stepped backward and faced him.

"You've come for the diamond necklace that Maureen O'Connor left in that drawer?" he asked.

"You've guessed right the first time. That's why I'm here."

"The one Renée Gautier stole for you from the dead woman's body was paste, I suppose?"

"It was a dud," replied Dias, and in spite of himself his face declared his astonishment as to the extent of Vereker's knowledge.

"Was it returned to the Colvins?"

"Yes, but they saw that it wasn't genuine, and the Portuguese police refused to pay Ribeiro the reward for its return. The police are always inconsiderate even when you help them."

"You knew it wasn't genuine as soon as you saw it?"

"Oh, yes. I know a good deal about precious stones."

"Well, I'm rather sorry I've robbed you of your prize, but that's neither here nor there. I'm not in the least concerned with the necklace, Dias, but with the person or persons who murdered Maureen O'Connor. Do you know anything about the latter business?"

"I had nothing to do with it," replied Dias immediately.

"You know who did it?" asked Vereker.

"It was none of my business."

"Possibly not, but I'm going to make you a fair proposal. You know a good deal about the matter which in other circumstances you'd keep to yourself. Any information you can give me will be useful. Now I've caught you red-handed in a burglary. If I press that bell beside you the butler will come to my assistance and we can hand you over to the police. You wouldn't like that. I think Scotland Yard know something about you, and Mascarenhas, the chief of the Lisbon police, would certainly like to lay hands on a gentleman called Cardozo. If you'll tell me all you know about the murder of Maureen O'Connor I'll let you go free from here. I'll give you two days' start before I say anything to Scotland Yard about you. Is that a fair deal?"

"Why do you want to tell Scotland Yard about me? I'm not wanted by the police of this country."

"Perhaps not, but there are international courtesies which must be observed. I may not mention the matter at all to them, but I can't definitely promise anything more than two days' start. Are you going to accept the offer?" asked Vereker, and advanced towards the electric bell-push.

"Very well. Must I keep my arms up? It's getting painful."

"Give me your word of honour that you won't try on any nonsense."

"I promise by the mother of God."

"Good. Take a seat," said Vereker and pointed to a low Minty chair from which it would be difficult to rise quickly without the disadvantage of a warning indication.

Dias lowered his arms and sat down. Vereker drew an ordinary chair facing him and pulled over a small table on which stood a decanter of whisky and glasses to the left, but clear of his unexpected guest. He poured out the drinks with his left hand and passed one to Dias.

"Thanks, I need one badly," replied Dias and drank his liquor at a draught.

Confident that his visitor was going to accept the situation without any attempt at violence or a dash for freedom, Vereker slipped his Colt into the pocket of his pyjama jacket and sat down.

"To begin with, Dias, I'm going to tell you all I've learned about your relations with the late Maureen O'Connor," said Vereker, and for some time was occupied with a brief but fairly comprehensive outline of that knowledge. Dias sat and listened to the story without interruption, and at its close remarked: "A fairly accurate statement. I must correct you on one point. I was in love with the lady. She was not merely a convenience."

"I'll grant you the point if it's any satisfaction to your sense of honour. Are you now in love with Renée Gautier?"

"Oh, no, quite a different matter. Renée and I are useful to one another. Ours is purely a business arrangement."

"You're going to marry her, I believe?"

"Not at all. Marriage is a convenient pawn when you have business dealings with a woman. I'm sometimes obliged to make use of it."

"You're not going to meet her at Barcelona?"

"I had no intention of doing so, but I had to keep the young lady in a good humour. It was absolutely necessary in the circumstances."

"You knew that Maureen O'Connor had been murdered?"

"Hearsay only. It came as a great shock to me, and I had determined to avenge her death."

"Like a gallant lover," remarked Vereker. "Now we come to the point of how you knew and who told you."

"I'll tell you the truth about the whole matter. As you've guessed, there was a guilty liaison between Maureen and Guillermo Mesado. Mesado had stolen my lover, so I was going to make him pay for the pleasure. Renée is an old friend of mine and we always confided in one another, but like a woman she doesn't know the value of silence and when it pays to talk. She became Mrs. Mesado's confidante and was genuinely fond of her mistress. In an outburst of frankness she must have told Mrs. Mesado all about her husband's relations with his sister-in-law. Women do such things. They cannot help themselves. There was a violent quarrel and Guillermo left his wife and returned to the Argentine. Mrs. Mesado then determined to make sure that the story was true and invited Maureen to this place, Firle House, for the weekend. She found out that Renée had told the truth, and at once related the whole story to her sister, Constance Colvin, and to Constance's husband. The latter is a vicious drunkard. One can admire a clever criminal, but a drunkard is contemptible. One can only spit on him and pass him by. Colvin knew that Guillermo's departure meant the loss of a good living for him. Guillermo paid him handsomely for the little and pleasant work he did for him. He has a violent temper, and being a weak man he can't control it. Infuriated at the loss of his income the poor wretch could think of nothing better than wreaking his hatred on the cause of it, so he murdered Maureen O'Connor."

"You heard this from Renée Gautier?" asked Vereker, unable to conceal astonishment at the information.

"Yes; she ought to know. She was in the house when it was done."

"It's difficult to believe, but how did he do it?"

"Unknown to Constance and Beryl, he was showing Maureen over the house after dinner. He took her down to the refrigerator to explain the working of it, ushered her in and banged the door. She was dressed in an evening gown and died of exposure to the intense cold during the night. It was a clever idea. I give him credit for some wit."

"This was on Sunday night?" asked Vereker.

"I forget whether it was Saturday or Sunday. It matters little."

"How did Beryl and Constance find out about it?"

"After locking Maureen in the refrigerator Colvin went upstairs and asked where Maureen had got to. His manner was innocent and disarming. They didn't know, but thought she had retired to her room. After a considerable lapse of time Colvin, expressing anxiety about the lady, asked his wife to go and see what Maureen was doing. Naturally she was not to be found, and there and then they searched the house, but never dreamed of looking in the refrigerator. Finally they came to the conclusion that she had found the family atmosphere uncongenial and had gone home. Towards morning Colvin pretended to remember that they had overlooked the refrigerator and roused his wife, for they had retired after their first unsuccessful search. They got up, wakened Beryl and together they went down to the cold storage chamber. Arriving there they found to their surprise that Renée Gautier had also remembered the refrigerator. She had slipped on a dressing-gown and gone down to investigate on her own. On opening the refrigerator door Renée had found Maureen almost unconscious. She dragged her out and gave her hot tea to revive her. She recovered sufficiently to tell Renée that Colvin had intentionally locked her in. With these words she succumbed. When the three others came on the scene Renée in an angry outburst accused Colvin of murdering his sister-in-law. Faced with the accusation, Colvin admitted he had locked her up in the chamber, but only with the intention of punishing her. Thereupon there was a hasty conference between the parties, and the three relatives tried to nobble Renée into joining them in a story that it was an accident. Renée refused to have anything to do with the conspiracy, but agreed to hold her tongue about the business unless she were directly questioned by the police or at an inquest. Further than that she absolutely refused to go."

"She didn't wish to be accessory to a murder," remarked Vereker.

"No. Renée has a lot of French caution; she's very hard-headed."

"What happened next?"

"After some discussion they concluded that the safest thing to do was to dispose of the body secretly, so they decided to take it with them on Monday morning on their pleasure cruise and get rid of it at sea."

"Whose bright idea was that?" asked Vereker.

"I believe it was Colvin's, but I'm not sure."

"This was not prearranged?"

"Apparently not, but if there was a separate conspiracy among the relatives, Renée was ignorant of it. There may have been, for after all Maureen was the black sheep of the family and they were all sick to death of her."

"But what was Maureen going to do on Monday morning if the accident, shall we say, had not occurred?"

"They had told her that they would take her up to London by car, leave her and proceed to Tilbury."

"How did they all travel that morning?"

"Colvin and his wife went up by an early train. Renée and Mrs. Mesado and the luggage, which was considerable and included the body, went up by a car hired in Eastbourne. They had got rid of their chauffeur with the other servants the previous week."

"So that's the story as you heard it. Have you told Colvin that you know about his share in this business?"

"No, it's no affair of mine. I never talk unless it's profitable to talk."

"It may be profitable to talk later?" asked Vereker pertinently.

"No, I hardly think so. Things are getting too warm for me on this side of the Atlantic and I shall try my luck in America next. It seems to be the only place where fortunes can be made rapidly if one has a little courage, some brains and not too much sentiment."

"I think that's all I want to know, Mr. Dias," said Vereker, rising from his chair to signify that the interview was at an end. "Which way did you enter the house?"

"By one of the drawing-room windows."

"Did you cut a pane?"

"It wasn't necessary; there is one with a faulty catch which responds easily to a little manipulation."

"Perhaps I'd better see you off the premises in case the butler wakes up and fills you with shot. He always keeps a loaded twelve-bore beside his bed when the house is empty."

"It would be better. Our conversation has probably roused him, and I don't like to run unnecessary risks. I leave that to fools."

"Before you go I'll just have a look in that drawer to see that Maureen's diamond necklace is still there," remarked Vereker as he quickly crossed the room to the chest.

"A wise precaution," smiled Dias good-humouredly. "I was rather surprised you didn't look before."

"I heard you turn the key to open the drawer when I switched on the light, and was pretty certain you hadn't time to extract the jewel-case," replied Vereker.

"Hearing is a very faulty sense. I never trust it too implicitly. I may have been locking the drawer instead of opening it. Still on this occasion you are right, but as a detective you ought to make sure."

"I see it's here," replied Vereker as he opened the jewel-case and, finding the necklace, returned it to its place in the drawer.

"Shall I lead the way?" asked Dias when he saw that Vereker was ready.

"Naturally," replied Vereker with a sardonic smile and followed Dias down to the drawing-room, where he slipped silently out of an open window and, making his way rapidly across the lawn, vanished into the dusk.

Firmly closing and wedging the drawing-room window, Vereker returned to his bedroom. He once more locked the drawer containing Maureen's necklace, got into bed and tried to sleep. His mind, however, was not in a sufficiently quiescent state for sleep. He lay awake far into the night pondering over the details of Dias's story. They were circumstantial enough to be plausible, but they conflicted with Vereker's theory of the crime, and the more he thought about them the less credible did they appear. Look at the matter in whatever light he might, he could not visualise Richard Colvin as the murderer of Maureen O'Connor. In his own mind he was now fairly certain who the culprit was, but before being positive he would see Heather again and hear the result of his work on the fingerprints and bloodstains in the refrigerating chamber. On the assumption that Dias's story was a fabrication he strove to find a motive for it, but at length, utterly weary of the task, gave it up and fell sound asleep.

Chapter Fifteen

The next three days Vereker spent on the Sussex Downs, tramping, sketching, loafing. He had completely detached his mind from the Pleasure Cruise Mystery, and found his change of occupation restful and invigorating. On the fourth day he was planning an excursion to Alfriston to visit the Star Inn, the reputed haunt of smugglers in bygone days, and was preparing to start after breakfast when he received a telegram. It was from Richard Colvin stating that he was returning to Firle House without Mrs. Colvin and would be home for lunch. It concluded by expressing the hope that Vereker was still resident there and that he would be present at the meal. Vereker at once informed Dobbs of his master's imminent homecoming and his own change of plan. He had to admit to himself that this unexpected news gave him a keen thrill of excitement. He was anxious to see Colvin and thrash out the whole business of the Mesado mystery with him. At the back of his mind he had felt certain that Colvin would take every precaution to avoid meeting him again, and that his generous offer of hospitality had only been another move in an audacious game of bluff. He had called Colvin's bluff by accepting the invitation to Firle House, and had been anxious to see how that move would be countered. He had not envisaged Colvin returning boldly to face matters out. At once he began to surmise that something exceptional had happened to urge him to this course of action. He spent the morning in elaborating some of his sketches of the previous three days, and at midday he heard the car which brought Colvin from the station whirl up the drive of Firle House and come to a halt before the main entrance. He laid down his sketching materials and looked out of the window only to see the car turning for departure. He was about to go down and greet the arrival when his door opened and Colvin entered. He looked haggard and ill and was evidently in great mental distress.

"I'm glad you're here, Vereker," he said and, after shaking hands, sank into an easy chair as if exhausted.

"You don't look up to the mark. Anything gone wrong?" asked Vereker sympathetically.

"Every damned thing has gone wrong!" exclaimed Colvin with weak exasperation.

"Yes, I agree. The game has gone badly against you from the very beginning," replied Vereker.

The remark caused Colvin to look up sharply, but on meeting Vereker's steady gaze he lowered his eyes and for some minutes was lost in deep thought.

"I've been wondering for some time now how much you knew, Vereker," he said at length. "Even when we were on the 'Mars' I had an inkling that you had probed unexpectedly deep into our secret. I was at first inclined to put the blame on my guilty conscience, but there was something in your attitude which warned me that you were on our tracks. It put me on the defensive and I naturally became more guarded than ever, but it seems as if I might have saved myself the trouble."

"I've an idea I know all about your secret, Colvin," said Vereker quietly, "but even now I'm not too cocksure. Before we discuss the matter, what has happened to Mrs. Colvin? Not met with an accident, I hope."

"Poor Constance, the strain was too much for her. I had to take her to a nursing home on our return from Spain. She has had a dreadful breakdown."

"A mental home?" asked Vereker.

"Yes. It's only temporary, I hope, but it's a bad business and the doctor in charge wasn't too sanguine."

"I'm sorry for her, but a murder and a suicide in the family are enough to unhinge any but the strongest brain."

"Then you do know," said Colvin. "We've played a desperate game and lost. For myself I don't care two hoots, but for Constance..." Colvin left the sentence unfinished owing to his deep emotion. There was an uncomfortable pause, but regaining his self-control he said, "Tell me what you know and I'll let you know if you've got the facts correct."

"To begin with your sister-in-law, Amy Diss or Maureen O'Connor, was the cause of all the trouble."

"Yes, to a certain extent. She has been the skeleton in the Diss family cupboard for years. Beyond the fact that her sisters, Beryl and Constance, would have nothing to do with her owing to the degraded life she was leading, nothing serious would have happened if that scoundrel Dias hadn't come on the scene. He's a man of the most dangerous type. He became friendly with Beryl's husband in the Argentine, and on landing in England began to dig into the Diss family history after somehow learning that there was some mystery about a third sister, Amy. Having with extraordinary pertinacity found out all about Amy, he continued his search until he found out where the woman lived in London. As you know, he's a handsome and plausible rogue, and soon he had Amy, or Maureen as she called herself, completely in his power. With a view to blackmail he introduced Guillermo Mesado to Amy. Up to this point Guillermo had never heard of the existence of Amy. The result of this meeting was disastrous. Guillermo pitied the woman and, being very susceptible to feminine charms, was soon making passionate love to her. She encouraged him. He spent money recklessly on her and became so careless of his behaviour that Beryl's suspicions were roused. Moreover, Guillermo became jealous of Dias and, finding that Dias was simply bleeding Amy of the money he was providing, he quarrelled bitterly with her and left her. Finding that no further money was forthcoming, Dias tried to blackmail Guillermo. This was ineffectual, and to revenge himself Dias got his tool Renée Gautier to tell the story of the whole sordid business to Beryl. I believe Gautier too was in love with the man, but of this I wouldn't be positive. In any case there was a terrible row between Beryl and Guillermo. They almost came to blows, for Beryl when roused was absolutely reckless and behaved like a maniac. Guillermo promptly left Firle House, and we haven't seen him since. I dare say he has gone back to Buenos Aires, but we don't know. Now came the most serious part of the sorry business..."

"Let me continue the story, Colvin, and if I'm wrong in my particulars correct me. Beryl Mesado, thinking that Amy had been the cause of her husband's infidelity and of her estrangement from him, decided to make sure of her facts. She probably did this in a fit of remorse, because she loved Guillermo and began to fear that she might have acted hastily in reproaching him. She invited her sister to Firle House and, finding that Gautier's story was true, decided to revenge herself on her sister. She inveigled her downstairs under pretence of showing her the refrigerating chamber and locked her in. In my investigation I surmised that you and your wife were not at home on Sunday evening. I should like to know if that's correct."

"Damned smart, Vereker. We were over at the Mortons to dinner and didn't return till midnight. When we arrived back at Firle House Beryl told us that Maureen had left the house after an angry scene between them. She didn't know where

"Where was Gautier?" asked Vereker.

"She had gone to bed early after laying a cold supper for her mistress and Maureen. Dobbs and his wife were up in London."

"It looks as if Beryl had planned this business."

"I can't say. She was a very difficult woman to understand. I'm inclined to think she acted on impulse and that circumstances were favourable by mere chance. I may be biased in her favour because I was very fond of her."

"How did you eventually find out what she had done?"

"Gautier, who was troubled with sleeplessness that night, came down in the early hours of the morning to make herself a glass of hot milk, and went into the refrigerator for the milk. She found Maureen unconscious and made her a cup of tea to warm and revive her. She recovered sufficiently to tell Gautier what Beryl had done and then snuffed out. Gautier promptly came upstairs and wakened Beryl first and then ourselves."

"I see, and then there was a council of the four of you to settle what you were going to do about it."

"Exactly. I was all for us agreeing to say that it was an accident."

"Certainly that was one way out of the trouble, though one of you might have weakened and made a mess of things at the inquest. There would naturally have been a lot of uncomfortable explanations to make and questions to answer. It looks a water-tight story at first glance, but I'm not so sure it wouldn't have sprung a leak. I take it that you and Constance were going to save your sister's neck at all costs?"

"Naturally. What else could we do? Constance and I would have gone through hell-fire for Beryl. In spite of her many faults she was one of the most fascinating women I've ever known."

"Gautier, I presume, was not so eager."

"Well, she said she would do all in her power to shield her, but she got the wind up when we began to discuss the inquest."

"Who suggested concealing the whole affair and getting rid of the body at sea?"

"Gautier. At first Constance and I and Beryl were dead against such a risky course, but Gautier pointed out the advantages of the scheme and Beryl was immediately won over. Everything seemed so favourable for its success. After a long discussion of ways and means Constance and I agreed to the suggestion. I was the last to succumb because I saw that the act of getting rid of the body would fall on me. When Beryl said she'd carry out that dangerous bit herself and twitted me with being a funk, I said I'd carry it out. After that we all set to work to arrange the details of the enterprise."

"I worked it out that you were to carry the body from Beryl's cabin and fling it overboard in the early hours of the morning. I also surmised that you had made some hasty arrangements to counter untoward happenings. If you were caught carrying the body up the companion you were going to say Mrs. Mesado had fainted and you were taking her up on deck for air."

"By jingo, that's good, Vereker. It's exactly what we arranged!"

"And on it being found that the lady had died of heart failure the real Mrs. Mesado was to be shut up in the duplicate trunk in your cabin and be taken ashore at Lisbon."

"Yes; it was a desperate alternative, but the whole plan was a desperate one. It meant that Beryl would have to lie doubled up in the trunk while the stewardess tidied up her cabin every morning, and as soon as possible Constance would return, bolt the cabin door and let her out. We had arranged an opening to allow for sufficient air; a very neat flap in the back of the trunk which took me all morning to make. She would only have to do this for three mornings at the most.

"You'd have had to run her through the Customs," remarked Vereker.

"That we foresaw would be the biggest risk of all, and we were going to nobble the Customs with fifty thousand escudos—about five hundred pounds—if the occasion arose. Our scheme might have failed, but we had to take our chances. On board it would have worked all right, I think, because Constance was going to feel seasick and keep to her cabin till we reached Lisbon. As long as she and Beryl kept the cabin door bolted they would have been safe against detection. Still we were now thoroughly worked up, and the more we thought things out the more sanguine we became. We didn't meet trouble half-way and all hoped for the best."

"It might have worked if you hadn't lost your head at the critical moment, Colvin. Ricardo happened to come round the corner of the promenade deck and you promptly dropped the body and returned to your cabin."

"Yes, it's all very well looking at the affair in retrospect; but I'm not blessed with nerves of steel. I ran down to tell Beryl she must vanish into the trunk in my cabin and that we must pretend that she—that is the body on deck—had died of heart failure. There was no one on board who could say that Maureen's body was not Beryl's except the Penteados and Dias, and we would not have allowed them to view it."

"It was your trump card and won the trick, but what went wrong? Did Mrs. Mesado lose her head?"

"She did. In spite of my efforts to persuade her and a violent struggle that followed she rushed up on deck and flung herself overboard. You can imagine my consternation when I discovered you had her necklace. I guessed she had thrown it in your open cabin window in mistake for her own."

"And Maureen's necklace had vanished from the body in the trunk?"

"Yes. Neither Constance nor I cared a damn about Maureen's necklace until Beryl found that it had been stolen from the body in the trunk."

"You suspected Gautier?"

"No, or rather Beryl was certain Gautier hadn't stolen it. Constance and I were not so sure. It was a horrible quandary, for if some one else had stolen it it was clear that our plan had been discovered by a stranger."

"When the necklace was returned to you at Lisbon it proved to be a paste duplicate?"

"Yes. That scoundrel Dias, whose tool Gautier was, got the disappointment of his life. Constance said that the real necklace must be the one Beryl locked up in a drawer in this room."

"It's here all right, Colvin. I took the liberty of opening the drawer in my search for clues."

"Let's see if it's the genuine one!" exclaimed Colvin with a faint show of eagerness.

"Your sister-in-law was careless about valuable jewellery," remarked Vereker as he extracted the key from the Satsuma vase and opened the right-hand top drawer of the chest. Taking out the jeweller's case he handed it to Colvin, who opened it and swiftly examined the necklace.

"Good Lord!" he exclaimed after a brief but careful scrutiny, "this is a paste duplicate, Vereker. How the hell...?"

His words were cut short by a burst of bitter laughter from Vereker.

"Well I'm damned!" the latter exclaimed at length. "Of all the fools in this world, Colvin, I think I must be the biggest!"

"I don't see what you're driving at," said Colvin slowly as he stood gazing at Vereker in blank bewilderment.

"Dias has substituted this paste duplicate for the genuine one after all. I didn't think he'd had time to do so. I was a simpleton not to take immediate steps to find out," replied Vereker, and then related in full to the astonished Colvin the story of his recent midnight encounter with Dias as a burglar.

"A clever devil," remarked Colvin with the first smile that had lighted his sunken features since his return. "You got the better of us, Vereker, and I must say I'm just a little pleased that for once some one has put it across you. I think he has earned that necklace, and he's welcome to it."

"I suppose it's good to get the conceit taken out of one at times," said Vereker, acutely chagrined at the neat way he had been tricked, "but it's an unpleasant experience."

At this moment the gong sounded for lunch and the two men descended to the dining-room. Over their meal they reverted to the topic of the desperate plan to conceal Beryl Mesado's crime, and Vereker pointed out to Colvin the curious fact that Maureen had only expired after he had left her body on the promenade deck of the "Mars".

"In spite of your mishaps your luck held," said Vereker, "for if she had been dead when you packed the body in the trunk Doctor Macpherson would certainly have discovered that your story of heart failure was all bunk, and then the fat would have been in the fire."

"We hadn't thought of that snag," said Colvin reflectively. "The words rigor mortis were never mentioned by any of us. They say all murderers make one silly blunder, and that was ours."

"And now I suppose you know you are guilty of being accessories after the fact to a murder," said Vereker gravely.

"Yes, yes, I know all about that, Vereker. I don't care a continental either. I only did what I could to help Beryl because I was fond of her, and because Constance loved her. I'd do it again if the occasion arose. You're the only man who knows the truth about our conspiracy, and you can jolly well do your damnedest for all I care."

"Chief Inspector Heather of Scotland Yard also knows," said Vereker.

"Then the sooner he gets on with the job of arresting us the better. Constance is in a mental home. God knows where Gautier is, but I'm here, and here I'll stay until the inspector turns up."

"You took a chance, Colvin, and apparently you've lost. I must say you're taking defeat like a well plucked 'un. I'm going to see Inspector Heather this afternoon. In the meantime I should keep my tail up if I were you. I'm afraid we've not arrived at our journey's end yet and no one knows what's round the bend of the road."

Chapter Sixteen

It was about a week after Vereker had returned to his flat in Fenton Street, W., that Heather found time to pay him an eagerly awaited visit. The inspector had been engaged on the case of a young woman of the demi-monde who had been brutally strangled with a silk stocking in her rooms at Maida Vale, and he had at last been able to take an afternoon off from his exacting work. He arrived shortly after lunch, and Vereker, who had been putting the finishing touches to a picture intended for one of the spring shows, promptly flung down palette, brushes and marl stick and at once broached the topic of the Pleasure Cruise Mystery.

"You've brought the photo-micrographs, Heather?" he asked eagerly.

"Yes, here they are," replied Heather, producing them from an attaché case, "and they fully bear out your theory. The finger-prints on the refrigerator door tally with those of the dead body on the 'Mars' and are indubitably those of Maureen O'Connor."

"Eminently satisfactory," remarked Vereker excitedly; "and these two stones, an emerald and a ruby which I picked up on the refrigerator floor, corroborate the assumption. They are the stones that were missing from the dead woman's marquise ring and were doubtless knocked out when she made frantic efforts to open the door or attract attention to her terrible plight."

With these words he produced a twist of tissue paper from his pocket and displayed the gems for Heather's inspection.

"And the finger-print on the sealing wax from Mrs. Mesado's envelope, does it tally with any of those from her celluloid comb which Mascarenhas developed for me?"

"It's a thumb-print, to be correct, and does agree," replied Heather. "The blood on the refrigerator door was human, and now we've got all the facts the question is, who murdered Maureen O'Connor?"

"We've come to that point at last, but before I ask you for your answer or give you mine, Heather, I must add two very important sections to the story," said Vereker and briefly narrated his experience with Dias at Firle House and gave an account of his recent interview with Richard Colvin.

"Let me see, Mr. Vereker—er—h'm—I'm feeling very thirsty—er..."

"Oh, damn, it's beer you want, I suppose. Ring the bell. Albert will do the rest; he knows your habits. In the meantime carry on with your yarn."

"From your very interesting narratives, Mr. Vereker, I'll first make an attempt to list the probables in the case. To begin with, Maureen O'Connor was Dias's mistress. Dias may have got all he wanted out of her in the shape of money and tired of her as far as affection is concerned. He's a nasty bit of machinery and from all accounts doesn't hesitate to kill, but if he's the culprit I can't see why the Colvins and Mrs. Mesado had anything to do with the disposal of the body. Besides, he wasn't at Firle House at the time as far as we know, and it's clear that the young lady met her death there. Secondly, Guillermo Mesado was in love with Maureen and probably sick to death of her extravagance as well as jealous of her love for Dias. She may have been Dias's tool in blackmailing Mesado, and the latter may have been driven to killing her to prevent his wife from discovering the story of his guilty passion. Mesado has vanished and no one apparently knows where he is. This looks very suspicious, and I'd like to know whether the gentleman was in the neighbourhood of Firle House during that week-end. Could he have entered the house and done the job without the occupants knowing he had any hand in it? In that case the disposal of the body was a conspiracy entered into by the family after they had discovered the author of the crime to save his neck and their own reputations. Colvin's story contradicts this, but it may now suit his book to keep Mesado out of danger of hanging. I can't see Colvin as a suspect unless there were relations between him and the dead woman which your story hasn't revealed. As for Dias's statement that Colvin committed the murder, I can only say that in my opinion it's pure bunk, but I'd like to know the motive behind the lie."

"Most important, Heather. I too want to know his motive in spinning such a yarn. I'm certain there is one," interrupted Vereker.

"Possibly, but let me continue. I'll take Mrs. Colvin next. According to your account she's a very religious woman, but I consider she's out of the running unless she has the spirit of the early Christians in her and made herself the instrument of the Lord in destroying a relative who had become a scarlet woman. It's difficult nowadays to understand the ardour which drove people to burn heretics at the stake, but those burnings definitely establish the possible revival of such ferocity in a human being. We now come to Mrs. Mesado. If she was the murderess her motive was a terrible jealousy, and as we know jealousy is a common motive in murder cases. It seems clear that her husband entered into guilty relations with his sister-in-law, and if Colvin's story is true the maid blew the gaff to the mistress. I also think it was a premeditated and carefully planned crime. The conspiracy to get rid of the body is easily imagined and to me Colvin's story appears true. I therefore put down Mrs. Mesado as the murderess of Maureen O'Connor. I think we can leave Gautier out of our reckoning. We know she's passionately in love with Dias, but again she knew that Dias had tired of Maureen, if indeed he had ever loved her. A woman doesn't murder a woman whom her lover once loved. She lets her live as a perpetual reminder of her own superior personal charms—a bit of flattery incarnate, so to speak."

"Heather you've put your case very clearly—I mean very clearly for you. I'm inclined to agree with your findings, but there's one big obstacle that sticks in my way. Let me explain myself. We'll take it for granted that Mrs. Mesado, having found out her husband's guilty relations with Maureen O'Connor, decides to murder the thief of her husband's affection. Mrs. Mesado is a clever woman with a most violent temper and resolute will. She thinks out the safest way to do the killing without being discovered and hits upon the plan of practically freezing her victim to death. I consider her idea a brilliant one if practicable. The temperature in that refrigerating chamber can be lowered to intense cold, and Maureen, physically none too strong and dressed in a flimsy evening gown, would soon succumb to exposure. The medical profession, in this country in any case, are none too well acquainted with the various factors connected with death by freezing for the simple reason that such cases seldom if ever come within their observation. One authority, however, says that exposure to great cold will kill an unsuitably clad person of average health within an hour. A night of such exposure would almost make death a certainty in our case. To my knowledge there is one authentic instance of an employee in a cold storage warehouse having been accidentally locked in a refrigerating room in the evening and been found dead from the effects in the morning. Having struck on this diabolical method of committing the murder, Beryl Mesado must have considered it carefully in all its aspects. Firstly, Maureen's death could be ascribed to an accident. The lady might have wandered by herself into the refrigerator in an idly inquisitive mood and shut herself in. Even a search party might overlook a refrigerator when hunting for a missing guest. The door of the refrigerator in Firle House can only be opened from outside, though the latest insulated doors to large refrigerators are fitted with an opening mechanism workable from within to obviate this very type of mishap. In passing, my deduction that the finger-prints on that door were made by a stranger arose from the fact that they were near the hinges and that the prisoner was ignorant of where the lock was. To resume, Mrs. Mesado in contemplating the crime must surely have thought of the possibility of removing the body to a wood in the grounds of Firle House and leaving it there. This would have been the plan I'd have adopted. A subsequent post-mortem could only have revealed that death had been caused by exposure. It was a bitterly cold week-end if you remember, Heather. Even the cut hands were not a factor contributing to her death and could have been explained away easily enough. Now, having committed the crime and being fairly confident that there was little risk of discovery, why did Mrs. Mesado suddenly alter her plans and under Gautier's suggestion decide that the safest way of avoiding detection was to dispose of the body in the sea? The scheme was not only bold, it was fantastic in its risk of falling to pieces. On the one hand we have an imaginary accident and no risks worth considering of it being construed as murder, and on the other an intricate if clever scheme that with the slightest hitch would break down and prove disastrous. Colvin's story is that Renée Gautier refused to enter into the conspiracy to declare Maureen's death as due to an accident. She is supposed to have got the wind up over the idea of being interrogated by the police or at a coroner's inquest. Yet she suggests this dangerous scheme of getting rid of the body at sea and is willing to become an accomplice. No, Heather, there's something radically wrong here, and it has been intriguing me for some time. Who discovered Maureen's body and heard the statement that Beryl had locked her up in the refrigerator? Renée Gautier. Who was the only other person in the house when Beryl locked up her sister-in-law? Renée Gautier. She is supposed to have retired after laying the evening meal for the two sisters, and knew nothing of the crime till she heard it from the dying woman's lips. This may be true, but I simply can't believe it. I'm almost certain that Gautier knew that Beryl had shut Maureen in the refrigerator and came down in the early hours of the morning to see if her mistress's plan for killing had proved effectual. You say Gautier had no motive for desiring Maureen's death. She too had the all-powerful motive of jealousy. Maureen as far as we know had still got Dias in her thrall. Dias himself confessed this to me. Maureen, moreover, had the advantage over Renée of being extraordinarily beautiful and capable of laying her hands on large sums of money for her lover's use. Again, she may have been instigated to murder by Dias himself, who may have had no further use for Maureen. You see clearly that I suspect Renée Gautier of having some hand in the crime. Let us return to our old difficulty of rigor mortis in connection with Maureen's body after it was discovered on the deck of the liner 'Mars'. I had a theory that she must have fallen into a cataleptic fit due to hysteria on finding herself locked up in the refrigerator, especially after Miss Marchant told me that she was subject to such fits. The only alternative to this was an overdose of some hypnotic drug. Now, as you know, I discovered a phial of nembutal capsules among Mrs. Mesado's belongings on the 'Mars'. The drug had doubtless been prescribed for her by a specialist. It's a drug fairly new to medicine and would hardly be prescribed by a general practitioner except under the guidance of an expert. Quite recently there was a case of nembutal having proved fatal, and in an overdose it would almost certainly produce prolonged unconsciousness prior to death. Now

Ricardo, who has been invaluable to me in this investigation, saw an empty phial labelled 'Nembutal' among Miss Gautier's things in her cabin. She hastily flung it out of the porthole on discovering it there. It seems likely that she had secreted the phial in her attaché case among some photographs and in the stress of that last morning at Firle House had forgotten where she had hidden it. Revert once more to the story of her coming downstairs in the early hours for a glass of hot milk to drive away sleeplessness and going to the refrigerator for the milk. She found Maureen unconscious in the chamber and made her some hot tea to warm and revive her. This is a tall story. On finding an unconscious person in the refrigerator she would hardly start calmly to boil water and make tea. She would have rushed for spirits. She knew where the decanters were kept. No, Heather, when Renée Gautier went to the cold storage chamber she found Maureen alive though probably chilled to the bone. She was terribly disappointed with the failure of Beryl's plan to kill her sister and decided to take the job into her own hands. She made Maureen a cup of tea and put an overdose of nembutol, the only poison she could lay her hands on, into it. Maureen, half frozen, greedily drank the tea and fell into a coma fairly rapidly in her exhausted condition. Convinced that Maureen was dead, Renée ran upstairs and wakened her mistress and the Colvins. To fix the guilt of murder on her mistress she concocted the story of a dying statement by Maureen, whereas Maureen was probably well on the way to recovery when she told Gautier how she had come to be imprisoned in the refrigerator. There then followed, as we know from Colvin, a dramatic council of four people, who discussed what had to be done in the circumstances. Colvin and his wife favoured the story of an accident and suggested letting matters take the course consequent on such. Beryl seems to have agreed with them at first. At this point Gautier appears to have taken an extraordinary stand against such a natural and plausible story through fear of the police and a coroner's inquiry. She persuaded Beryl and then the

Colvins to dispose of the body at sea during their pleasure cruise on the 'Mars'. Her suggestion had the deadly quality of being unusual and feasible in spite of its risks, but its cardinal asset as far as Gautier was concerned was that it obviated a post-mortem examination and the discovery that Maureen had been deliberately poisoned. She carried her point, but I have still the pleasure of knowing that I frustrated Maureen's burial at sea and that the body still lies in the Os Cyprestes, the English cemetery at Lisbon, in case we need an exhumation."

"So you have finally decided that Renée Gautier murdered Maureen O'Connor by poisoning her with nembutol!"

"That's my verdict, and as the 'Mars' arrived at Tilbury this morning the hour for action is at hand. Gautier will return to Firle House, where she'll get a chilly reception, and I expect Ricardo to turn up here any moment and let us know all the news of his pleasure cruise."

A few minutes after Vereker had spoken these words the electric bell of his front door began to ring, and continued to do so incessantly.

"That's that devil Ricky. I know his irritating trick of keeping his thumb on the bell-push until some one arrives to let him in!" exclaimed Vereker.

There followed the sound of Albert's measured tread to the front door, and a few seconds later Ricardo burst unceremoniously into the room.

"Hello, hello! What's all this, what's all this?" he asked boisterously. "A secret meeting of the Big Two? Perhaps I ought to say the Big One and a Bit considering your bulk, Heather. Please ring that bell for another glass, Algernon. I'm feeling a perfect hart for cooling streams at the moment. You've got to congratulate me, Algernon!"

"You've solved the pleasure cruise murder?" asked Vereker eagerly.

"Murders be damned! I'm engaged to Rosaura Penteado!"

"Engaged?" asked Vereker, looking at his friend incredulously.

"That's the word, Algernon. It has a finite sound about it that's not very pleasant, but there you are!"

"When are you going to be married?" asked Heather slowly.

"An altogether irrelevant question, Heather. An engagement's a major phenomenon with me because I seldom get so far in my relations with the fair sex. The lady in the case is an heiress, which is a desideratum, if I may say so. Altogether I'm blissfully happy—I think that's the correct expression."

"But tell us about your work, the results of your investigations, Ricky. We can talk about your footling engagement later," said Vereker impatiently.

"Haven't got much time, I'm afraid," said Ricardo, glancing at his watch. "I have a date with a peach, as the Americans say. Sounds like a fruit salad, but you'll understand."

"God bless my soul, but you haven't left the lady more than an hour ago!" said Vereker.

"My dear Algernon, you don't understand. It's not Rosaura. There are other peaches as well as pebbles. The date was fixed prior to my starting on the 'Mars' cruise. It's therefore ancient and must be respected. I keep my engagements at the risk of breaking my engagements. It's moderately safe, because the Penteados left us at Bordeaux, where the plums come from, and are now on their way to Buenos Aires."

"Can't this other lady wait?" asked Vereker irritably.

"She does as a matter of fact—in a West End tea-shop. Still, if there's anything colossally important you want to know I might stretch a point by telling her the 'Mars' had to wait for the tide."

"Then sit down and let us hear the result of your investigations," urged Vereker.

"Well, I haven't made any since we left Barcelona."

"Great heavens, didn't I predict it!" exclaimed Vereker. "You've simply wasted your time and my money for a passing love affair. Ricky, you're unspeakable!"

"Don't be peevish, Algernon. There was no need for further investigation after we left Barcelona, and by that time I was glad because I'd reached a very critical point in my relations with Rosaura. I had a slight difference with her about her mother. She insists on her mother living with us, and as you know the mother is a futurist portrait of Rosaura..."

"Damn her mother! Why was there no need for investigation after your leaving Barcelona?"

"Because I had learned all there was to be known of the murder of Maureen O'Connor—not Beryl Mesado, mark you, Algernon—shortly after leaving the Spanish port."

"Renée Gautier told you?" asked Vereker eagerly.

"Yes, poor girl. I was very sorry for her. It was a dirty trick!"

"More of your love affairs?" remarked Vereker, fearing that Ricardo was once more about to diverge from the main subject.

"No, no, Renée and I became great pals on board. She very kindly aided and abetted me in making Rosaura as jealous as the devil, and this brought my affair with the heiress to fruition. Competition is a powerful fertiliser. It was Dias, whom she loved madly, that played Renée the dirty trick. He was to have met her at Barcelona and taken her to Paris for her marriage. He never turned up, but wrote her a letter saying it was all over between them and that he was going to America. I had been very friendly with her—no nonsense, you understand, simply friends—and I was the only person she could confide in. She wrote me a long letter telling me the unhappy story of her love affair with Dias, of her jealousy of Maureen O'Connor, of Maureen's death, and of how she stole the necklace from the dead woman's neck for that noxious vermin Cardozo, alias Miguel Dias."

"Did she tell you how Maureen met her end?" asked Vereker with suppressed excitement.

"Yes. On that Sunday night before the cruise the Colvins went out to dinner and there were only three people left at Firle House: Beryl Mesado, her sister Amy, or Maureen as she preferred to call herself, and Renée Gautier. Renée laid the table for the two ladies' supper and said she would turn in. Something or other made her change her mind—it might have been one of my serials in a Sunday paper. In any case she sat down in the kitchen and began to read. About an hour later Beryl and her sister came downstairs and made their way to the refrigerator. Renée knew the refrigerator was the show piece for guests looking over the house, especially the women, and paid no heed to the business. From the kitchen, however, she could hear every word that was spoken, and as she sat reading with her ears unconsciously at the half-cock the refrigerator door suddenly slammed violently and she heard Beryl Mesado exclaim viciously, 'That'll cool down your passions, you dirty sewer rat!' There followed the sound of Mrs. Mesado's footsteps hurrying back as fast as she could to the dining-room, and as she sat listening there came the dull thud, thud, thud of fists beating frantically on the refrigerator door."

At this point in his story Ricardo paused in thought.

"That would make a stunning chapter for a serial..." he began, but was cut short by Vereker telling him to proceed.

"The letter then gives an amazing account of how bitterly Renée herself had hated Maureen O'Connor, and the reason why. She describes in vivid language how she went to the refrigerator door and gloated over the cries from within, which she could hear faintly, though they must have been piercing shrieks of agony. At short intervals throughout this ghastly script there runs Beryl Mesado's pregnant phrase, 'That'll cool down your passions, you dirty sewer rat!' It is repeated *ad nauseam*, a morbid chorus and a vivid gauge of the intensity of Renée's hatred. You see, Maureen was Dias's mistress, and she had taunted Renée that she was only a poor, disappointed lover and would never be any more than that. This had so nettled Renée that she had done everything in her power, even surrendered herself to Dias to win his love. This was her hour! Revenge had come at last. She could easily have freed Maureen, but she wanted her to die and stood with her ear to the door and heard the frantic pummelling of the prisoner's bloody fists grow weaker and weaker till at last they ceased. She then remarks that her legs were aching with the fatigue of standing listening to her rival's agony and that she began to feel hungry. After eating a slice of brown bread and butter she went to bed and slept soundly till three o'clock in the morning. To cut a long story short, at three o'clock Renée, bitten by curiosity, came down to the refrigerator to see how the captive was faring. All was silent, so she opened the door and stepped in. Maureen was lying on the floor of the chamber, her face deathly white and her evening frock all stained with the blood that had flowed from her smashed knuckles. She was still alive. Renée even then could easily have saved her life, but she had no intention of doing so. She was going to destroy any chance of her returning to Dias's arms, but a streak of pity entered her hard heart. She decided that she should die in a painless sleep. She made a cup of tea, put in the contents of a phial of nembutol and handed it to the woman to drink. Maureen, half dazed, managed to get the stuff down her throat, and not long after sank into a deep sleep. Confident that she had made death absolutely certain, Renée was just going to leave Maureen when Beryl Mesado appeared on the scene with Colvin and his wife. By this time Maureen was apparently beyond recovery..."

"Thanks very much, Ricky. I think we know the fest of the story," said Vereker, and gave him a précis of events as they had happened.

"Well, Heather, what do you think of it all?" asked Vereker, turning triumphantly to the inspector.

"Not half bad for an amateur. In the Polo Ground Mystery I scored one over you, but I'll give you best this time. You deserve it because it has been a most complicated case. This beer..."

"What happened to Renée Gautier after she received Dias's letter at Barcelona and wrote to you confessing that she had murdered Maureen O'Connor?" asked Vereker suddenly of Manuel.

"I wondered if you two fellows would let me finish my story after you had grown weary of patting one another on the back.

Well, the whole business so preyed on Renée's mind that in a fit of terrible depression she took her own life. She shot herself the day before we touched at Ceuta on our way home. You should have heard Captain Partridge's language! He said it was the last pleasure cruise he'd ever skipper. What with a sudden death, a suicide, a baby swallowing its dummy and Lady Hildenborough asking him to sew a button on her boots, old Partridge's cup of bitterness was filled to overflowing. But if you don't mind I really must keep my appointment with Judy. I shall be ten minutes late if I rush off now. I'll see you to-morrow, Algernon. Lunch with me at Jacques' at one o'clock. If there's anything more you want to know I shall be in a happier frame of mind to talk. I also want you to come and help me to choose a ring."

"Help you to pay for it, you mean," remarked Vereker as the gay Ricardo vanished out of the door of the flat. Turning to Inspector Heather he asked, "Well, old friend, and what's the next step? Of the four conspirators two have committed suicide. They were both equally culpable of murder, though Gautier was the actual culprit. One is in a mental home, in danger of becoming a lunatic, and poor Colvin is at Firle House, a worn and sick man."

"I think the best thing to do is to leave the matter as it stands, Mr. Vereker. Besides, there's this mysterious strangling case in Maida Vale that needs all my attention. If you've got the time why not come and do some real detective work?"

"No thanks, Heather. I'm going down to Firle House to see Colvin and put him wise as to the truth about Maureen O'Connor's death. Then I'll have a good month or so of painting on the Downs as soon as the weather turns warmer."

"Very good, Mr. Vereker, and while you're down there you might find out which pub in Sussex keeps the best beer. The Downs may be able to whisper..."

Heather left the sentence unfinished in order to drain his pewter tankard.

THE END